BOOK 2 OF COURAGE ON THE OREGON TRAIL SERIES

FAITHFUL TRAIL

A.T. BUTLER

FAITHFUL TRAIL

An Oregon Trail Western Adventure

A.T. BUTLER

As she walked home in the early afternoon, Olivia Greenwood pulled her coat closer against the chill. Though it was rather too thin for the winter weather, she wrapped her scarf around her neck once more to try to preserve as much warmth as she could. Thankfully, Olivia thought, it hadn't snowed yet. Where they lived in the hilly inland of Virginia, they could expect a storm any day. With the shorter days of December, the winter sun was already halfway down in the sky.

Following behind her aunt and uncle on the wide gravel road, Olivia couldn't help but overhear when they mentioned her name. The three were returning home after church one Sunday.

The morning at church on that particular Sunday had been a refreshing change. Usually, Olivia simply enjoyed the sabbath as the one day that she wasn't expected to be doing chores on the Drysdale farm from dawn until dusk. But this week, a traveling preacher had come to Charlottesville. Younger and more captivating with a fresh point of view, he was exactly the kind of man the First Church of Christ needed that week. The sonorous voice of Luke Montgomery as he extolled the lessons of Jeremiah 29 reminded Olivia of why she had always loved those old Bible stories. As Mr. Montgomery preached, she had felt as though he were talking directly to her.

The sermon that day had been about each person fulfilling the role that God had created for them. Now that she had some quiet on their walk home, Olivia was thinking over all the ways that she didn't seem to fit into her role at all. And all the ways she wanted to change that but didn't see how she could.

"But what about Olivia?" her aunt Bea said in a harsh whisper.

Olivia's ears perked up, and she was pulled out of her reverie. She strained to hear how her uncle Raymond would respond.

"She knows her place," he muttered back.

Aunt Bea looked back and caught Olivia's eye. The girl ducked her head, embarrassed to be caught eavesdropping as she slowed her steps to allow her guardians to get farther ahead.

He was right, though—Olivia did know her place. It had been deeply ingrained in her since she had first realized that they were not her parents. She had come to live with Uncle Raymond and Aunt Bea after her parents had died, not long after her first birthday. Of all the things that Olivia wished for, memories of her mother and father were at the top of the list. Instead, she had grown up as an extra, a leftover, a burden on her guardians, and she had been constantly reminded of that fact.

Olivia sighed. Whatever place that they wanted her to keep, they didn't have to worry. She was well used to her role in this household.

She made sure to stay behind them for the rest of their walk home. Not so far that she would be accused of dawdling, but not so close that she could eavesdrop on whatever they wanted to say about her. For the last two decades, she'd had to maintain this delicate balance. Olivia reminded herself that she was twenty years old now; she could take care of herself, and if she got married or had a way to support herself, she wouldn't need to acquiesce to her uncle's controlling ways.

But in the meantime, Olivia didn't know what else she could do. There was a small family trust that she was supposed to come into when she got married or when turned twenty-one, but she wasn't clear if it would be enough for her to live on. No one had told her anything. As far as Olivia knew, she didn't have any options at all.

When they reached MapleRose, the Drysdale family farm, Olivia was immediately given her instructions. She hadn't even hung up her coat and scarf before she was expected to attend to a task.

"Heat up that soup and take it up to Billy," Aunt Bea told her, pointing to the large, covered pot on the stove.

Olivia murmured her acquiescence and obeyed without further comment. She knew perfectly well that her cousin Billy had been faking being ill that morning to get out of having to go to church. It seemed far too convenient that he had been plenty well enough to go ice skating with Robert Grady and Gilbert Moore the previous evening, but then had suddenly become bedridden on Sunday morning.

But he was Raymond and Bea's only child, Olivia's only cousin, and the only heir to the once sizable Drysdale estate. It was no wonder he was coddled.

A few minutes later, Olivia was carefully balancing the full bowl of soup on the one serving tray the family owned and walking up the stairs. Billy's bedroom was the large, east-facing room under the eaves, far larger and more luxurious than any of his friends slept in, but then, Billy was far more spoiled than any of his friends were either. She gently knocked on the door before letting herself in and found her cousin sitting up in bed, reading yesterday's newspaper. He made to hide it under the covers as she entered but changed his mind when he saw who it was.

"Oh," he said. "Hello. You all back already?"

"I brought you some soup if you're hungry." Olivia crossed the room. She set the tray down on the seat of the wooden chair that sat next to the bed and stood behind it.

"Thanks." Billy turned back to the newspaper. "Did I miss anything good?"

Olivia's memory flashed to whatever her aunt and uncle had been discussing about her on the walk home, but she knew that Billy wouldn't care about that. "That traveling preacher Mr. Montgomery gave the sermon this morning."

"Oh yeah?" He seemed disinterested.

"He's quite..." She searched for the word she meant. "...captivating. Listening to some of the folks talk afterward, I think maybe he'll stick around for a week or two.

Everyone seemed to really like him. Probably through Christmas, I think."

"That's good." Billy still hadn't picked up his soup.

Olivia waited another long moment in silence, but her cousin seemed disinclined to conversation. "Well," she said as she took a half step toward the door, "I suppose I'll be up again later to collect the bowl."

He nodded, without looking at her, and she returned to the kitchen to help her aunt.

"Finally!" Bea exclaimed when Olivia entered the room. "I need those potatoes peeled. I only have two hands."

"I'm sorry, Aunt Bea. I'll take care of it now."

The two women worked in silence for a few minutes. Olivia preferred it that way—quiet allowed her to focus on her task. It wasn't long, however, before her aunt burst out with news she couldn't wait to tell Olivia.

"The mayor and his family are coming for supper tomorrow," Bea said as she continued shelling the beans. "You are to help cook and serve, of course, but you'll have to eat your portion in the kitchen."

She glanced at Olivia, as though checking how the girl would take the news without giving her too much attention.

Olivia merely nodded and kept peeling potatoes. If she looked at her aunt Bea, she would be furious, though she was also annoyed at herself for not expecting such a development. It was only by avoiding her aunt's eyes that Olivia was able to stay quiet, stay in this role that Providence had made for her.

"You understand, I'm sure," Bea continued. "The mayor's niece is visiting from Richmond, and we think she would be overwhelmed with too many young people at the table. Billy will be the ideal host, and he is part of the family, after all." She coughed as though choking on her own words. "Not that you are not part of the family, Olivia, but... well... as I said, I'm sure you understand."

Olivia didn't look at her aunt. She took a deep breath and went back to peeling potatoes. The two women continued working in silence. Olivia had stopped allowing herself to hope she would be included when they had guests. When she was twelve, the schoolmaster had come for supper; Billy had been so jealous of the attention his cousin had been shown. He acted as though the schoolmaster was his own very special friend, and Olivia was stealing him.

Though she had cried and protested that she hadn't done anything, other than being a better student than Billy, her aunt Bea had been infuriated that her beloved son had been so overlooked and hurt. Olivia had not been fed supper with the family for three days afterward, having to eat bread and a little meat by herself in the kitchen. Little by little, since that moment, Olivia had been treated more like a servant and less like a blood relative.

Her own relatives hadn't been the only ones to start shutting Olivia out. The other families in town had slowly gotten the message that the girl wasn't to be included. By the time she was eighteen, she was no longer invited to social events in Charlottesville.

This supper with the mayor was just one more example in a long list of ways Olivia had been made to stand on her own two feet outside the warmth of a loving family.

She was interrupted in her musings when the porch door slammed open.

Uncle Raymond entered the kitchen carrying an armful of firewood. "Did you hear the Markham place is for sale?"

"Is it?" Aunt Bea looked up from her vegetables. "Such a beautiful farm. It's a shame Mrs. Markham has to sell it."

"But since she does, it's too bad she didn't do this years ago. The whole place has gotten so rundown she won't be able to get a good price for it."

Olivia said nothing, but her heart soared. The Markham farm had always been the property she had most admired. Though it seemed impossible that she would be able to buy the farm with her meager savings or even her parents' trust, she let herself dream a little. Imagining being mistress of her own home. Imagining being out from under her uncle's controlling thumb. Imagining being able to take care of herself and not be a burden to anyone.

"Olivia!" her aunt called, pulling her out of her daydream. "That is quite enough, girl! What am I going to do with that many potatoes?"

The younger woman looked down at the pile of peeled potatoes in front of her. Indeed, she had kept working long past when she should have, and now some of this food would have to go to waste.

"I'll eat them," she told her aunt, blushing with the embarrassment of failing at this minor task. "I'm sorry."

Aunt Bea shook her head and huffed as she hurriedly gathered all the peeled potatoes into her largest pot.

"Just... go. I will fix this. I must do everything myself, it seems."

Olivia didn't have to be told twice. She could feel her uncle's eyes on her as she exited the kitchen out to the stairs, but she didn't look back. Sunday afternoons were the only time of the entire week that she had any time to herself. If her aunt didn't need her help with supper, Olivia could be perfectly happy alone, quiet, and daydreaming in her small bedroom upstairs.

CHAPTER TWO

The next morning, Olivia was up before the sun, carefully braiding and pinning up her heavy dark brown hair to stay out of her way for her long day of work. When she showed her face downstairs, she knew that her aunt would have a long list of chores for her. There would be all of her usual winter morning chores—from mucking out stalls to baking bread—along with any number of things Aunt Bea would come up with to ready the house for distinguished guests.

In as many years as Olivia had been living with the Drysdale family, never once had the mayor of Charlottesville consented to have dinner there. It was certainly tied to the mayor's young, beautiful niece visiting from Richmond. Uncle Raymond had made it clear long ago that he expected big things from his son, and marrying into such a powerful family seemed to fit. It was a momentous occasion, and there was no doubt that Olivia would be expected to make the place shine as though they were hosting royalty.

And no doubt that Billy would have virtually nothing expected of him.

Once her hair was in place, Olivia tied yesterday's apron over her gray dress and headed down to the kitchen to make herself useful. If she got her dough mixed first thing, they could have a fresh loaf of bread in time for dinner. Fortunately, and in spite of everything, Olivia enjoyed many of the chores that were expected of her. She resolved to do whatever her aunt needed and stay out of the way.

When Olivia was a child, Aunt Bea had been one of her favorite people. Her mother's sister, Aunt Bea was always ready to teach Olivia a new crocheting stitch or to make a special treat for her. Olivia was the only other person her aunt had to pass down family recipes and other traditions to.

"Just us girls," she would say as she pulled her niece close.

Aunt Bea had been the one to teach Olivia to cook, to sew, to find the joy in keeping a house running efficiently. For most of Olivia's childhood, she hadn't even realized that most other girls had mothers to teach them such things; Aunt Bea had been everything she needed. Aunt Bea had, of course, always coddled Billy, who was two years Olivia's senior. But as long as Olivia had been small, she hadn't been any kind of competition for Billy. She was loved.

Now, however, Olivia sometimes wondered if the Drysdales even remembered that she was related to them. As soon as Billy did get married, Olivia would be swiftly replaced in Aunt Bea's affection by his new wife. She couldn't pinpoint when the turning point had come, but she spent most of her time now simply trying to avoid attention.

"Finally!" Aunt Bea exclaimed when she saw Olivia walking halfway down the staircase. "We have no time to lose."

And, just as Olivia had predicted, for the next eight hours, she was on her feet, cleaning every nook and cranny of the old farmhouse, washing every plate, platter, and bowl in the house, helping prepare no fewer than four different dishes that would be served to the guests later—to say nothing of everything Aunt Bea was also doing.

It wasn't until well into the afternoon that she got a moment to herself. Olivia had been sent out to the front of the house with instructions to make the home presentable to anyone approaching from the road. She had already gathered sand to scrub a handful of grease stains off of the front steps and now was busy raking up the last of the fallen leaves from the stone walkway to the front door.

In spite of everything, she did enjoy the accomplished feeling of getting so much done. Olivia would sleep well that night, knowing that she had done good work and made good food that nourished another person's body. She was humming to herself and daydreaming about the old Markham home. Someday she would have a place like that, a place of her own. Someday this satisfaction of a job well done would be because she had tended to her own home, her own family. Her own future.

Olivia blew a loose strand of hair out of her eyes and redoubled her grip on the rake. The sun was almost set.

She needed to get the front yard as tidy as possible before she lost all the light. Their guests would be arriving shortly afterward, too, and Olivia still had to set the table before she shut herself away from curious eyes.

"Do you need help with that, miss?"

Olivia was startled into dropping the rake.

"Oh!" she gasped and looked up to see the traveling preacher, Mr. Montgomery, standing on the flagstone path leading up to the house.

This was closer than she had been to him at church the previous day—she hadn't realized how very blue his eyes were. She hadn't realized how young he was. He couldn't be more than a few years older than she was. He smiled kindly at her, his bright eyes twinkling under his black hair, as though they were sharing a joke just the two of them.

"I'm sorry," she responded, almost in a whisper. "I was supposed to be done with this before anyone arrived."

He chuckled as he checked his pocket watch. "Oh, I'm certainly early. I had nothing else planned this afternoon and thought I might see if I could be of any help."

He took a few steps forward to close the distance between them, stooped to pick up the rake where it had fallen in the grass. He held it awkwardly for a moment, as though unsure if he should be taking on the chore for her or giving the tool back. Olivia smiled and saved him.

"I'll take that," she said. "If Uncle Raymond looks out the window and sees you doing yard work, I'll never hear the end of it. Let me show you inside, and then I can finish."

Mr. Montgomery chuckled. "Yes, ma'am. Lead the way."

Olivia walked ahead of him to the front door. She opened it, called for her uncle, and made sure he had seen that a guest was standing in the doorway before she ducked out again. There was still so much to do, and now even less time than there had been before. She couldn't be caught dawdling, especially when she wasn't supposed to be meeting the guests in the first place.

The time until supper flew by. After the run-in with the pastor, Olivia hurried through the last of the raking, making sure to be hidden away in the kitchen before any of the rest of the guests appeared. The laughter and chatter from the mayor, his wife, his niece, and Pastor Montgomery floated through the door that stood slightly ajar. Everything was ready and waiting for supper to begin. All Olivia had to do was serve food, and then she could disappear again, away from the criticism and disappointed looks of her aunt and uncle.

She had a quiet moment to herself and stood leaning against the large worktable in the middle of the kitchen where five platters and giant bowls were waiting to be served. Taking a deep breath, Olivia closed her eyes and listened to the conversation that she was not a part of.

The guests all talked over each other; there seemed to be three conversations going on at the same time. Chairs scraped the wood floor as they were pulled out, and each person took their seat. It was a pleasant hubbub of social niceties that lulled her into a comfortable feeling.

She was jolted out of that when the pastor's voice cut through the crowd.

"What about the young woman I met as I came in?" Mr. Montgomery said. "Is she not a member of this family?"

She stood upright again and crossed the room to the door.

Olivia couldn't see her aunt and uncle from where she perched on the other side of the doorway, but the stark silence that fell over the room was telling. She could imagine the frantic or desperate expressions flitting across Uncle Raymond's face, even as he tried to hide them. Now that each person was seated, she was supposed to bring in the biscuits, fresh out of the oven, but she knew if she did, it could go very badly. She would be drawing attention to the fact that she was in the house and not invited to sit at the table.

"Young woman?" Uncle Raymond said, clearing his throat. He seemed to be stalling for time. "I'm not sure..."

"The young woman who was raking up the leaves and sticks and things at your front gate. I stopped to help her, and I'm embarrassed to say I don't believe I caught her name. Surely you must know who I'm referring to."

Olivia peeked through the small gap in the door and watched the pastor look from one face to another, the earnestness in his expression unmistakable.

Billy snickered.

Uncle Raymond glared at his son, but his shoulders dropped dejectedly. He seemed to know he wouldn't be able to come up with a convincing lie, seeing as the other man had already met Olivia.

"Oh." He cleared his throat. "Yes. My niece. Olivia. She's..." He looked to his wife.

"She was just about to bring in the biscuits," Aunt Bea said, her voice louder at the end of the sentence to be sure the young woman heard her in the other room.

Olivia felt cold all over, shocked that she was actually being invited to come into the room with the mayor and his family and this new traveling preacher. But her aunt was right. She was just about to bring in the biscuits, and it wouldn't do any good to pretend otherwise. They were getting cold as she procrastinated. Catching up the platter, she tucked a strand of hair behind her ear and took a deep breath. Squaring her shoulders, she entered the dining room, carrying the food to the guests as she was expected to.

"Finally!" Uncle Raymond exclaimed, as though he hadn't just almost denied her existence.

Olivia smiled at the group sitting around the table and set the dish on the end near her aunt, where a space had been cleared. She had intended to then make her exit and go back to the kitchen, leaving the Drysdales with their guests, but she hesitated. Not long. Not obviously. But just enough for Mr. Montgomery to be able to speak up on her behalf.

"But, Mrs. Drysdale, forgive me. I must be quite dull to miss it, but I don't see a chair or place setting for this young lady."

Olivia couldn't bring herself to look at the traveling pastor even as he stood up for her honor. It had been so long since she had eaten with guests that she almost couldn't remember how to behave. Should she make her excuses?

There was an awkward moment of silence as all the guests looked to her aunt Bea to take care of the situation. The older woman turned a bright red, and her mouth spread wide in a forced smile.

"Oh, heavens," she said brightly. "I don't know how we missed it. Must have slipped my mind. Billy, why don't you go out to the sitting room and grab that extra chair. We can fit in another place setting right here next to Mr. Montgomery."

Olivia's mouth hung open in shock, but her surprise was nothing compared to how Billy must have been feeling. His frown grew more and more pronounced as the realization that he was being asked to wait on his cousin became confirmed.

"But, Mother—"

"Go, boy," Uncle Raymond commanded, bitterly.

Olivia didn't dare look at her uncle. Instead, she murmured an excuse to go back to the kitchen to retrieve another dish. She dawdled as long as she thought she could get away with before finally returning to sit at the table with the family and their guests.

By the time she had finished bringing in all of the food, Aunt Bea had maneuvered all the rest of the pieces in place so Olivia had a spot to eat supper with them. She didn't dare say a word throughout the meal, but she didn't need to say anything to see how Pastor Montgomery kept looking at her.

CHAPTER THREE

Pastor Luke Montgomery must have seen something in the quiet young woman that he liked. He came calling for Olivia the following day, and the one after that, and the one after that. In between his visits to other members of the congregation, he continued to make time for Olivia. Though Uncle Raymond had at first tried to stop her—to manufacture another chore or excuse—even he wasn't able to refuse the pastor what he asked.

At first, their time together felt forced and awkward. He was so earnest in his interest in her that it overwhelmed Olivia. She had to learn to get used to attention all over again. He seemed to never tire of asking her questions about herself, her childhood, her hopes. Olivia had never been good at small talk and the inanities that most of their neighbors indulged in; somehow, having Mr. Montgomery immediately assume an intimacy felt more welcome than indelicate. It took the pressure off of her.

Olivia treasured every moment she spent with this man. Not only was he one of the few people who had ever shown her attention, but he was kind and charming along with it. She didn't ask for much, but Mr. Montgomery more than delivered.

"And what will you do with this windfall when you do turn twenty-one?" he asked her one evening in the second week of their acquaintance. He had come to call after supper, and they were now taking a walk through the Drysdale orchard.

"Well, I ..." she demurred. The fact of her waiting trust had somehow slipped out. She couldn't recall ever revealing such a personal detail to anyone else before.

"Go on." He nudged her shoulder gently with his own.

Olivia grinned.

"I admit, I have been thinking about it more recently. My birthday is just a few months away. Of course, I'll also get it if I get married first, but that has not even been a remote possibility yet, so I had no thought of it."

"But, you have thought about what you would like to do with the money?"

She nodded. "There's this house— I... Well, I've lived with my aunt and uncle since I was a baby when my parents died. I wasn't old enough to really remember the home I had with them, but I like to imagine it. Living here, I have never really felt like I belonged.

"I guess I just... I want a home," she continued. "There's a house that we pass by occasionally that always makes me feel so happy when I visited. Mr. Markham died, and it sounds like Mrs. Markham will be selling the farm soon, and I would just... She was my Sunday School teacher a few years ago. She always made me feel safe and welcome, and I just love that home so much."

"So, you'd spend your money to buy a farm?" His tone made it sound so easy, so matter-of-fact.

Olivia glanced at him. "I think so. Yes. I want a home," she repeated with a self-conscious shrug.

Luke smiled at her, and Olivia could feel herself blushing. In that smile, she could see his compassion, his support for her dream, his wanting her to feel safe to tell him the truth. She opened her mouth to speak again but didn't know what to say. Instead, it was enough to just walk at sunset with him.

Putting her desire into words like that had spurred Olivia's imagination. Soon, she couldn't go more than an hour or so without dreaming about what it would be like to be mistress of her own kitchen, make her own choices about who came to supper, or what vegetables she planted in the spring.

Though she told herself over and over it was likely not enough for the dream she was building, Olivia resolved to ask her aunt about the details of her trust. Exactly how much money was waiting for her when she turned twenty-one. If it was enough, or close, maybe she could talk Mrs. Markham into waiting a few months to sell the house to her.

These plans and possibilities consumed her until she found the right moment to broach the subject.

The men were out repairing the fence between the Drysdale farm and the Barrys' farm. Olivia and Aunt Bea were in the sitting room, each working on a piece of sewing while they stayed warm by the fire.

Olivia had been watching her aunt for the previous half-hour, waiting until she seemed most relaxed and open to what might be a distressing conversation. Finally, she could wait no longer.

"Aunt Bea," Olivia said, getting her aunt's attention. She set her quilt square aside and crossed the room in a few long strides to sit next to her aunt on the sofa. The look of surprise on Bea's face was unmistakable, but Olivia pressed on. "I'm not sure if you remember, but my birthday is in just a few months. My twenty-first birthday. I'd like to be able to start making plans, and I wonder if you can tell me how much money is in the trust my parents left for me."

Aunt Bea paled and looked away.

"Oh, goodness," she said. "I really couldn't say. I'll have to check with Mr. Pendleton at the bank."

"I see," Olivia said, though she couldn't pretend she hadn't noticed her aunt's expression. "I am remembering correctly, aren't I? It's my twenty-first birthday when the proceeds are transferred to me?"

"Yes, dear, yes." Bea was busying herself inspecting a non-existent speck of dust on the arm of the sofa. "Or if you get married before then, of course. Your father wanted to..." Her voice broke, and she trailed off, then cleared her throat.

The two women sat in silence; Bea turned away from her niece as Olivia's heart pounded faster.

"What?" she asked, almost a whisper.

There was a short beat of silence before Aunt Bea finally turned to look at her.

"I..." She closed her mouth as though stopping herself from continuing.

Olivia didn't know what to say. She didn't even know what question to ask. Instead, she simply waited.

"There is..." Bea cleared her throat. "There was a provision as part of the trust that your guardian could use the funds for your upbringing. That we could borrow from the balance as long as you still lived in our care."

Olivia could guess where this was going. She felt her face flush in anger.

"You know when we rebuilt the barn a few years ago... Your Uncle Ray went to the bank for a loan, but Mr. Pendleton pointed out that we could use the money in the account from your parents."

"My money?" Olivia clarified. "Mr. Pendleton said it was all right if you used *my* money?"

"Well, you understand, of course, that we wouldn't have ever if he hadn't... that is, we thought he was most knowledgeable... so we... Well, in point of fact, we borrowed the money from your trust. A little at a time, here and there over the years, to improve the property. Which you have also benefitted from, of course."

She looked as though she were expecting Olivia to agree, but the young woman was too furious to trust herself to speak. How could they possibly think that *she* had benefitted from the barn getting a new roof?

"And so," Aunt Bea concluded, "at the moment..." She cleared her throat. "There is not currently any balance left in the trust, but I know your uncle is planning on paying back every penny just as soon as he is able."

Angry tears ran down Olivia's cheeks faster than she could wipe them away.

She had nothing. Everything had been taken from her. All Olivia had wanted was to be able to live her own life, and now that one narrow option had been stripped from her.

As Aunt Bea made this claim, she reached for Olivia's hand, touching her in kindness and compassion for the first time in the girl didn't know how long. But it was like her skin was burning. To be so used. To be so betrayed like this. Olivia wasn't going to try to assuage her aunt's feelings.

She stood up.

"Olivia—"

"No." Olivia cut her off in a harsh tone. "You..."

But she couldn't say it. She couldn't tell her aunt that she'd ruined her life. That she'd destroyed the one small piece of hope she'd had. Olivia looked down at where Aunt Bea still sat, pleading with her eyes to be forgiven, though she hadn't even yet apologized.

She took a deep, steadying breath and wiped the tears from her face.

Olivia's strength and her anger carried her out of the room, out of the house, down the front path, and into the grass before she froze. Her hands shook, but she pushed away her heartbreak. It would do no good to cry over the loss of her dreams, her promised independence, and her very sense of self.

She was stuck. She would be the Drysdales' maid forever.

CHAPTER FOUR

Olivia barely held herself together, taking deep, anguished breaths to calm her pain and fury. Only moments earlier, she had learned that everything she had pinned her hopes on was gone. She had no idea what she should do next.

In this lost state, she heard footsteps approaching. Olivia looked up, hastily climbing to her feet from where she had kneeled in the grass, smoothing out the skirt of her dress and wiping the tears from her face as best she could all at the same time. Clenching her fists to keep her hands from shaking, Olivia tried to put the news of her loss from her mind.

But when she saw who it was that had come visiting, she almost ran back inside rather than speak to him. There was a brief moment where she still had the choice, but something inside her told her to stay. She couldn't say for sure why she thought this, but Olivia felt certain that this man would understand, that this man would let her be vulnerable and admit how hurt she had been.

It was part of his job as a pastor, after all.

She opened her mouth to greet him, but he spoke first, saving her the effort of false cheer.

"Why, Miss Greenwood," Luke Montgomery said, hurrying to her side, "you are upset! It pains me to see that you've been crying. What is it? How can I help?"

At that, she burst into tears again, in spite of all her efforts to tamp down her stronger emotions.

"Let's..." He looked around as he took her arm to lead her away. "Let's go inside."

"No!"

"No? All right."

She was grateful he didn't question it.

"Then let's go to the pond, to that log you showed me that is just perfect for watching the water."

Olivia nodded and let herself be led. Away from her aunt and uncle, and in the quiet of one of her favorite places was the best option at this moment. The pond was a short walk away, on the border between the Drysdales' property and the Barrys'. The two new friends spent it in silence. She kept her head down, watching where she stepped, but she could feel the man's eyes on her. He kept glancing to the side occasionally as though assessing her state of mind.

She knew he wouldn't press her if she didn't want to talk about it, but... maybe she did want to. Olivia tried to imagine how this man of the cloth would react to her being so upset about losing mere material possessions, wondering if he would truly understand.

They reached the log that sat near the eastern side of

the small pond, where they had before spent many hours talking about their lives and becoming better friends. Where better for Olivia to reveal her greatest vulnerability?

"Now, then," he began as they took their seats. Olivia still couldn't look at him. Instead, she watched a heron that had landed in the shallows along the far shore. "I'm sorry you're so upset, Miss Greenwood. Is there anything I can do?"

She shook her head.

"I'm rather good at listening," he prompted gently.

Olivia sighed. She looked at him and tried to keep her voice steady.

"I received some distressing news." She cleared her throat and tried to sit up straighter. "I... When my parents passed, our family home was sold, and the little money they had saved was all put in a trust for me. I was to receive that sum when I turned twenty-one, or when I married."

"I see..." He nodded, waiting for more.

"I..." Her voice cracked, but she pressed on. "My aunt and uncle... They took it. They spent it." Olivia was barely louder than a whisper now. "Aunt Bea says the bank manager suggested that they borrow from my sum when they needed money over the last few years, but... they've not been able to pay back a penny of it."

"Oh, no... Miss Greenwood," he murmured.

"I have nothing." Tears spilled down her cheeks. "I've lost my only hope at a life for myself," she said through her tears.

She hung her head, looking intently at her hands in

her own lap and trying to make herself as small as possible.

He was silent after that, and she dared not look at him. Quieting her sobs was her priority. She was so ashamed; how frivolous he must think her, to have set such a store on mere money. Surely a man of God like he was didn't care so much about physical comforts like having her own kitchen and not having to do chores for her aunt. Why, now that she thought about it, Mr. Montgomery must think her very un-Christian to not want to serve others forever like she had been doing.

Olivia's face burned. Her sobs overtook her, and she dropped her head to her lap, wishing she could curl up into a little ball of shame and disappear.

"I'm sorry," he said gently. "I won't tell you I understand completely, but there is a small part of me that empathizes. I haven't ever had the kind of security or home you're talking about, so I can't imagine what it must be like to lose it."

Olivia nodded. She sat up straight again and took deep breaths, filling her lungs with cleansing air. Just knowing that he didn't think her foolish helped her feel better about the whole situation, though she still couldn't meet his eyes.

"I just... I don't know what to do now," she said helplessly. "I know it sounds like I'm complaining. I probably am. But I have endured much over these last several years, not only losing my parents. This money... I know, it's only money. It can't solve all my problems. But it was something... This money was—"

"It was a chance," he finished for her.

"A chance. Yes. That's exactly it." Olivia nodded

vigorously. "It was a *chance* to make my own way and my own life. It was a chance to start over fresh. To be on my own and not be a burden to anyone else. It was exactly what I needed after living on my aunt and uncle's charity almost my whole life. And now I... I guess I'm just stuck. Living on my relatives' pity until... Until I die."

Much of the pain must have left her tone because he softly chuckled at her hyperbole. She smiled. Just being understood had helped her feel better.

"Well, let's hope that you don't go seeking out that escape," he teased. Luke gently nudged her shoulder with his. "What would you like to do? If you had the money. What would be your first choice?"

She took a deep breath. "I would buy the Markham farm. And I would figure out a way to support myself on it. Even as I say that I know it's... I know how difficult that would be. Maybe it's for the best that the money is gone. It forces me to find a more realistic option."

"Don't say that. Don't ever say that. After all, technically, the money is still owed, right? Maybe you'll see it again one day."

"Maybe."

"But what I'm hearing—and maybe I'm wrong—is that you want ... freedom. You want to escape. You want a different life than the one that has been dealt you here in Charlottesville."

"Yes," she replied with a sigh. "That's exactly it. I want independence."

"Well..."

He took her hand. Olivia looked at him, startled but happier than she had been in days. If not weeks.

"Olivia..."

He had never before used her Christian name. Her heart beat frantically in fear and in hope of what such an intimacy foretold.

"My heart breaks that you have been so hurt. I'm sorry that I cannot offer you the money and inheritance that has been lost. I cannot promise you that everything will always be comfortable or easy or even happy. But what I can do is promise to protect you. I promise to give you a fresh start, and I promise to do everything in my power to help you have the life that you love."

Olivia was speechless, her heart hammering in her chest. This was so far beyond what she imagined when she had seen him crossing the grass to her that afternoon.

"Olivia Greenwood," he said, offering her that same kind, intimate smile he had the day they met, "please do me the honor of becoming my wife. Of spending your life with me. Of letting me give you the freedom you so deserve."

She almost laughed in relief. Here was a lifeline. Though she had not thought to look for a second chance in a marriage to a man she had only known a couple weeks, it seemed that she had found the best option possible, given all her circumstances. She took a deep breath and stepped bravely into her unknown future.

"Of course. Mr. Montgomery—Luke... yes. I will."

"Thank you," he whispered as he cupped her cheek.

Olivia felt a tingle at his touch, a jolt through her entire body. This was the man that she would spend the rest of her life with. She closed her eyes in contentment as he leaned forward and kissed her.

CHAPTER FIVE

After she said yes, everything else happened quickly. Family was informed. Dates were set. Plans were made. Olivia wanted to be married—and free of her relatives—as soon as possible.

Luke and Olivia Montgomery's wedding was a small affair. The groom didn't have any family nearby. He had one much older sister in Vermont that he had not seen in years and told Olivia he would send her the news in his next letter. Any guests they would invite would be the local families. Through the month that Luke had been preaching in Charlottesville, he had won the affection of many families—especially the matrons—of the community. Uncle Raymond and Aunt Bea didn't contribute more than a pie to the newlyweds' supper, but the other families of the church more than made up for it.

Consequently, the young pair found themselves at their wedding dinner on a Thursday afternoon populated by a dozen families that Luke knew better than Olivia did, despite the fact that she had grown up in this church. Pastor Lyons and his family were there. Mrs. Lyons had arranged for the women in attendance to bring a dish or three to feed all the guests. For perhaps the first time since Olivia could remember, she hadn't had to lift a finger and was given a seat of honor near the head of the table that groaned under the generous feast from their neighbors.

All three of the Drysdales were there, but Olivia felt as though they were avoiding her. She kept feeling someone's eyes on her, watching as she mingled with her guests after the ceremony. But whenever Olivia checked, Aunt Bea seemed to look away immediately. She told herself that they felt guilty about how they had let her down, spending her money, and not supporting her marriage. Though she couldn't quite believe that was true, she kept thinking back to their initial reception of the news of Olivia's engagement.

After the two young people had officially become betrothed, there had been about half a day of anxiety as they wrestled with the unknown. Olivia always felt more secure when she knew what to expect. But when they had returned to MapleRose hand in hand to tell her uncle and aunt about their upcoming marriage, everything she had subconsciously counted on disappeared. There was no joy, no hugs, no promises from either of her guardians. Instead, Aunt Bea looked to her husband for how to react to the news that their niece would be marrying and leaving them. He had merely nodded, shaken Luke's hand, and left, making an excuse of some horseshoe that needed replacing.

After Aunt Bea had remained conspicuously quiet

about wedding plans, Olivia had plunged into a maelstrom of stress. Where would they get married? How would she be able to do everything that needed doing all by herself? This was no way to start married life together. Luke merely kissed her hand and promised he would take care of it. By the end of that first night, he had secured an invitation from Mrs. Markham to host their wedding meal at her home.

Now that everyone in town who loved Luke was gathered together to support them, Olivia could breathe again. Spending this most important day in a place where she had such fond memories had turned out to be the best after all. Far better, in fact, than if they had married in the home where Olivia had had such an unhappy childhood. It had been so thoughtful of Luke to manage it, and she was grateful to start out their life together so happily.

It hurt Olivia to know that this might be the last time she got to be in the house that had meant so much to her—goodness knew her husband didn't have the money to purchase it, and it would soon be in the hands of a stranger. In spite of that impending loss, however, she walked through the rooms slowly, talking to her guests, thanking them for their generosity, and reveled in the promise of her own new home that seemed just around the bend in the road.

Olivia looked around at her wedding guests and sighed. She missed her parents. She regretted that she hadn't ever made the kind of bosom friend that she would have wanted by her side on this important day. So much of her life to this point had been spent alone.

Now, though, she had her new husband and the potential of a new family.

It wasn't the same, but it had to be enough.

Olivia put the thoughts from her mind. There was no point in mourning what she had never had and never would have. Better to focus on what was right in front of her.

Across the room, Luke Montgomery—her husband—stood listening attentively to Mrs. Markham. The older woman gestured wildly with her hands, as she always did when telling a story. The look of patient compassion on Luke's face made Olivia smile. This was a good man. This was a man she could build a future with.

After a few hours, before they got too tired, the newly married couple made their way out of the throng of well-wishers to where the horse-drawn sleigh sat waiting for them. The mayor of Charlottesville—a friend of Luke's since that first supper at the Drysdales'—had sent his driver to take the couple to where they would spend their first night together. He was one of Luke's biggest supporters in Charlottesville, after all, and took great pride in lavishly gifting them on this day.

Luke had told Olivia many times that he would take care of everything they needed as soon as they were truly married, and that included where they would spend their first night together. He resisted all attempts at prying out information and merely smiled mischievously when she tried to guess where they were going.

"You would not believe me if I told you," he murmured in her ear. "All our friends who helped with our wedding dinner have also helped with this. Trust me, Livvy. You deserve all the niceties in life, and I intend you should have them."

It wasn't until the sleigh slowed to a stop in front of the largest, fanciest hotel in town that Olivia actually believed him.

Though Olivia had driven by the Rivanna Hotel many times, she had never dreamed that she would stay there, if only for one night. Her eyes were starry as she clung to her husband and looked all around the lobby at the immeasurable luxury that surrounded them.

When the two were shown to their bedchamber for the night, Olivia had thought she would be shy. What would Luke expect of her? But he immediately put her at ease, casually and matter-of-factly talking excitedly about their day as he ordered them hot water and towels.

Olivia sat at the vanity, unsure of how to approach this luxury that she had never seen before in her life. What kind of woman had such comforts in their bed chambers? She smiled, satisfied, at her reflection in the mirror as she undid the clasp of her necklace.

"Well, it's probably best that this was a small affair," Luke said as he took off his coat and hung it in the wardrobe. "We'll be hitting the road again soon, and the less we have to travel with, the better."

Olivia felt like her stomach had dropped into her shoes. She paused while taking the combs from her hair.

"Hitting the road again?" She tried to make her voice sound normal, but she was shocked. Though she knew how he made his living, she hadn't thought to be torn from what was familiar to her quite so quickly.

"Yes. I'm not sure there's much sense in us staying here any longer." He seemed completely unaware that she was panicking inwardly. "I'm thinking we'll start making our way west. Maybe stop in Waynesboro. Go all the way to Kentucky? I don't know."

"West."

"But actually..." He had removed his shoes and pulled down his suspenders. "Now that we're talking about it in earnest, I had an idea that I'm leaning toward."

"An idea." Olivia was far too stunned to do more than just repeat what her husband—her husband! She was now tied to this man—was saying.

"Being on the road for so long is starting to wear on me. And seeing as I have a wife now, and maybe a family soon, I've been thinking about where the best place for us might be to settle down where I can plant a church."

"Plant a church?"

He seemed finally to notice then how wooden his wife was.

"Olivia?"

He sat on the edge of the bed next to her and leaned forward on his elbows.

"Are you okay?"

She turned to him, smile wide, hoping she could make up for the lack of sincerity. "Yes. Yes, thank you. But... I didn't... That is, are we really leaving so soon? For some reason, I thought..." She gestured helplessly, praying that he would interpret in her silence the mountain of questions and objections and thoughts that were whirling through her mind.

"Well, yes. One of the things I've learned over my years doing this work is to leave a place before I've overstayed my welcome." He smiled at her, tenderly, as though she were a child who needed things explained to her simply. "I probably would have left Charlottesville already if I hadn't met you. But now I have you by my side, to go with me into the world, to help in my fight against the powers of darkness."

Olivia nodded numbly. What else could she do? He was right that she should have known. Why had she thought that when she told him her dream of a home, he would take that to mean giving up his own dreams?

"What do you think about Oregon?"

That word jolted Olivia back to sense. "Oregon?" Her alarm was apparent.

Luke nodded and pulled her hand to his lips. He turned it over, pressing a kiss to the inside of her wrist as he whispered. "We can have anything we want in Oregon. We can plant a church where we can lead people to the Lord for years. There can't be many pastors making the journey; we could find land and build the home you've dreamed of."

"Oregon," she repeated, still stunned.

"Oregon!" He laughed as the joy bubbled up inside him. "The Oregon Territory, my love. Just think. Away from any disappointments or bad memories you have in this place, to a territory where a family like ours can really find all the resources we need to succeed. Of course, it won't be without its hardships. The trip is at least four months long, and we'll have to do without a lot of the luxuries we've become used to. But all in all, this could be exactly the new beginning we both deserve."

"How long have you been thinking about this?" He

seemed to know an awful lot about it, considering this was the first time she had heard about this plan.

"Not long. Maybe only a year"—her eyes widened—"but I never really felt like I had what it took to take that risk until I met you."

"But—"

"Of course, if you want to stay here in the states, we can. But we'll have to keep on as I have been doing. I make my living going from church to church, Olivia. I will take care of you, but you will have to understand there are limitations to such a nomadic life."

"Yes, I can imagine."

"But if we take the chance... if we emigrate to the territories, we won't have to travel ever again. You can have the home you've wanted. A garden. A community. A place for our children to grow up."

She took a deep breath.

"So," he continued, "will you do it? Will you join me on this adventure and travel to Oregon to plant a church and build our home?"

"I... I suppose."

What else could she say? What choice did she have?

CHAPTER SIX

Now in late March, Olivia Montgomery stood alone at the edge of the street and held up the hem of her dress, so it didn't drag in the thick mud. Springtime in Independence, Missouri, meant two things: torrential rain and immense crowds of pioneers heading to Oregon.

She and Luke were finalizing the last of their plans before they, too, jumped off from this frontier town into the wilds of the west. With only a couple of days left to prepare, Olivia had been tasked with visiting Hancock's General Store to confirm that everything they had ordered was ready and to pay for the delivery of the order. Once that was done, they could pack their wagon and prepare to leave. Luke was finding a wagon train to link up with, in hopes that they could start their journey west by the end of the week.

They had been in Missouri for four weeks already, getting their wagon built and collecting supplies. Though Olivia was ready for this stay to be over, she certainly didn't feel prepared to continue on to the next part. Maybe she would never feel prepared for it. Everything was so far away from what she had grown up with and was used to. Every day was a new challenge, even getting this far.

For three months, she had traveled west with her husband, moving from town to town, stopping only long enough for the pastor to make enough money to push them the next leg of the journey. Olivia felt dizzy by how fast he could charm, make friends, and request donations before leaving them again and forgetting all about those people. The first time it had occurred, she had been shocked to hear Luke describe his dismissal of previous congregations as merely a way to protect himself.

"I likely will never see them again," he had explained. "I need to leave room in my head and in my heart for those that will be investing in our lives for the long haul."

Maybe it was because Olivia had such precious few friends of her own that the idea of deliberately forgetting someone felt so foreign to her. As it was, she wasn't sure anyone in Charlottesville would miss her now that she was gone. In fact, Pastor Montgomery was far more likely to be missed than his wife.

There was one consolation Olivia could take—her aunt Bea had tried to repair their relationship before Olivia left.

"I know this doesn't make up for all of it, and it's certainly not what you were expecting to get upon your marriage," Aunt Bea had begun, "but I have a gift for you."

Olivia and Luke had made one last stop to the Drysdales' on the morning they left town. Luke was preoccupied with Uncle Raymond, and Aunt Bea guided Olivia to come stand behind their wagon with her, out of sight of the men.

Aunt Bea directed her attention to the bundle in her hands. A thick towel had been wrapped around something that seemed heavy, and she cradled it as though it was a beloved child. After looking around the corner of the wagon, Bea turned back to her niece and lifted the edge of the towel to show it had been wrapped around her large cast iron pan. The one pan that they used when cooking virtually every single meal for as long as Olivia could remember. This pan was more than essential to the family—it was a treasure.

"What is this?" Olivia asked, bewildered.

"I want you to have this. My mother gave it to me on my wedding day, and I thought... well, we know Billy won't care. And I don't have anything else that will—That is, I know it won't make up for anything."

"You said that already," Olivia said quietly.

"I'm sorry," Aunt Bea whispered, forcing the bundle into Olivia's hands. "You can use this. It will be ideal for your journey. Please. Take it."

Olivia didn't respond, but she tucked the pan into the wagon before they left. She would have to mull over what she thought about this attempt to buy her forgiveness.

Now that she was in Missouri, the last bastion of civilization before the Pacific Ocean, Olivia was grateful for that heavy pan. Luke had looked askance at it, muttering about the weight on the wagon, but in the end, he acknowledged that they would need something to cook in, and a pan they already owned was far preferable to spending money on one.

Olivia stepped out of the muddy street into the doorway of Hancock's General Store. The crowd here, on the very edge of the states, was far bigger and far busier than she would have expected. Luke kept reminding her that this was the most popular launching point, during the time of year when it made the most sense to go. If there was a crowd to be found west of the Mississippi, it would be in Independence, Missouri.

Still, she kept her head up, eyes ahead, looking for anyone who might resemble the "Mr. Hancock" she was supposed to be meeting to confirm her husband's order. Olivia kept the cash she would need for the purchase inside her reticule, which she clutched with one hand, and held her hem up off the dirty floor with the other. Though she had to wade between families and ill-washed men to reach the counter, Olivia finally found someone who at least appeared to work at the store.

"Mr. Hancock?" she asked timidly.

"That I am," the man replied heartily as he turned toward her. He was a short, round man with a face like a moon and arms like cannons. The broad smile that flashed at her from under his blond-gray mustache put Olivia at ease. "What can I do for you, Missus...?"

"Mrs. Montgomery. I'm here to take care of our order of supplies and food for Oregon while my husband sees to the wagon."

"Yes! Of course!" He clapped his hands once in excitement. "Your husband was a great pleasure when he was in the other day. I told him, 'Pastor Montgomery, you just see if ol' Hancock doesn't find you everything your heart desires,' I said."

"That's very kind of you," she responded with a small smile.

He came around the counter and beckoned to her to follow him into the storage at the back of the shop. There was a wide double door, propped open, and more piles and stacks of supplies in the room beyond. From where she stood in the doorway, Olivia noticed a single scrawny young man, maybe not older than sixteen, consulting a list as he counted the bags of something in front of him.

"Over here," Mr. Hancock indicated, leading Olivia to the corner.

At first glance, it seemed like an enormous mountain of food. Olivia's mouth dropped open in surprise. Flour, beans, dried apples, cornmeal, sugar, coffee. Rope, tools, blankets, ammunition. And so much more. She had taken for granted that such things had always be available, but now they had to transport their entire supply of everything they needed for the next six months.

At that thought, Olivia took a step closer and began to count the items, rather than be overwhelmed by the volume. She didn't get very far before she frowned.

"I thought... didn't my husband order several hundred pounds of flour? I count only... This seems to fall short of that, doesn't it? And the dried apples as well. There should be more of the beans... The rice..." She counted again, then consulted the list she had grasped in her fist, flustered. "I believe there should be more rope, too. Mr. Hancock, is this maybe not our order? The Montgomerys. Maybe you can check again?"

She noticed what seemed to be a flash of anger cross his face before it disappeared to be replaced by his wide welcoming smile. "Oh, no, this is for the Montgomery family. No question. Maybe your husband just didn't tell me as many as he claimed to tell you."

Olivia blinked at him in surprise. "Are... Are you accusing a pastor of lying to his wife?"

"No, of course not, Mrs. Montgomery. No. I just wonder if maybe you are mistaken about how much food he ordered. Even this pile comes to quite a bit of money. Maybe he didn't have the funds for what he told you."

She felt her face flush at the implication but held her tongue. After all, it was true that they had been living virtually hand-to-mouth since their wedding day. That night in the Charlottesville hotel was the last night of luxury she may ever have again.

"Well, maybe," she allowed. Then something caught her eye, and she crouched down, letting the hem of her dress hit the dust so she could take a closer look. "Is that...? Mr. Hancock, I do believe this bacon is already starting to rot! I will not be paying for food that we cannot eat."

He looked closer alongside her and grumbled. "Yes, all right. I see that. I'll replace it."

"And the rest of my missing goods?"

"The truth is, Mrs. Montgomery, that prices have changed since your husband originally placed your order. The food you see before you," he gestured carelessly, "will cost what I quoted him. If you have more than that, I'm happy to add what stores I have to your order."

Olivia looked down at the reticule still clutched in her hand. Though she didn't know exactly what their financial resources were, she had enough of an idea to not commit to anything beyond what she had with her.

Again, she wished her uncle hadn't been so quick to "borrow" from her account. It wouldn't be the last time she regretted that.

She had a decision to make here and now, given what she had and what she knew—which wasn't much.

After heaving a deep sigh, Olivia said, "All right. Thank you, Mr. Hancock. Let's settle this order now, and I'll speak to Mr. Montgomery about if we need to supplement it at all before we leave for Oregon."

"Wonderful." He rubbed his hands together. "Mind you don't wait, though, Missy. Prices are going up all the time. More folk that are here to buy, the less supplies we have to sell."

"I understand."

She let herself be led back to the sales counter, where she handed over her dollars and provided Mr. Hancock with the address to deliver the food and supplies that would have to last the Montgomerys through the entire summer. In exchange, he handed her a receipt, detailing precisely what she had purchased. Olivia made a mental note to compare the two lists with Luke when she returned to their room. If they were going to find themselves short of coffee or beans at the end of July, she needed to know now.

As she stepped out of the store back into the muddy street, Olivia forced herself to ignore her dread, to shut off her feelings of uncertainty and anxiety.

There were things to do, and emotions about it wouldn't help anyone.

CHAPTER SEVEN

In spite of how crowded the town of Independence was this time of year, Luke and Olivia Montgomery had managed to retain a private room for just the two of them. The pastor had joked about it being their miracle, a sign that God approved of their plan to plant a church in the Oregon Territory. Through their encounters with other soon-to-be emigrants, Olivia had learned that many of the families staying in town, waiting weeks for their wagons to be built, had been split up, crammed into sleeping quarters with strangers. Fathers and sons offered a mat on the floor wherever there was room; mothers and daughters sharing a bed in the same room as other women.

Through luck or guilt or generosity, it usually happened that once Luke mentioned he was a pastor, their prospective landlady seemed to free up an entire room just for the two of them. Here in Independence, their quarters could barely be called a room—there was space for a narrow bed and a tiny washstand and nothing more. But it was certainly better than sharing any space with strangers.

After leaving the general store, Olivia made her way back to that boarding house. She was to meet her husband there in time to have supper together and go over the final plans they had to make to be ready to leave town.

The boarding house, however, was several blocks outside the center of town. That was the price they had to pay, she supposed, for the luxury of getting a private room. On her way back, Olivia had a chance to watch and observe the strange cross-section of people who had somehow found their way to this small frontier town in the middle of North America.

There were the big families, small children dawdling and following behind the parents. Mothers seemed harried and overwhelmed; fathers seemed focused on the next step.

There were the gangs of single men—brothers or friends who had banded together to seek new fortunes in the west. Without any hope of inheritance from the family, many men had no better choice than to start over completely in a place where white men were scarce.

There were also the natives, clad in leather and hung with feathers and beads. Olivia tried not to stare when two bronze-colored men with long black hair passed her. She had never seen a member of an Indian tribe before they got west of Tennessee. She tried not to show them she was scared, and so she averted her eyes rather than look.

All this and so many more: women with skin the color of acorns with baskets looped over their arms, following after a white woman who was likely their master, teenage boys dirty and tanned from months outdoors driving teams of oxen and mules down the middle of the street, vendors yelling at passersby to come to look at their wares.

It was a lot for Olivia to take in. They had been in Independence for weeks already, and she still felt like she had so much to learn and see. Her walks to and from the main street were both exhausting and exhilarating in her exposure to so many new people. Charlottesville had never been such a hubbub as this.

When she arrived at Mrs. Case's boarding house, Olivia spent several minutes trying to scrape as much of the mud from her boots as she could. It wouldn't do to make any more of a mess than she absolutely had to, not when the woman was so kind to them. Olivia knew what it was to have to track down all the muddy footsteps that somehow got throughout a house. Billy Drysdale had probably never scraped off the sole of his shoe in his life.

When she finally entered the house, Olivia was greeted with the smell of garlic and onions, somewhere between just chopped and cooked through for whatever meal Mrs. Case was making for her boarders. The front parlor was mostly empty, other than a school-aged boy sitting on the floor near the window with a small workbook open in front of him.

He looked up and grinned. "Welcome back, Mrs. Montgomery!"

"Hello, Lawrence," she said. "Working on your writing again?"

He nodded. "My mother and aunts made me stay

behind today. They said everything is just about set for us to leave soon, and once we're on the trail, I might not get a chance to practice that often."

"Your mother is a smart woman." Olivia hung up her coat on one of the dozens of hooks near the door. Judging by how empty they were, she imagined most of her fellow boarders were also out in Independence running errands.

"Yes, ma'am," he replied before focusing back on his work.

Olivia couldn't remember all the details about Lawrence Hudson and his family coming west from Virginia, but she did know this boy had only learned to read and write in the last year. Before that, who could say how he spent his time. For certain, Olivia could not judge any young man who worked outside of a school-room to support his family. But the fact that he was working so hard at it now spoke volumes as to his character. She had been quite impressed with him ever since they met a few weeks ago.

"Mrs. Case?" she called into the rest of the house as she left Lawrence to his studies.

"In the kitchen, dear!"

As Olivia made her way to the small, hot kitchen, the sting of onions in the air made her eyes water. She picked up the scent of roasting potato and some kind of meat; whatever Mrs. Case was making for their supper would be delicious.

"Can I help you with anything?"

The older woman had tied her wide, calico apron over her dress and was busy whipping up something in a medium mixing bowl.

"Oh, hello, Mrs. Montgomery." She kept whipping but nodded her greeting. "Did you have a productive afternoon?"

"I think so." Olivia stole a green bean out of the bowl that was sitting near the stove. "That is to say, I think I did as well as can be expected, but we'll see what Mr. Montgomery says. You're sure I can't help here?"

"Oh, no, dear. Everything is in hand. This should all be ready in the next hour or so, which will give your Mr. Montgomery time to return."

Olivia smiled her thanks and made her exit. She still wasn't used to Luke being called "hers" and felt a small thrill each time she heard it. As she climbed the stairs to the small room over the kitchen where they had been sleeping, Olivia thought more about what it meant that that man belonged to her. True, she hadn't known Luke all that long before agreeing to marry him, and also true that she had discovered rather quickly that he wasn't perfect. Still, he was a good man. Everyone said so.

When she reached their small bedroom, Olivia took off her boots and lay back on the bed. Her chances to simply rest in the middle of the day had been few and far between for much of her life and would only become rarer as they lived day to day on the Oregon Trail. Though it made her feel a little lazy, Olivia knew this was a luxury that was so unlikely to present itself again that she should not feel bad this once.

She *did* feel bad; she just told herself not to.

With her eyes still closed and her hands crossed over her belly, Olivia heard the front door open and close and the murmur of male voices. It wasn't long before the sound of footsteps darting up the stairs made her sit up.

Her husband burst into their room a moment later, face lit up at seeing her.

"Livvy!" he exclaimed. "Lawrence told me you were here. I'm so pleased to get some time with you to myself before supper."

He toed off his shoes and climbed onto the bed next to her. This side of Luke—this playful, almost boyish enthusiasm—was one of the most pleasant surprises about being married. This was a side of his personality that he didn't share with anyone other than her. And now, after a long day apart, he seemed genuinely grateful to see her.

He crawled carefully along the length of the narrow bed until he sat beside her, leaning against the headboard.

"Now, Olivia Montgomery. Tell me everything. How was your day?" He absentmindedly began playing with a loose curl that had fallen out of her hairpin onto the pillow.

"Luke, did you happen to be at Martin's Wagons when our food order was delivered?"

"No. Why?"

"Well..." She hesitated about how to tell him. It wouldn't do to make him feel as though he had somehow done something wrong. "It seems that prices have raised since we originally indicated to Mr. Hancock what we wanted to buy. The money you gave me didn't buy everything we were hoping for."

He frowned, still playing with her hair. "So, then, what does that mean?"

"It means that we need to buy more supplies."

"But... Olivia, my dear, you know how difficult that

will be. Everything we have to spare is already being spent on the journey. Maybe we can earn more, or be given more along the way, but we have to make sacrifices—"

"I know," she assured him. "I do know. And maybe it will be fine. But, just as an example, I believe you ordered three hundred pounds of flour? We only got just under two. That might not be enough to get us all the way there."

"Oh, well, if that's all, I'm sure we can manage."

"But, Luke, that's not all. I think we were also short cornmeal, dried apples. Rope, I think. And that's just what I noticed right away, before Mr. Hancock explained to me the change in prices. I have the receipt; I can show you where the differences come in."

Luke's frown deepened. "Well, I'll see what I can do. Maybe I'll go try to speak to him in the morning. Or maybe the trip won't take that long. You know that can vary by months, depending on the weather and such."

"That's true." But Olivia was not convinced. Given that they would have to transport all the finished goods they would ever own all the way to Oregon, it seemed far better to be more prepared than they thought they would need to be.

Still, she wouldn't argue with him. Surely her husband had thought this all the way through and knew better than she did what they could expect. He wouldn't let her starve after all.

"But I have news for *you*, my dear."

She rose to be sitting next to him. Luke caught her hand and held it in both of his to his chest.

"We have been accepted into a wagon train."

"Goodness! Already?"

"Of course! Our wagon will be ready by mid-day tomorrow, and the Sullivan-Mills Oregon Company will be heading out the day after that. We'll have just enough time to get all our ducks in a row before we join our future friends and neighbors."

Olivia didn't know what to say. After so many months of working toward this very moment, it seemed almost too much to bear. The idea of not only meeting so many new people but also having to befriend them overwhelmed her.

Olivia knew what was expected of a pastor's wife. Over the past few months, since they left Charlottesville, she had learned more and more that she wasn't as suited for the role as she ought to be. Now, she had to step into a more permanent leadership position; many of the families in the wagon company would be church members when they finally reached Oregon. They would all be looking to her. She was determined to do her duty.

"Two days," she said in wonder.

"Two days. And then we'll be on our way to our new life. I'm so grateful you're here with me, Livvy."

He wrapped his arm around her shoulder and pulled her to him, planting a kiss on her cheek.

CHAPTER EIGHT

Accordingly, less than forty-eight hours later, Olivia had packed the last of the Montgomerys' new purchases into the wide, canvas-topped wagon that was to be their home for the next several months. She still wasn't at all convinced that the food they had managed to purchase would last them the whole way. Having grown up on a farm, Olivia had at least a passing idea of how to find sustenance outside of a store shelf. Hopefully, she wouldn't have to use it, but she felt better with that knowledge.

Luke hadn't made time to try to purchase any more. Instead, the previous day he had gotten a head start on getting to know what he hoped would be his future congregation while Olivia finalized the last of their belongings. She tried not to resent him for this choice. She knew perfectly well that their future survival depended on the kindness of these strangers and others they may meet in Oregon. Such was the life of a man of the cloth, Luke kept reminding her. Their very livelihood was dependent on their likability.

But that left more of the household's responsibility on Olivia's shoulders.

Responsibility to see that their oxen team was ready. Responsibility to visit the blacksmith for new tools and three more trips to the general store for last-minute items that Luke hadn't thought to order.

Though completing all these final tasks on her own was exhausting, Olivia tried to remind herself how much work being a pastor's wife would be. It wasn't as though she expected to live in the lap of luxury. She told herself she had just gotten too used to her husband's undivided attention on their travel west from Charlottesville. Now that they were in one place, part of a community, working behind the scenes to support his work was something she would need to get used to.

And as such, she began by helping him hitch up their team of oxen. He had driven the team to Martin's Wagons, and they had just finished yoking the animals to the vehicle.

Their money hadn't gone very far, but they had just enough for a team of four oxen that Luke had named: Shadrach, Meshach, Abednego, and Nebuchadnezzar. Olivia had laughed when he told her. It was just like Luke to make even their draw animals a bit over the top. But she didn't object. It didn't do any harm, and it made his calling to them as they walked down the main street of Independence more fun, if ridiculous.

Every last barrel was in place, every rope tightened, and every animal fed and watered just before midday. There was nothing else to wait for, and so Olivia stood back and held her breath, watching as Luke prodded the oxen forward.

"Gee!" Luke called to his team.

The animals leaned forward, pulling the wagon wheels to rolling for the first time since the several thousand pounds of supplies had been loaded.

Luke laughed in delight to see his dream of heading west finally beginning. Olivia smiled to herself as she stayed back and watched her husband take care of it all.

At the main street, their wagon joined a line of other emigrants leaving.

Olivia walked on the other side of the wagon from Luke, slightly behind the animals. Many of the other members of the Sullivan-Mills company were heading out of Independence at the same time, all making their way to the campsite just outside of town. The Montgomery wagon was one in a long line of emigrants, cheering and hustling their way west. There was even a crowd of onlookers lining the street, waving the travelers on.

As she walked alongside her wagon, Olivia looked around, taking in the sights and saying a final prayer before they had left civilization altogether. Several families waved to her husband—he'd been even busier than she had realized.

On and on they walked, out of the main street, out of the town altogether, out to where the dirt track headed west and seemed almost to be only westbound. How many folks would come along that road coming back east, Olivia wondered?

The walking alongside the wagon became almost lulling to Olivia. Her boots were sturdy enough; all she had to do was put one foot in front of the other, on and on, and let her mind wander. It was April in Missouri, the very end of the rainy season. The scent of the new grass reminded her of the previous spring back in Charlottesville. The purple, red, yellow, and orange wildflowers popping up all over the plains surrounding them reminded her of the church picnic she had helped plan the previous June back at home. The laughter and games of the children running through those same wildflowers reminded Olivia of the Porter children that lived just a mile down the road from her aunt and uncle and who she had sometimes helped take care of when their parents had other responsibilities.

That life was all behind her now. But the memories of it helped make this new adventure feel more like home.

After an hour or so of walking along the trail and thinking to herself, Luke called to her over the animals.

"Mrs. Montgomery, could you come here, my dear?"

She smiled in answer and crossed behind the wagon to walk alongside her husband.

"Do you think," he asked, "you would be up to driving our team?"

Her mouth dropped open in surprise, though only moments later she realized that she could. "I... Yes, I think so. If you need me to."

"Wonderful!" He handed her the rein and the whip. "I'll just be a few moments. I see Mr. Gladwell's wagon up ahead, and I wanted to get in a word before we get too far."

With that mysterious explanation, Luke darted off, leaving his wife in charge of four two-thousand-pound animals that she had only met that morning. Olivia reminded herself that she was far more used to farm animals than her husband was. How difficult could it be to simply follow the trail behind the next wagon?

But Luke's promised few minutes grew into another hour.

And then another hour beyond that.

Olivia was hot under the afternoon sun. Her bonnet protected her skin and shaded her somewhat, but the unrelenting sun still beat down on the fabric over her head and shoulders. Her arms ached from the strain of trying to keep the oxen in line, not so much because they were uncontrollable, but more because she wanted to be extra vigilant just in case. She could already tell her legs would be tired as soon as she stopped but counted it a blessing that she didn't seem to be developing any blisters from all the miles of walking. Not yet, at least.

Wherever Luke had gone off to, she hoped he was accomplishing what he had set out to, but she was rather put out that he had been gone so much longer than he had promised her.

As the sun set behind the horizon, the Sullivan-Mills wagon company finally arrived at the campsite. Olivia looked around, confused, and wondering where she should lead her team. Already there was a sea of white-topped wagons spread out across the prairie, enough families to populate several wagon companies. Where should she go?

Just as her frustration was mounting, Luke appeared at her right elbow.

"There you are!" he exclaimed.

"Where have you been?"

"I was looking for you. Come, let's make camp over this way."

Before she could further question him, he deftly took the reins from her and led the team off toward the edge of the campsites to their right. Olivia vaguely recognized some of the children of the families nearby but was too frustrated with her husband, too tired from her day, and too focused on what she needed to do next to think any more about it. She told herself she would do better about being a friendly neighbor next time. It couldn't be expected of her now.

"If you could get supper ready, my dear," he kissed her sweaty cheek, "I'll take care of the team."

She nodded but wasn't sure he had seen it before he was busying himself with their harnesses.

Olivia took a deep breath. She untied her bonnet and fanned herself for a couple moments as she looked under the canvas into the back of their wagon. The Montgomerys' supplies had fallen from their previous places; a barrel had turned over and rolled to the far end. She had to take a moment to figure out what she wanted to pull out and where it might be.

This was to be her home for the next maybe four or five months, she reminded herself. She would need to organize it as such.

With the sun almost set, Olivia hung her bonnet on one of the hooks on the inside of the wagon, climbed in, and found the tools she was looking for. She would need to gather water, make a fire, decide what to make for supper, and at the very least organize the wagon enough so that what she would want for breakfast in the morning was handy.

She would also have to ask Luke about plans to leave the campsite the next morning, find out if they could expect water before the next campsite, and if she had any more time after that, try to get clean as best she could. Even if it was with cold water from the spring, Olivia wanted to sponge herself down.

As she climbed back out of the wagon with her arms full of food and her arm looped through the handle of their bucket, she gasped at what she saw. For what seemed like miles around, the landscape was peppered with campfires, smoke rising into the violet sky. The air was full of the sounds of girls laughing, men murmuring, mothers scolding, and from somewhere not far off, a fiddle playing a lively tune.

Though Olivia couldn't imagine who would have the energy to dance after the day they had had, she was grateful for the sound. Music had always felt like an otherworldly luxury, something she was lucky to be near, even if she could never create it herself.

That sound, that sight, this whole small makeshift city on the plains of Missouri anchored Olivia in her new circumstances. Up until this day, the idea of spending the summer making their way to the territories had just seemed like a theoretical future plan. She couldn't really envision herself walking along the dirt trail, living out of a wagon, learning to rely on strangers. But now, as she made her way down to the spring to get the water she and her husband needed for their supper, Olivia saw there was far more to this journey than she had expected. Any illusions of preparedness vanished as she considered the immense task ahead of them.

CHAPTER NINE

Olivia's first night sleeping in the wagon was a rough one. At first, Luke had intended to sleep on the cornhusk mattress with her, inside the wagon bed and under the protection of the canvas cover. Neither of them had realized how cramped that would be, however. After a couple hours of both of them tossing and turning and trying to find space for all their limbs among the sacks of sugar and barrels of flour, he gave up.

"It's fine," he whispered as he pulled an extra blanket out of the trunk that had been under the coffee. "All the men sleep outside under the wagons. I wish I had thought to buy a tent, but it's perfectly fine. We both need our rest."

She didn't argue with him; she was that grateful for some undisturbed sleep.

Olivia had certainly needed the rest. That first night, she slept like the dead and didn't wake the following morning until Luke had poked his head into the wagon and called her name.

"Livvy? Sunshine of my life, are you awake?"

She cleared her throat and rubbed her face. She hadn't even sat up yet when he continued.

"I didn't want you to worry," he said. "I heard from Mills that we'll remain in camp today to let the final stragglers join us from Independence, so I'm going to use the chance to make sure the rest of our new neighbors know who I am. I might get invited for dinner or supper, even so, don't wait for me. You might want to use this time to reorganize," he gestured, "all of this. So it's exactly how you want it. All right? All right."

And with that, he was gone. He hadn't waited for her assent or anything beyond confirming that she was conscious.

Olivia supposed it was just as well. She yawned and stretched, trying to worry out the kinks in her neck. He was correct that she did need to organize their things, and she would get far more done when he wasn't underfoot. Luke Montgomery was a good man; she knew that. He was kind and thoughtful and generous... but he was also sometimes utterly exhausting.

Getting his energy out by making friends with the other members of their wagon company would be the perfect way for him to spend the day. And she would have a chance to rest and spend some much-needed time by herself.

Though it had only been just over a day since they left, Olivia was beginning to realize exactly how much work would be required of her to be supportive behind the scenes. Growing up on the Drysdales' farm, she had seen firsthand what was needed to make a home. All four members of that household had had plenty to keep them busy throughout most of the day, and that had been with them staying put. Now, with the daily chores of maintaining the wagon itself and having to walk who-knew-how-far for fuel, the sheer volume of work seemed daunting.

And it was beginning to look as though Olivia would be the one doing it all. She was the one expected to keep their home running while her husband was off being charming.

But, she had to admit, he *was* charming. And he had given her an escape from Charlottesville. And she would always be grateful for that. She would run Luke Montgomery's household as well as any woman could.

But first, she needed coffee.

And to do that, she needed water, a campfire, a kettle, the coffee, a mug, and, goodness, she must be forgetting something.

Olivia squared her shoulders and set to work.

Twenty minutes later, she was walking back to their campsite. Tucked under one arm was a big stack wood and sticks to get her fire going, and the other arm carried a full bucket of water that she had managed to collect from the spring. As she was getting her water, no fewer than half a dozen different women had introduced themselves to Olivia, recognizing her as the pastor's wife and telling her their own names in return.

Though she didn't know that she'd remember any of them the next day, Olivia found herself immeasurably grateful that there would be at least a few friendly faces in the community she had just joined. Maybe the task of making friends wouldn't be as difficult for her now as it had been growing up. But at the same time, she wanted to soak up her quiet alone time now while she could.

When she reached her campsite again, she set to work.

Another hour later, Olivia had a fire going and was cooking a batch of biscuits they could eat for a midday meal or snack throughout the day. She had already made her coffee, her breakfast, and cleaned the dishes. Without Luke underfoot, she could be far more efficient.

Again, she felt a stab of disloyalty, and again, she pushed it down. She had far more things to worry about now than the feelings of a man who hadn't even made time for her yet that day.

By the end of the day, however, all thought of what she might owe to Luke was gone. While he had been gone for nearly twelve hours, she had remained alone at their campsite, cleaning, organizing, sorting, and in general readying their store for the journey ahead. Though she couldn't be sure what precisely they would encounter—storms, Indians, drought—she did her best. They had picked up a guidebook to Oregon in the last big city before they reached Independence, and Olivia had already read it cover to cover two times. The more she knew, the better prepared she could be.

But no amount of knowledge could prepare her for doing the work of two people while her husband was off somewhere else making friends.

Luke finally showed up at their wagon again at

almost dusk, after Olivia had given up waiting for him and put their supper away. She was sitting by the campfire, listening to the people around her and thinking about the trail ahead when he came striding into the circle of firelight.

"Well," he exclaimed, "I did it. I managed to meet each and every person on the Sullivan-Mills wagon company."

"Did you?" She noticed he hadn't asked about her own day.

"I'll allow that my task was made a bit easier, seeing as some of these folks, like the Hudsons, I had already met in Independence, but I did it."

"The Hudsons are here?" Olivia asked, looking around as though she would see them from her perch. "I didn't know that!"

"Oh, yes, I thought I had said. Or that Louisa had told you. Feels like that woman is always offering advice. Didn't I tell you it was her that led me to Mills?"

Olivia frowned and shook her head.

"Oh, well, yes. That woman has connections. But there's also a woman who is far enough along in the family way that she'll likely give birth before we reach Oregon. There's a doctor *and* a teacher in the company. There are at least two couples that I imagine will not be able to help themselves and will want to get married before we reach Oregon."

Olivia smiled. "And, of course, you will help them."

"Of course. And there are also several well-off businessmen who I think will be instrumental in our church planting when we get to Oregon. We won't be able to do it without the support of the influential. I think we have a really good chance, Livvy. I really do."

Olivia smiled. "I'm really very happy for you," she said, standing. "Did you eat?"

"Did I eat?" He laughed. "I ate at practically every single campsite I stopped at. I tell you, the people of this wagon train are generous. I'm gladder than ever that I had the idea to come west, I tell you."

He placed a hand on her shoulder and took a deep breath.

"And I'm beat," he continued. "Mills wants us out at dawn, so I'm going to catch some shut-eye."

She nodded but wasn't sure he had seen; he was already walking away from her. Olivia sat back down again and watched the fire, thinking about her day. She was quite proud of everything she had gotten done that day, but she could admit now that she missed her husband. Missed having him to talk to, to cook for. She supposed she should be grateful that so many of the members of their wagon company so adored him, but instead, she just felt left out.

But, she reminded herself as she made her way to the wagon to sleep, this was only the first day. There were still two thousand miles to go, and there should be plenty of time to find her place.

The following morning, Olivia was up early, brewing coffee and fixing bacon for them to eat quickly before the wagon train left camp.

There were almost fifty families in the Sullivan-Mills company, even more wagons, and all of them were getting ready to leave camp at the same time. Luke had requested—and received—permission to be near the back of the train. He told Olivia he felt better able to keep an eye on everyone in the wagon company from the rear.

They were up and ready at seven in the morning but didn't actually pull out of their campsite until almost noon.

"Here we go!" Luke shouted excitedly to his wife.

CHAPTER TEN

Olivia wasn't sure what she should have expected, but that first day on the Oregon Trail started out much like their day leaving Independence had been—monotony, sun, prairie grass, and plenty of time to walk and think.

As with the previous day, Luke led their team of oxen while Olivia walked along next to him. This day, however, her husband had much to say about the families he had met and broken bread with. He was full of plans to start a regular Sunday service and get these men and women used to seeing him as their spiritual guide, as an integral part of their lives. The sooner he was that, he explained to Olivia, the better foundation for the church they would plant in Oregon.

She nodded along. Though she had some ideas and suggestions, she already knew her husband well enough to recognize that now was not the time for that. Luke could be a good listener, but he needed to *choose* to be. That first morning that they spent with the Sullivan-

Mills wagon company was far more about him telling her what he had learned.

And Olivia could recognize that he needed her for that. She just hoped Luke could recognize what she needed from him.

The wagon train didn't stop for a meal at noon—George Mills had wanted them all to get a strong start to the journey. Setting the example at the beginning of the journey of how difficult it could be seemed like a wise way to manage the expectations of all the families under his care. Olivia had been prepared. It took her a couple tries, but she managed to pull herself up and climb into the wagon while it was still moving. Once there, she dug out a small snack for herself and Luke. Leftover biscuits and bacon, along with a few slices of dried apples. She also strode off into the grass towards the line of trees in the distance to find more fresh water. After growing up on a farm, Olivia knew far better than her husband what could happen to a person who didn't drink enough water under a hot sun like this, and she intended to do her part to keep him healthy.

It wasn't long after she had rustled up their food that the wagon ahead of them slowed almost to a stop.

"What is it?" she wondered out loud.

Without answering, Luke handed her the reins and ran on ahead to see what the hold-up was. Olivia sighed in frustration, grateful there bwas no one to hear her. She shook off her exasperation. It wouldn't do for the pastor's wife to be seen having selfish impulses.

The wagon train inched forward slowly, and Olivia occasionally had to redirect her team. Nebuchadnezzar kept getting distracted by the lush grass along the side of the trail. If they weren't moving forward, he acted as though it must be time to eat.

Finally, after twenty minutes of barely moving, Olivia noticed the train was being redirected off the main trail, around an obstacle that had landed in their way. She nudged her team forward, following the wagon in front of her, and kept her focus on the rough terrain. It wasn't until her team was even with the obstacle that she looked up to see what had redirected them.

Her stomach dropped.

To the right of the trail, a wagon had overturned, and a man was trapped under the heavy wheel. Several families had stopped to try to help, and one young man was directing the rest of the wagons to carry on past the wreckage. Olivia kept her team moving past, even as she noticed her husband nearby, comforting a woman not much older than he was. She was flanked by two small children, wailing and sobbing. The company's doctor had already made his way back to this accident and was kneeling over the broken man, but even from this distance, it seemed clear that nothing could be done.

As she led her team around the overturned wagon, her husband caught her eye. There was just a short beat; she saw his expression. His pain was written all over his face as he tried to soothe the new widow, but then he looked away.

Olivia felt a sob stuck in her throat, but she kept putting one foot in front of the other. There was nothing more she could do than what she was doing. It was her duty to take care of their home while her husband did his work.

She knew this. She kept telling herself this, even as

she turned back to watch him with that other family as she kept walking farther and farther away.

In spite of the Sullivan-Mills wagon company suffering through a horrific death of a member of their own, they kept moving the rest of the long day. Olivia had to spend hours walking under the sun, leading their team of oxen all alone while her husband tended to the needs of the new widow. In those hours, Olivia had plenty of time to think—about how she needed to make more friends among the company, about how she didn't see how she would have the time if she ended up being the sole person in charge of driving their wagon, about how she didn't even know the name of the woman whose husband had died.

She remembered fondly the pastor's wife from her home church in Charlottesville. Mrs. Lyons was the most hospitable woman in their entire congregation, always having families over for supper or taking food to the afflicted. Olivia could admit to herself now that at least a small part of her desire to marry Luke was a subconscious desire to be more like Mrs. Lyons.

There was still a chance, but not as long as Luke put so much responsibility on her and paid so much attention to everyone else.

Olivia could feel herself getting angry and resentful. And the more time that passed without her husband seeking her out, the more resentful she grew.

Finally, not long before dusk, the wagon in front of her slowed again, pulling to the left off the trail toward a campsite. Their long first day was finally over. As exhausted as Olivia was from her day of walking, she still needed to feed and water her team, as well as feed herself and possibly Luke. She took a deep breath and set to work. As bone-tired as she was, Olivia knew what her duty was, and she would do it. There was a lot on her plate, but it wouldn't get done unless she did it.

Olivia took a chance and cooked up a dinner for two people, hoping that her husband would show up any minute. With all the time alone she had, though, she had a hard time keeping herself from stewing over all the ways he was not the partner that she'd hoped for. It didn't matter how she tried to reason with herself; she simply grew angrier and angrier the longer she was left alone.

"I found you!" Luke said as he stepped out of the gathering dark into the circle of their campfire light. "Heavens, what a day, huh?"

He pulled out a handkerchief from his coat and wiped his brow as he sat. Without a word, she brought him a dipperful of cool water to drink.

"Thank you, Livvy," he murmured. He took a deep drink. "I don't suppose supper is ready, is it?"

"Just one more minute or so."

She turned her back to him and fussed with her pans over the fire. None of the food cooking needed that much attention from her, but she thought if she tried to speak to Luke, she might lose her temper. She just needed time and—

"A shame about Mr. Buchanan, isn't it?" Luke said, cutting into her thoughts.

"Hmm?" She pulled the pans off of the fire and began dishing up two plates for them: beans, cornmeal patties, and coffee.

"Mills's son Daniel and the doctor and I all stayed

behind to bury Mr. Buchanan by the side of the trail. Poor Mrs. Buchanan still hadn't stopped crying when I finally left her camp to come find you. And those children..." He shook his head. "I think she'd greatly appreciate a visit from you, my dear, just to—"

"How on earth could I do that?"

For the first time since he had returned, for the first time that day, even, Olivia stood up straight and looked him full in the face, unable to hold her tongue any longer.

"What do you mean?"

"Luke, I understand that this is your life, that this is your work and presiding over the burial of a man in this company is what you need to do."

"Thank you, but—"

"But you have to recognize where that leaves me." She gestured to their campsite.

He frowned, confused. "I don't understand. You're my wife, Olivia, and—"

"And as your wife, I recognize that I also have certain responsibilities." She felt that she should maybe stop interrupting him, but couldn't stop now. "I know it is my job to keep us both fed. I'm happy to do it. But I can't do that and drive the team and also find the time to make friends with the couple hundred people that are part of this wagon company. I'm only one person, and there is only so much time in the day!"

"But why don't you just ask for help?" He sounded genuinely confused.

"Who am I supposed to ask for help, Luke? I don't know a soul here!" Olivia could feel a sob welling up, but she shoved it down again. "It's just me, on my own.

Everyone else has plenty of their own work to do—no one is going to come wandering over to our campsite just to check on me. The one person I thought I had— *you*—is too busy with everyone else."

He gaped at her, as though shocked that she had an opinion different from his own. She could see the anger start to gather behind his eyes, but she plowed ahead.

"And not only that, Luke, but all this time you're spending shoring up your relationships with these strangers is time that you're taking away from me. From our marriage. From your relationship with your wife. I just... When do I get to be a priority in your life?"

Olivia could feel tears threatening to spill over. She was finally giving voice to thoughts she hadn't let herself acknowledge. She was finally allowing emotions she had kept tamped down show themselves.

"I've *never* been a priority." Her voice cracked. "Not since my parents were alive. I thought... I thought marrying a man who seemed to so cherish me would give me that, but it seems as though I will always come last, behind every single other person who could possibly ask for your time."

"Now, Olivia," he began. His voice had a steel tone she had never heard before. "You knew this was my work."

"I also know you promised to love and protect me," she spat back at him. Olivia couldn't remember ever being this angry before. Hurt, yes. Frustrated, of course. But angry?

"Lower your voice."

Olivia wanted to scream. Who was he to tell her how

to manage her feelings when he spent all day, every day, comforting other people?

She held his angry gaze for one more beat before letting out a sobbing huff and stalking off toward the wagon. He could clean up their supper himself. She needed to be alone.

CHAPTER ELEVEN

Olivia barely slept after her first fight with her husband.

She lay in bed for hours, alone in the wagon long after when she had hoped to be asleep. As she tossed and turned, the rustle of the dried husks in the mattress under her sounded loud in the otherwise quiet night. First, she lay listening to Luke clumsily move around their campsite, thudding and dropping and then sitting quietly. She strained her ears, hoping to hear a clue or an indication that he was taking her concerns to heart. Then once it was clear he had gone to bed, she lay listening to the quieting families and animals all around her, still unable to sleep. Soon it felt like she was the only one awake in the whole world, just lying there, staring at the canvas above her, wishing for the rest that her body so desperately needed.

Somehow her exhaustion—both physical and emotional—from the day must have caught up with her. The next thing she knew, she was waking to the pre-dawn sounds of neighbors starting their own day. She opened her eyes to the growing light. In a flash, Olivia remembered her fight with Luke. Emotions surged through her as the anger and hurt reared up again. She sat up, still tired, still worn, still angry.

Though she waited and listened, Olivia didn't hear Luke stirring on the other side of the canvas. When she finally climbed out of the wagon, she noticed he wasn't anywhere nearby. There was a small fire going, so he must have at least done that. Olivia felt a burst of gratitude that he had helped her in this small way, but she refused to let it color her memories of the preceding days. Besides, he was gone now. There was no other indication of her husband. Where he had gone, before sunrise and before breakfast, she had no idea. With nearly fifty different families to befriend, her husband could be anywhere.

It was probably better that Luke was nowhere to be found when she awoke, Olivia thought, as she made her way to the spring to wash her face and collect a bucket of water. She was still so angry they were liable to have another argument all over again. She averted her eyes from her neighbors and tried to complete her chore as quickly as possible so as not to be pulled into any conversation.

It wasn't until she returned to camp that she noticed that her husband had left the dirty pans out. The night before, Olivia had stormed off to bed after dinner, not considering what still needed to be done and Luke had not touched any of it. She seethed. It seemed she couldn't count on him for anything. He had left their valuable pans just sitting in the dirt by the campfire overnight. The heavy, wide cast iron pan that Aunt Bea had given her was practically overrun by ants as they surged and swarmed to carry off the bits of bread and bacon that had been left.

"Gah!" Olivia exclaimed in frustration. She caught up the pan and hit it hard against the dirt. What she really wanted to do was throw it. Or hit it against the wagon. She wanted to break something to release the anger that was becoming a constant with her.

But she didn't have time for that, did she? No, she had to clean up Luke's mess, and put Luke's home back together, and get ready to follow Luke to Oregon.

Olivia was furious.

But she was also responsible.

Though, that frankly made her even more livid.

She took a deep breath, shook off her frustrations, and got to work.

As she set about cleaning her pan and making herself coffee, Olivia tried to remember the last time she had been this angry. She was usually much better about taming her temper and quieting her stronger emotions, but this had really gotten to her.

The sun was just over the horizon when Luke returned to their campsite without a word. He didn't look at his wife. He didn't offer to help her put the cooking things away or tell her where he had been. He didn't acknowledge her at all.

She watched him move to the back of the wagon, put his blanket back in there, and withdraw a pair of gloves, pulling them on as he walked away again. She sat by the smoldering campfire and watched as he moved about, hitching up their team of oxen.

The Montgomery wagon was ready before they

needed to roll out onto the trail for the day. Still, neither husband nor wife spoke to the other while they waited.

Although Olivia knew she shouldn't have lost her temper, she still could not admit to being wrong. And it seemed as though Luke wouldn't either.

In fact, she found herself feeling grateful to him for being there to drive the team and then mentally scolded herself. That was what he *should* be doing. Why be grateful to him for the bare minimum?

As the wagons began to leave their campsites into the long train of white-topped prairie schooners for the day of travel, Olivia had an idea.

Without acknowledging Luke, without even a glance, she hurried ahead to the wagon that had been in front of theirs the last few days. She glanced back briefly to make sure Luke had seen her go—so he wouldn't abandon their team assuming she would take care of it—and then turned her attention to the trail.

This would show him. Give him a taste of what the last couple of days had been like for her *and* do what he considered her duty to befriend their future congregation. She barreled on, fighting her natural inclinations to not bother others, and forced herself to interact with the new neighbors.

"Hello?" she called to the man driving the team of oxen.

He didn't seem to hear her over the lowing of his animals and the shrieking laughter of the children in the grass on his other side.

"Excuse me!"

At that, he turned, surprised, to see who was yelling. He was a tall, broad man, with dark brown hair that hung loosely around his shoulders. When he saw it was a woman approaching him, he doffed his hat.

"Why, Mrs. Montgomery, how nice to see you."

She smiled awkwardly. What had she been thinking? Now she had to make conversation with this stranger. Maybe spiting Luke wasn't worth it. "Ah, yes, so you know me, then? I'm so sorry, but I don't believe we've met." As she said this, she closed the distance between them, hurrying her steps so she could walk with the man along the trail.

"Your husband pointed you out to us the other day. I figured it would be just a matter of time before you and us crossed paths. Name's Morris Carter." He returned his hat to his head. "The missus is back in the wagon bandaging up a scrape. I'm sure she'd be happy to make your acquaintance as well."

"Oh, well, that's very sweet," Olivia said. She was torn between being grateful to Luke for at least mentioning her to the other families and again being angry at herself for the gratitude. But, as she was well used to, Olivia forced herself to push those feelings aside and focus on what was required of her here and now. "So, then you must know my husband's line of work and a little bit about us. I'm sorry, but he didn't say a word to me about you, though. But, then, I get the feeling there's a lot he's not telling me." Olivia gave a self-conscious laugh.

"Really? Well, he must have a lot on his mind, I'm guessing. We're from Maryland. My folks had a small family farm that just kept getting smaller and smaller as the years passed. We had debt to pay. Finally, this last fall, the wife and I decided we wanted more room.

Neighbors were getting too close, you know? So, we packed up the children and came out to Independence, hooked up with Sullivan. Probably a pretty common story, truth be told."

"Oh, yes, Mr. Sullivan is one of the captains of this company, right? I haven't met him yet either."

Mr. Carter seemed even more surprised at this news, and Olivia silently scolded Luke for leaving her on her own so completely.

Before he could respond, they heard a woman's voice from behind them.

"Hello?"

Olivia turned to see a woman with a bright smile, maybe twenty years older than her, hurrying toward them. A young boy, around eight years old, ran off into the tall prairie grass. Olivia watched him meet up with a crowd of at least a half-dozen other children who were all too old to ride in the wagon and too young to be expected to do chores along the way.

Mrs. Carter greeted her with a hug. "Oh, my dear Mrs. Montgomery, I'm so pleased you're in the wagon right behind ours."

Olivia's eyes widened. She was shocked at such familiarity. She supposed she would need to get used to it. This was the job of a pastor's wife. Being friendly and available was her duty.

It didn't matter how many times she reminded herself; it never failed to surprise her.

"Thank you, yes, I thought it about time I came over to introduce myself. Your husband has just been telling me a little bit about your family. You have just the one son then?"

"Oh, no." Mrs. Carter looped her arm through Olivia's and guided her a few steps away from the team of oxen, and thus out of the small cloud of dust that was beginning to kick up. "We have two children older than Amos, too. Rose and Jefferson, but they're off..." She looked off to the horizon shielding her eyes against the sun, and pointed when she found what she was looking for. "There. They're in charge of herding our cattle along the way."

"Oh, my, that must be so helpful for you."

Mrs. Carter laughed. "I'm not saying that is why we had the children, you understand, but it certainly helped."

Olivia laughed along with her, and not for the first time felt the pang of loneliness. Though the idea of having children had always been a vague future goal, in all the rush and bustle of getting ready to travel to Oregon, she had completely forgotten that she was married now, and it was a very real possibility. She had never had such a close family like the Carters must be. Could she have it now?

She resolutely put that thought aside again.

"And you will be farming again when we get to the territory?"

"Yes. We're hoping for a big stretch of acreage and room for an orchard, our cattle, maybe even a mill. Morris keeps dreaming up bigger and bigger plans, but mostly I'm just happy to give our children a better opportunity."

"Of course."

There was an awkward pause. Olivia felt silly. What had she been thinking, charging off to show Luke what it was like to be left alone? She had never been good at small talk and making friends. Thank goodness for Mrs. Carter, content to chat away, answering her questions.

"Tell me, Mrs. Carter—" she began.

"Oh, you can call me Dolly."

Olivia smiled. "Dolly, tell me, please... My husband has been so busy I am sure he has much to tell me but hasn't gotten a chance. Who else are the important personages I should make sure to meet?"

"Oh! Well!" Dolly grinned. "Now, I pride myself on not being a gossip, of course, but between the children and myself, we've managed to at least hear about most of the families in the wagon company. First, have you met Dr. Martell?"

Olivia shook her head, and Dolly Carter proceeded to illuminate the pastor's wife about as many of her future neighbors as she could think of. The Van Andas, the Schmidts, the family of boys and their widower father, the socialite from New York. The more detail that Dolly told her about the families that were part of the wagon train, the more overwhelmed Olivia became. The more overwhelmed Olivia became, the more excuses she could think of for staying close to her wagon in the future and not venturing out to make herself vulnerable to any of these people.

Without Luke to act as her protection and her introduction to this new life, how could she possibly find her place?

CHAPTER TWELVE

In the middle of their first week on the trail, the train of wagons crossed into Indian territory. From here almost constantly until Oregon, they were at risk every moment. Not just from attack, but from the very land and weather trying to destroy them. Olivia reminded herself that the men and women that lived on these plains had done so for centuries, that their wagon company would be fine. That it was possible to thrive here, and it was lack of experience that left her people struggling for survival, but that only made her feel less safe. Every man that traveled in the Sullivan-Mills wagon company would do everything they could to protect the families in it. Still, she felt as though it were only a matter of time before they had a confrontation with the natives of whose land they were crossing.

The wagon captains—William Sullivan and George Mills—quickly established strict rules and discipline to ensure the safety of all the families under their care. Each evening when they stopped to camp, the wagons would be pulled into a large circle as tightly as possible. The wagon tongues would be overlapped and the hubs chained together, with the cattle and other animals corralled inside. This would form a secure barrier, a veritable wall against invasions. In addition, each man over the age of sixteen would have to take their turn standing guard against Native Americans.

Somehow, though, Luke was not part of the guard duty. He and Dr. Martell apparently were so valuable in their services to the company that they were spared the overnight commitment. And yet, in spite of this, the pastor *still* couldn't find time for his wife. Olivia *still* found herself maintaining a home for a man who wasn't there. Olivia wasn't sure if he was trying to prove he was worth it or some other reason, but Luke seemed to only be at their campsite for supper one out of every three nights. Occasionally he would comment about her joining him to visit such-and-such a family, but he never insisted on it.

Worse, he never warned her when he would be gone. She was running through their food stores faster than necessary simply by cooking for a man who never showed up.

And given how much work she had to do to keep their home running—cooking, cleaning, repairing, sewing, even driving the team—she never was able to find the time to go with him. If she wasn't working, she was exhausted. Being alone suited her. It was how she had always lived her life, after all. Chores and solitude. Why had she thought being married would make any difference?

And so, Olivia spent her days alone walking ever

westward alongside the trail, her time filled with the same tasks over and over. She got a perfunctory kiss on the cheek from Luke before he went off to help Mr. Alden shoe a horse, or to read a Bible story to the Buchanan children, and then didn't see him again until dusk. It seemed that he had simply dismissed her complaints and trusted Olivia to take care of their home without needing anything from him.

There weren't many other women driving their own oxen—the Hudson sisters notwithstanding. Olivia imagined the other women judging her for not being able to keep her husband at the home hearth, the men judging her for doing something so unfeminine as to drive her own team of oxen, for not reaching out to be part of the community of emigrants.

But what could she do? What other choice did she have?

Though Olivia still didn't seek them out, she couldn't help but pick up some more information about her new neighbors. Every morning before they left camp, and every night as they made camp again, she was in charge of getting the water she needed for cooking. As such, she followed the crowd of women and girls to whatever stream or spring that was nearby, with a bucket in each hand. It was a fellowship of a kind, though Olivia was never truly drawn into the fold.

One night at the camp's spring, she could feel more eyes watching her than usual, and she wondered if there was some story or other going around about her. She felt her face burn, self-conscious that she was somehow failing, both as a woman and as a pastor's wife. It wasn't that she was shy; it was just that she seemed to lack whatever natural inclination toward overt friendliness that other women had. Or perhaps she had never learned it.

Since she had lived almost her entire life in the same town where she was born and where her parents had been born, Olivia had never had any need to learn how to make friends.

And then Luke had made it so easy, inviting all the people who loved him to see them be wed.

But now, he was still making friends and leaving her far behind.

Olivia kept her head down and didn't take her eyes from the buckets or the water. Pretending that she was busy, that she was focused. Keeping her eyes down let her act as though she didn't see all the women watching her. Let her listen to the conversations nearby without having to participate.

Keeping quiet and listening was her armor, and she would keep it up as long as she could.

A few days later, the wagon company took the whole day to cross a shallow, rocky river. Luke stuck with his wagon and his team to make sure it got across the water safely, though even with him nearby, Olivia couldn't find anything to say to her husband.

Instead, she watched the others in the wagon company, making note of who Dolly had told her about or who she had heard gossip about in the small moments when she had found herself in a crowd.

The family ahead of the Carters in the wagon train was the Larsons, formerly of Wisconsin. They were a large family, with six children on the trail to Oregon, and that was after leaving their oldest behind with her in-laws.

The family behind the Montgomerys' wagon was the Sheldons, dairy farmers from Connecticut who were also driving their stock all the way across the continent. They had four children, similar in age to the Carters. Olivia often saw one boy or another running back and forth past her to the other family's wagon.

She watched the children make friends. She watched the young girls braid wildflowers into each other's hair. She watched the men loan tools, and the women trade extra food. She watched all around her as the community of emigrants became more tightly knit and friendly.

As she watched, she felt more like an outsider.

One afternoon, the wagon company was taking the day to cross a small tributary of the Missouri River. Letting the oxen cross the water slowly was the best way to keep them from panicking, and some families also had horses and cattle to coax through the stream. After her own wagon was led through to the other shore, Olivia made camp. For the first time since they had left Independence, she gave herself the rest of the afternoon off from chores.

There wasn't all that much that needed to be done that second, and Luke had disappeared to who-knew-where, so Olivia instead walked back down to the shore of the stream to watch the rest of the crossing.

Watching and observing had always been one of Olivia's favorite pastimes—when she had time to spare. She sat alone, just seeing how each man, woman, and child was handling this obstacle along the way to Oregon. Some with pride, some with fear. Some of the children seemed utterly unconcerned and splashed in the shallows. Even though she had yet to meet any of these families directly, Olivia felt like she was getting to know them as she watched.

As she was sitting in the grass, watching the teams and wagons cross, Olivia realized she recognized the person driving the team that was then in the middle of the water. She climbed to her feet, brushing off loose bits of grass, and called out.

"Miss Hudson!"

She waved wildly above her head, then immediately regretted it. Olivia felt embarrassed at being ignored, but then even more ashamed when she realized why. How selfish of her to think that Louisa could pay atten-tion to her. Louisa Hudson was having a difficult time convincing her oxen to continue putting one foot in front of the other to get all the way across the shallow stream. She couldn't afford to let her attention be stolen by someone who merely wanted to say hello.

The other Hudson sisters, however, were wading through the water on their own and had noticed Olivia on the shore.

"Mrs. Montgomery!" Margaret Hudson called with a broad wave.

The relief that Olivia felt over finally being recog-nized and wanted was almost palpable. She couldn't help but grin widely as the other woman came running over to her and enveloped her in a big hug.

"How is this the first time we're seeing you?" she

asked Olivia with a laugh. "Where have you been hiding yourself?"

"Oh, well, you know. There's just always something that needs doing."

"And Mr. Montgomery didn't tell you to come find us?"

Olivia felt her smile falter, but she recovered quickly. "He might have, but then you know how excited he can get. He's made a lot of new friends these last few weeks." She hated talking about her husband as though she were indulging a child, but neither was she prepared to admit to Mrs. Hudson that she couldn't remember the last time her husband had had an actual conversation with her. "But, you're here now."

Mrs. Hudson looked over her shoulder to where her son Lawrence was helping her sister-in-law Louisa bring their team hauling two wagons up onto the riverbank.

"I am, but I should go help them set up camp." She impulsively gave Olivia another tight hug. "But now that you know we're here, you come find us whenever you get the notion. I was thinking about making an apple pie the next time we stop for more than a few hours, and you'll have to come snag a piece before that boy of mine eats it all."

This last she called over her shoulder as she walked away from Olivia. The other woman waved her thanks and stayed where she was, at the edge of the water but somehow feeling less alone than she had before.

CHAPTER THIRTEEN

Olivia and Luke continued in this uncertain, nearly silent, stalemate for days. Still putting one foot in front of the other. Still resolutely making their way west, but not so much together as she wished for. Everything that Olivia had hoped was waiting for her when she said yes to marrying him now seemed even farther away. With each new day, she suffered under the growing expectations of her, and her resentment of her husband didn't abate.

Instead of relying on him any more than she had to, Olivia did what she could to take matters into her own hands—she started reading again through the guidebook Luke had bought in Charlottesville before they even headed west. She had never been much of a reader; only the Bible had ever held her attention. But with the risk of actual death or disease every day as they ventured farther into the wild, Olivia knew she had to make sure she was prepared. For all she knew, something terrible could happen to her during any one of the many days that Luke was off assisting another family.

And so, she read. She read and learned—and grew more worried about the shortage of flour and other foodstuffs that they had set off from Missouri with. She prepared herself for the stress and strength of a prairie storm that could be waiting for them any day. She wrestled with the knowledge that she was alone and unprotected nearly every day. Without being able to rely on Luke, whose idea it was to come west, Olivia turned further inward.

The guidebook wasn't particularly stimulating reading, but it was informative. It was through this reading that Olivia realized the Kansas River would be coming up soon, and she would have to figure out how to get her wagon across it, possibly without her husband's assistance. She pored over the recommendations of the guide and worried about every possibility that could befall them.

Finally, when the wide, slow river appeared on the horizon, she was as anxious as she could ever remember being. Though she had crossed over a great many streams and rivers in her lifetime, particularly since leaving Virginia, she realized she had no idea what to expect here. Whatever image had been in her mind of what the Kansas River would be didn't come anywhere near the reality.

Late one morning, the wagon train climbed a low hill and came over a ridge that overlooked the water. From that height, Olivia could see hundreds of white-topped wagons funneling into one narrow point. The row of wagons snaked around in a long line, all leading to the same single spot where each one could cross the water. The Kansas River was more than six hundred feet across in this spot, and still the safest place for the emigrants to cross.

Olivia had learned that getting settlers across the river was a lucrative business for a couple of enterprising men. A few years earlier, they had seen the need for a safe, reliable ferry when the real travel across the continent had begun in earnest. They set up their business to charge emigrants a small fee to get them over safely.

Though a man may choose to swim over his team or caulk his wagon to float it across, at this spot on the river was a small ferry. Dugout canoes for flotation were lashed to a platform large enough to carry two wagons plus their teams over to the other side. The men guiding the platform pushed it—and the thousands of pounds it had to carry—across the wide river with long poles. Then they had to return to the first bank. With only the two wagons over at a time, it was no wonder the traveling was so delayed.

Under these circumstances, the Sullivan-Mills wagon company would take two days to get over the river, making camp while they waited.

This was all in the guidebook that Olivia read almost religiously. Where Luke pored over his Bible, his wife pored over the instruction manual that would get them to Oregon safely.

As the wagons slowed to a crawl leading down the trail to the ferry, George Mills made his way down the line of waiting wagons.

"When you all get to the shore," he yelled to the three families gathered, trying to give instructions as efficiently as possible, "do everything the ferrymen say. Everything." Olivia thought he had glared at *her* for a split second, as though expecting this mere woman to defy him. "My son Daniel will be there helping, as will several of the other teenage boys who have volunteered."

"Jefferson Carter, I think," Luke whispered to Olivia.

"We'll go over the water two wagons at a time. Get your team and wagon into position on the ferry, careful about the weight. Talk with your neighbors," he pointed to the wagons on either side of the Montgomerys, "to coordinate. Be sure to chain your wheels, so they don't roll. Be careful! Ask those boys for help if you even suspect you might need it. I don't want anyone going into the water this day."

"Mighty kind of them," Luke told Mills. "We're grateful for any extra pair of hands that can be spared."

Mills shook his hand, nodded, and kept walking to the next group.

Olivia had been sitting on the wagon seat listening to the instructions, though she knew none of the men expected anything of her in this. Once Mills had moved farther down the train to give other families the same instructions, she sat thinking about what Luke had said. There were extra hands, extra help, peppered throughout the company. Maybe Luke was right that she could ask for help when she needed it. Well, she told herself, whether there was a person around to ask for help was not quite the same thing as her being willing to ask. Thank goodness for the boys tasked with helping the wagons over the river. She wondered if they had volunteered for such a position.

As Olivia looked across the broad Kansas River and

at the sea of canvas wagon tops on either side, she wondered what each of those travelers had thought when they had left home. If they had been excited about what they were heading west to do or if they, like Olivia, merely were trying to escape from something else.

The Montgomery wagon was in the back half of the wagon company; they had to wait until the second day on the shore to have their turn crossing. Their half of the emigrants pulled their wagons into a defensive circle and enjoyed a longer afternoon in camp during what remained of that first day at the river. As such, Luke also had fewer people in the company to occupy himself with, and Olivia found him at their campsite well ahead of supper that first night.

She had assumed she would be by herself—as usual—all afternoon. Given what she knew to expect the next day, Olivia had been baking, setting in a store of extra biscuits for the following day, and trying to distract herself from the fear of what danger waited for them. But then, to her surprise, hours before sundown Luke came back to their campsite and sat in the dirt on the other side of the campfire from her.

"Good afternoon, my dear," he said pleasantly. "Whatever that is smells delicious."

Olivia had been experimenting with different ways of making her biscuits. Anything to break the monotony when every meal was made up from the same half dozen ingredients. This batch was not only being cooked up with bacon grease—in the cast iron pan she had been given by her aunt—but she had also cooked a few slices of bacon, torn it into smaller pieces, and mixed those pieces in with her dough. The resulting bread could be almost a full meal on its own.

"Thank you," she replied curtly. She continued to study what the guidebook said about crossing the Kansas River.

They sat in silence for a few moments longer before he tried again. "How was your day?"

She looked at him then and took a deep breath. "Well, to be honest, Luke, I've been worrying over our crossing tomorrow. I don't know that I can keep the team calm and get our wagon over all on my own."

He looked surprised at this veiled accusation, though she didn't know why he should. She could count on one hand the things he had helped her with over the last few weeks. His shock was quickly replaced by his charming smile that he must use on everyone.

"Fortunately, you won't be alone. I'll be right there alongside Shadrach and Nebuchadnezzar. And you know, of course, that Daniel Mills has been standing by to help anyone who needed an extra hand. Jefferson Carter. Maybe Lawrence Hudson as well. Everyone in this company is always so eager to help, we'll be just fine."

Olivia shook her head slightly, though she wasn't sure he had noticed. He was always so quick with a positive word about other people while she toiled away for him without notice. The more she had learned about the stress involved in crossing the Kansas River, the more she feared what they would have to do the following day. And the less he took it seriously, the more she had to take on herself.

But in spite of that very real fear, Olivia could not bring herself to have that fight with him again.

She had now gone so far down the path of not needing him—or letting him believe she didn't need him—that she wasn't sure she could find her way back. Instead, she looked away and said coldly, "We'll see."

As she stood to go somewhere, anywhere but here, Luke stood with her.

"Wait, please." He came around the campfire to her, reaching for her hand.

She didn't have the energy to pull away. She didn't want to make this a fight; she wanted to save her energy for things more important. For her very survival.

"Thank you, Livvy," he said in a low voice, "for everything you've done to take care of me and take care of us. Please know I see all of it."

She scoffed. "You can't possibly see all of it, Luke."

"Well, you're right, of course. I know. I see a lot of it, at least. I know I never go hungry or am want of clean, neat clothes. I know I never have to worry that the team is kept watered. I know... Oh, my love." He tried reaching for her again, and this time she let him. "I know how hard you must be working, and I can't tell you enough how grateful I am."

Olivia took a moment before she responded. It wouldn't do either of them any good for her to come at him with as much anger as she had been feeling. But at the same time, she couldn't let him think this was enough for her.

"Thank you. But more than your gratitude, even, Luke... I need you to be there with me tomorrow. When we cross. Please. I can't do it on my own, and I need you to help me."

"Of course!" he agreed readily. He cupped her cheek with one hand and pulled her close to him by the waist with the other. "Of course, Livvy. Of course I will be there. I'll take care of you and we'll cross the river, and be one more stop on the way to Oregon together."

Though it was exactly what she needed to hear from him, Olivia somehow felt like it wouldn't be enough.

CHAPTER FOURTEEN

The next morning, Olivia made their breakfast with a little more care than usual. She had the time, after all, since they would just be waiting around until it was their turn to cross the Kansas River. Luke raved and exclaimed more than once over the bacon-biscuits she had made. Even eaten cold with his coffee, they were remarkable.

But his attention didn't last long. Even before Olivia had finished her own coffee, before she had a chance to pack up and put away the last of their things into the wagon, Luke had headed off to talk to someone or other about something that Olivia apparently had nothing to do with.

She watched him go, bitterly, though told herself that he'd be back when it was their turn to cross.

That turn came sooner than she expected.

"Come along, Mrs. Montgomery," the younger Mr. Mills called to her.

He was around her own age, the unmarried oldest

son of one of the company leaders. Without a family of his own to take care of, Olivia imagined he must have been a great help to his father in leading the company. Already this early in the day, however, Olivia could see his skin paling in the chill of the current. He had been waist-deep in cold water all the previous day and now again, helping every single wagon cross the treacherous river.

Olivia nodded to him and began to lead her anxious team over to the ferry. She looked briefly over her shoulder, but Luke was nowhere in sight, no hurrying with apologies for tardiness or his charming smile. He had left her on her own—again. Her anger was beginning to rise, though she tried to hide it. Her wagon would be crossing with the Sheldons' wagon, the family that usually followed them on the trail. Thank goodness Daniel Mills was there to help. He nodded encouragingly and took the reins from her as the first wheel of the wagon jostled onto the platform.

Junior Sullivan was on hand and also appeared pale, as though the cold had sucked all his color away. He trudged in and out of the running water helping hold the platform steady for the terrified animals. Though the water of the Kansas wasn't terribly deep, it was fast, and it was cold. Even from this distance, Olivia could see the way their clothes clung to the men and boys that were helping guide the wagons. She shivered unconsciously, thinking about how hard they must be working, dawn till dusk.

"Easy now," Mills said. "Why don't you step out of the way for a moment while we get things settled?"

Mr. Sheldon had hurried forward to help Mr. Mills.

Olivia looked around, back to the shore, just in time to see her husband running up from somewhere. He was sure to have some story, some excuse of why someone else needed him right at that moment.

But now was not the time to have that argument.

She needed to stay calm for the team of draft animals at the very least. Shadrach, Meshach, Abednego, and Nebuchadnezzar were looking to her, just as they had every day.

Olivia moved to the side, where the Sheldon children had been directed. The ferry was getting more full and more heavy as they maneuvered and arranged and balanced and brought all the animals on board.

The platform was full, edge to edge, with the Montgomerys' wagon and oxen team, the Sheldons' wagon and oxen team, and all the members of both families, not to mention Daniel Mills and the several men tasked with guiding the ferry across the water. Jefferson Carter had chained their wheels. Everything was set. Olivia's hands were clenched in tight, anxious fists, but the men in charge seemed to have it all under control.

All she had to do was hold on.

The ferrymen began to push the platform away from the bank, and Olivia felt it shift underneath her feet. Though the men had all urged her to stay out of the way, when the oxen began to protest the movement, she couldn't just stand back and watch. Nebuchadnezzar and Shadrach in the lead both stamped their feet, sliding, trying to back away from the edges of the ferry. Each step they pushed back upset the balance of the platform.

Olivia felt the level ferry tilt slightly as the oxen stamped their complaints. She shot both her hands out to try to balance herself. The wagon slid toward her enough that Olivia's stomach lurched. The team was panicking; the huge three-thousand-pound wagon slid—right toward her. If she didn't do something, she—and the Sheldon children standing near her—could get crushed or thrown into the cold water.

The platform tipped so far toward her side that a splash of water wet her boots. Her shoes would be fine, but it was still far too much.

And still, Luke did nothing.

Though her husband had told her to step back, though he had claimed he would take care of them, all he was doing now was panicking just as much as the animals were. Olivia shook her head in frustration, watching him. Why did she keep believing him when he told her that he would take care of things? There was no room for mistakes here.

And Luke Montgomery was the biggest mistake.

"LUKE!" she yelled sharply, directly.

Olivia immediately regretted her loss of temper, but what could she do now? The man was going to get himself trampled by panicking oxen if he didn't get himself together. She stepped carefully on the tilting platform, one step, then another, until she was next to Shadrach.

"Shhhh," she cooed, barely louder than the rushing water and the yelling ferrymen. Olivia put the palm of her hand flat on the beast's nose. "Easy, now. Easy." She leaned forward and placed her forehead against the animal's, slowing her breathing, trying to stay calm even as chaos reigned around her.

Shadrach was the lead oxen; the other three took

their cues from her. As they heard Olivia's soothing words, their stamping abated.

Olivia could feel her husband's eyes on her, but she couldn't be bothered to try to calm him down at that moment as well. Her first responsibility was to the animals—the eighteen-hundred-pound creatures of pure muscle that could destroy everything and everyone on that platform if they had a mind to.

She reached out to Shadrach next to her.

"Easy, now. Easy, girl. Shhhhh..."

Time seemed to freeze, and all she had in front of her was her team of oxen that she had depended on, day in and day out. Now they depended on her to get them back on solid ground. She breathed in and out. In and out. Willing the animals to stay calm.

Soon Olivia felt the platform butt up against the small dock on the other side of the river, and she looked up. When she met Daniel Mills's eyes, he nodded approvingly at her, offering a small smile.

"Thank you, Mrs. Montgomery. Can I—"

"I'll handle it," she said shortly, still not looking at Luke.

Once the platform was in place, once the chains had been removed from the wheels, Olivia called her team, urging them to step the final few feet off the ferry. Once the two lead oxen felt the dirt under them, they hurried forward eagerly, easily pulling the heavy wagon behind them. Olivia almost laughed at their apparent joy but didn't allow herself a moment of relaxation.

It wasn't until her team was safely on land and calm again that she turned to find Luke following behind, seemingly eager to help however he could now.

She tried to keep the accusation and disappointment from her eyes but could not manage it. He flinched almost imperceptibly under her gaze, so she looked away.

"Here," he said softly. He took the reins from her and guided their team away from the shore.

After a few moments of walking in silence together, Luke finally spoke.

"I'm so sorry, Livvy. I just got caught up." He laughed self-consciously. "You know how I get. I was talking to old Mr. Goldman about one of the finer points of theology in the Torah and just... You know. I'm sorry. I meant to help. I really did. Please don't be angry."

"I'm not angry you were late," she said, surprised to realize this was true.

"Oh, thank goodness—"

"I'm angry that I can't trust you. I can't count on you. When the oxen were panicking, you just..." Her voice broke in the wave of frustration that had overcome her.

She stopped speaking, as they were soon weaving in between other families and campsites to find where they would stay for the evening. Luke didn't try to comfort her or excuse himself. He didn't try to say anything, in fact, and soon they reached the plot of land near the Carters where they would make camp.

He began to unharness the oxen without another word while Olivia gathered fuel to make their fire, and pull her sewing out of the wagon. They worked side by side in silence like that for hours.

Olivia began to wonder if she was being unreasonable.

"Alexander!" she heard from the McKinnon campsite nearby.

Olivia glanced at Luke, who had also looked up at the mother's call. They caught each other's eyes and smiled. Olivia's anger had mostly abated, and with the distraction of Mrs. McKinnon, she couldn't help but laugh to herself. So many of the children in this wagon company were ecstatic to be let loose on the prairie. Overhearing Amos Carter beg his mother to be let go or David Sheldon to ride one of their horses always made Olivia immensely sympathetic toward their parents.

"Alexander!" the voice called again. "Alexander McKinnon, it's supper time! Where are you?" She sounded slightly farther away, venturing out to find the boy.

"I think I'll go see if she needs help," Luke said, as he got to his feet. "Is... Is that all right? Or do you need me here?"

Olivia was so taken aback that he even seemed to be considering her opinion that she didn't have the heart to tell him no. She paused. She wanted to tell him no. She wanted to tell him to stay. No, Luke, Mrs. McKinnon will be just fine without you. No, Luke, you don't need to rescue everyone. No, Luke, you're not the hero.

But of course, she couldn't say any of that. Not as a pastor's wife.

She let out a sigh and waved him away. "Fine."

Then she heard him calling for Mrs. McKinnon before he had even left his wife's side.

Olivia shook her head at him. She didn't know what else to do. She didn't know how else to get through to him what she needed and how he let her down.

She turned her attention back to the buttonhole she had been working on as the shouting voices looking for Alexander McKinnon heated up. From where the Montgomerys' camp was set up near the crest of a low hill, Olivia could see much of the rest of the camp stretching into the darkness and toward the river. Mrs. McKinnon had left her own camp behind as well, and she walk tentatively into the darkness, calling for her son. The silhouette of Olivia's husband stood out in the twilight, and he trailed slightly behind the mother.

How far could the child have gone?

Olivia had just lowered her head to look more carefully at the needle and thread in the dim light when she heard a blood-curdling scream. She stood up straight, letting Luke's shirt fall to the dirt. Even in the little sunlight left, she could see all the way to the river. All the way to the tragedy.

Mrs. McKinnon was knee-deep in the coursing Kansas River, with her skirt billowing up to the surface. She seemed bent over and cradling something in the water. From Olivia's distance, she just watched. Dozens of others were closer than she was, including her husband, who had left her side for this very thing.

The mother's heartbroken cry pierced the air, and Olivia realized what must have happened. The small child wandering off by himself. The little boy finding joy in playing in the river. A current or cold or injury or any number of dangers drawing him down, down, down, into the water.

A child had died, and Olivia was doing nothing to comfort the grieving. She was just watching from the comfort of her own campsite.

Women surrounded Mrs. McKinnon, wrapping her in a blanket. Someone took the body of the child from her. The mother was enveloped by the love and comfort of her neighbors and her pastor, and Olivia was nowhere nearby.

CHAPTER FIFTEEN

After Alexander McKinnon drowned in the Kansas River, Olivia didn't see her husband at all that night. She tried to go to bed, tried to tell herself she would need her rest and her strength for the following day, especially seeing as Luke would have pressing matters elsewhere. But instead, she found herself lying wide awake inside her wagon, listening to murmured conversations, men on guard against the natives, animals lowing.

And in all that time, Luke never came home to her.

As soon as dawn seemed close, Olivia forced herself to get up. Her whole body ached from her lack of sleep, but that couldn't stop what she needed to do that day. For the first time in a week or more, she actually took care with her appearance. She dug through the small trunk for a clean dress, pulling out the darkest, nicest one she owned. One of only two that had not yet been darned and repaired.

She made breakfast for two in the quiet, cool morning, every second expecting her husband to show up and tell her everything she had missed. Perhaps at the least, she could expect him to come looking for his wife for support after yet another death in the wagon company.

But he never appeared.

He never came back to his own wagon.

Olivia spent the morning alone, as she had so many other hours since heading west.

Without anyone to inform her what was happening, Olivia had to take her clues from her neighbors. No one thought to tell her where her husband was or what was expected of her. She could only watch what was going on around her. Soon Olivia noticed that no one else was packing up their campsite to leave for another day of travel. Everyone seemed to be holding their position.

At their nearby camp, the Sheldon family seemed to be getting ready for something. Olivia, trying to be surreptitious, watched them. A part of her was embarrassed by how much time she spent watching other people rather than engaging. At the same time, she couldn't bring herself to just walk over to them to ask what they were doing.

She watched the Sheldons leave their camp together as a family, walking down the low hill and through the other collected wagons. As they passed other campsites, more families joined in, walking toward the edge of the copse of trees that stood just outside the Sullivan-Mills camp.

Though she hadn't been specifically invited, though she only had a vague guess of what was now happening, the only thing Olivia could do was follow.

Following the Sheldons, following the other families, the walk was plenty of time for Olivia to try to remind herself of the names of all the families. Luke would undoubtedly know. As his wife, she would be expected to know.

How could she do this?

When she reached the group of people standing under the trees, the first thing she noticed was her husband, the pastor, speaking quietly to the McKinnons as they stood over a small hole in the ground. In the hole was a bundle the size of a small child, wrapped in a quilt. Olivia's stomach clenched. How could that be Alexander McKinnon? How could a child with so much life in him be so small in his grave?

She considered crossing through the crowd to stand at her husband's side, but just before she made the decision to go, he caught her eyes. The coldness in his eyes stopped her. He looked away again almost immediately, his expression inscrutable. Olivia twisted her wedding ring around and around her finger, trying to decide what to do. If she knew Luke Montgomery, the last thing he wanted at that moment was to have to attend to her.

She couldn't put that on him. She couldn't be a reason he wasn't able to comfort these poor grieving parents.

Olivia spent the whole of the service in the middle of a crowd of strangers instead.

Again, she watched instead of participated. Once the service was over, she wanted to offer the mother her sympathies, but she couldn't make herself do it. Maybe she was too proud. Maybe she was too embarrassed. All she knew is that Luke's expression had seemed like a wall between them.

This was his world, his work, and he didn't want her to have any part of it.

After so many days in the sun, after the cold and danger of the Kansas River, the company seemed dejected. The death of Alexander McKinnon was one more millstone around the neck of these kind people just trying to find a better life for themselves.

But even with all they had been through, there was no chance for a break.

Just a day after leaving the shores of the Kansas River, the sky opened up, and torrents of rain fell on the wagon company. Luke had foreseen such a possibility and had purchased two oilskin wraps from Hancock back in Missouri. Even walking in the rain and mud was preferable to the bouncing discomfort of riding in the wagon. Olivia was grateful that she could keep mostly dry and walked on.

The company had two full days of rain and mud. Mills and Sullivan pushed them forward. Though they only made five or six miles each of those days, that was more than none, and Olivia had had it drilled into her mind long ago that no time could be wasted on this journey.

There was no telling what unexpected obstacles might come up to delay their progress, so if any miles could be walked, they must take that chance.

The emigrants were at the whim of nature, but none of that changed the essential goal—get to Oregon before the snow fell.

After several days under heavy gray rain clouds, the sun finally reappeared.

The bright, drying day fell on the same day the company arrived at a new campsite on the banks of a narrow river. They would finally have a chance to rest for a full day. Many of the men needed to make repairs to their wagons, caulk up the cracks where water had seeped into the bed, and allow everything they owned to dry.

Ever since the McKinnon boy had died, Luke had been absent from their home even more. Whether there were real spiritual crises he needed to deal with or if he was just manufacturing reasons to not spend time with his wife, Olivia did not know.

She tried to bury herself in work to keep from dealing with the thoughts and feelings that came along with the very real possibility that her husband was avoiding her. But she could only come up with so many tasks to fill her time.

Finally, just after midday, Olivia gathered a clean dress, a towel, and her bar of soap and made her way down to the river. A couple of the other women had hung sheets across some of the trees that stood along the edge of the bank to allow a modicum of privacy for the women and children. Olivia was surprised to find that she was actually pleased to not be the only one who had thought to luxuriate and bathe.

For the first time on the journey thus far, she was happy to find herself in a crowd.

As she approached the water, she could count at least

five women and their assorted children in the shallows of the river, but even more of a crowd was gathered on the shore. Some women were combing out their wet hair. Some were tending to their children. Some seemed to be simply sitting and chatting with friends, enjoying a brief moment of rest in this long trek. Safe behind the privacy of the hung sheets, there was a small campfire burning with two buckets positioned above. Olivia recognized a woman Luke had pointed out as Mrs. Stephens, bending over the buckets. This woman looked so much like her aunt Bea that Olivia couldn't help but feel tenderly toward her, regardless of the fact that they hadn't yet spoken. When she got close enough, she cleared her throat, and the other woman started.

"Heavens!" She placed a hand on her chest. "Mrs. Montgomery, you startled me."

"I'm so sorry, I didn't mean to..."

"Oh, dear, no, it was me. I should be paying better attention." She glanced at what Olivia was carrying. "You take your time, enjoy your bath." She smiled. "And when you're ready, you yell for me or my daughter, and we'll bring you lovely warm water to rinse off with."

"Really?" Olivia's surprise at such generosity morphed into a wide grin. "I haven't had a hot bath in..."

"I *know,*" Mrs. Stephens said meaningfully. "You'll feel like a new person. Trust me."

"But, surely this water must be for someone else. I couldn't impose."

Mrs. Stephens looked at her as though she was crazy. "Impose? Mrs. Montgomery, this is precisely why me and Rebecca decided to do this. To do something nice for everyone. Please." She nudged Olivia gently toward the river. "Take your time."

"Thank you," she said, her voice thick with emotion.

At the river's edge, she undressed self-consciously, looking over her shoulder. No one was paying her the least mind. No one cared. No one was watching her. Each of these women was far more concerned about their own relaxing and cleaning than to bother an extra thought to critique Olivia's hair or figure. With her bar of soap clutched in one hand, Olivia walked into the river, lowering herself in the chilly water up to her shoulders.

She stayed a bit outside the busiest, most gossipy group of the women, watching and listening as she scrubbed at her skin. Olivia took her time getting at all the dirt that had been under fingernails. Even though the river was a bit cold, the speed and pressure of the current felt wonderful against her worn muscles. With her eyes closed, Olivia let herself wander farther into the water, farther into the current. She could stay in the water like this for hours, she thought.

Olivia had just begun to wash her long, dark hair when she heard her name—or, rather, her husband's name.

"Pastor Montgomery said he'd talk to them. I don't know if that man can work miracles or not, but I'm at a loss what else to do at this point."

Olivia used the heel of her hand to wipe the water out of her face, and she looked to see who was speaking about Luke.

"I don't know if I would call this a miracle," an older woman with almost fully white hair said, "but both

Robert and Beth are doing much better than I would have thought since their boy died. I'm sure it's all on account of how much time Pastor Montgomery is giving that family."

"The McKinnons?" said the first woman, a petite blonde a bit older than Olivia. She thought her name might be Mrs. Thompson. "Little Lizzie McKinnon came over to play with my Sarah and told us all about it. Pastor Montgomery has been reading to those children, taking them off their parents' hands at times. He's been nothing short of a godsend if you ask me."

Olivia sank back into the water, away from the speakers and back toward the shore. She didn't want them to know she had been eavesdropping on them. She didn't want to have to pretend she already knew how her husband had been spending his time.

Alone again, Olivia took her time with her hair. It was getting so long and heavy; wet as it was, it weighed her down. She scratched at her scalp as she thought over what she had heard and how her husband was changing the lives of those around him. She was surprised to realize that this was just as she had thought he was when she agreed to marry him.

How far they had come from that day...

CHAPTER SIXTEEN

After that quiet campsite, the company didn't come across any other usable water for days. As the wagons continued westward through the plains, each stream, rivulet, and even spring they passed was alkali. One drink of such stuff would cramp a man's stomach or kill a beast that drank its fill. Instead, each person had to be excruciatingly careful, carrying all the water they needed with them and rationing accordingly.

Luke and Olivia filled every usable container they had with water—pots, canteens, even her laundry tub. Each one seemed precariously balanced throughout the interior of the wagon, and Olivia even slept outside one night to avoid having to move any of their precious stores. Though the uncovered dishes jostled as they rolled over dips and rocks, some water was better than none, and the Montgomerys didn't complain.

Olivia almost made it a game with herself, trying to see just how long she could go without a sip of water. Trying to see how long she could get her full canteen to last. The oxen needed water; the cooking needed water. How much could Olivia herself save? Luke would slurp from his own canteen greedily, then remove his hat and drip more water onto the top of his head. Though she didn't say anything out loud, inwardly Olivia gloated at her own restraint, as though there were some prize for suffering that she was going to win. She endured the deprivation far better than her husband. *She* wouldn't be the reason they ran out of food or water on the journey. She knew from her guidebook that until they got to Oregon, there would always be stretches like this without enough water, but Olivia was up to the task.

As they walked through the dusty stretches of terrain, Olivia kept turning over her memories in her mind. The chance to bathe had been a small miracle—having both the time and the water to do so had been a luxury she didn't know when she would see again. That last chance of fresh, clear water was a memory that Olivia would live on for a while. She couldn't help it, really. Having to ration the water meant that Olivia was thinking about water constantly. Her thoughts kept traveling back to that last day by the river when she had the chance to bathe completely, and the currents of cool water wrapped around her body.

And thoughts of that day reminded her of what she had overheard the other women saying about Luke.

In the days after Olivia had accidentally eavesdropped on that conversation, she had tried to pay better attention to where her husband went and what he said to her when he returned. It always took her a while to think over something, to consider all the angles, and now she was starting to wonder if she had been too harsh on her husband. Maybe she hadn't fully realized what kind of responsibilities he was taking on.

One afternoon, just a couple days away from reaching the Platte, Luke led their oxen and drove the wagon. Olivia walked along the edge of the trail on the other side of the team. She glanced at him sideways, watching as he seemed lost in thought. He had been around to help her more often—why she couldn't say, but she had to admit it was a pleasant change to not be in charge of every single thing for once.

It was one of these times that Olivia snuck a glance at Luke that she got caught. He saw her looking and grinned at her over the backs of their oxen.

She smiled back, surprising herself. She couldn't stay mad at this man.

"Livvy?" he called. "Can I ask you a question?"

She nodded eagerly and crossed behind the wagon to walk next to him.

"I've been thinking about something," he started as soon as she was within earshot. "I'd like your opinion."

"Me?" She couldn't hide the surprise from her tone.

"Of course you. You know me, and I see the way you observe the rest of the company. You know them too. You notice a lot more than you let on."

Olivia considered this, recalling how she had learned some of their neighbors' names before even meeting them. Maybe it was true.

"I've been thinking—and, mind, I haven't asked the captains about this yet. But I've been thinking I might start a Sunday service for the rest of our journey. Probably not every week, but I could get these folks used to hearing me preach before asking them to invest in our church in Oregon and give them sustenance for their soul. I know a lot of them have been reading their Bibles all along the way, but maybe they're ready for something more."

She nodded thoughtfully. "I can see how that might be a good idea." She thought back to her bath in the river at their last long campsite, about what a difference the small change had made. Mrs. Stephens's gift of that hot water to rinse her hair and wash the river water from her body raised her spirits for days. A worship service might be able to accomplish the same thing. "Seems like folks might like to have a little something to take them out of the wilderness."

He frowned. "How do you mean?"

"Well..." She hesitated. She didn't want to sound accusatory. "Most of us, men and women alike, spend all our days merely surviving. Before dawn until well after sunset, there is always something to do. Driving the wagon and cooking and cleaning and mending and more cooking and more mending and the animals and hunting on and on."

He chuckled. "Monotony. I understand."

"Right," she nodded, "and so a church service could be a treat. Maybe some music? I think I heard Annie Hudson say she used to sing in their church choir. And you know someone around here plays the fiddle."

"That's true. Martin Jameson." He looked off up ahead and grew quiet. After a moment longer of think-ing, he looked back to her. "What about you?"

"What about me?"

"Would you be willing to help out if I held a service? Maybe you could take the littlest children off for story time... or, I think I've heard you singing once or twice."

"I... I'm not sure, Luke. There's always so much to do every day, and I surely don't get enough rest as it is. I don't know that I'm up for such a commitment on Sundays as well."

"All right," he responded lightly. "It was just an idea. If you can find some time—if I do end up doing this, of course—I'd be mighty grateful."

"I know and..." She looked down, embarrassed at her own selfishness. "I want to help. I do, but... you know. There's the cleaning and the cooking—"

"And the mending," he completed with a smile. "I know, Livvy. And I thank you for everything you do for me. For us. But..." He cleared his throat and looked squarely at her. "Forgive me for saying so, but you do far more than you need to. To tell you the truth, I don't need every single one of my shirts to be clean all the time. And I could do with a cold lunch some days if that meant that you had more energy to join me in leading the Sunday service."

"Really?" She frowned, thinking about if she could even bring herself to leave a chore undone when she had time to do it. What would the other women think?

He nodded. "Think about it. Please. I'll talk to Mills and Sullivan. Hopefully, we can start this coming week. Maybe once we get to the Platte."

Two days later, they reached the Platte River. The trail curled up onto a low ridge that looked down into the valley where the river cut through. When they reached the top of the hill, Olivia stepped off the trail and stood gazing out at the view as wagons passed her.

The river did truly seem to be a mile wide and a foot deep as it had been described in her guidebook. The river even seemed so shallow that in places the bottom looked like steppingstones to hop across. The water seemed so muddy and so shallow it almost didn't look like a river at all, but merely a low water table.

By then, the company had spent so long rationing water that Olivia's initial temptation was to run down the trail, fill her canteen, and drink her as much as she could. But she had read the guidebook, over and over. She knew the risks. All that water, all those gallons of flowing river, were too dangerous to drink. It was chalky and thick and could kill a person who drank it. She hoped there were none of the men or boys who imagined themselves strong enough to handle it.

Olivia stood watching the river from this vantage point almost long enough for the rest of the wagon train to pass her. She considered the life she had left behind and the life she was still walking towards. How fitting it was that Aunt Bea had gifted her a tool to make her work easier. It seemed as though the work was never-ending, and yet here was this man—her husband—who was able to find opportunities to care for his neighbors and offer them comfort. Now that they had reached the Platte, he would be setting about hosting a worship service, trying even harder to offer their fellow emigrants a break, a rest, and something to look forward to.

Maybe, Olivia thought, there was another way than what she had been doing. Maybe her husband's way was better. Maybe she was a coward for hiding herself in chores rather than making friends with the very families who would be her neighbors and congregation for the rest of her life. She didn't know how to reconcile this; she only knew what she had in front of her right then. The western frontier stretched out toward the horizon. It reminded her of the palm of her hand—seemingly flat from a distance, but when a person looked closer, it was full of curves and cracks and scars that made it beautiful.

Olivia took a deep breath, smelling in the grass that stretched in all directions, the musk of the draft animals that passed her on the trail. She felt the ground underneath her and closed her eyes to listen to the chatter and laughter of the families that walked up over the ridge of the hill near her.

Finally, feeling better, she ran on ahead to catch up with her husband, eyes on the Platte River as much as possible. She was mesmerized. The current seemed strong, though shallow, and the way the rivulets wove over the terrain was gorgeous.

The trail followed the edge of the Platte River for more than a week; each day, Olivia had to remind herself the water was not safe to drink, thirsty though she may be. She did, however, take one opportunity to remove her boots and walk into the water up to her ankles, reveling in the cool, tiny break she was allowing herself. Though muddy, the river water was soothing on her muscles, refreshing for a few moments of rest. Yes, she thought, maybe Luke's way could be right after all.

CHAPTER SEVENTEEN

After days of the Platte River running alongside the trail, it forked, and the company had to cross the wide water. There would be no perilous ferry crossing this time. It was shallow enough for Olivia and Luke to lead their team across without much trouble, though they both got wet above their knees. The rocks and muddy bottom forced them to go slowly, but it was far better than the tilting platform they'd had to endure crossing the Kansas River.

Once the group was across the Platte River, they continued along the trail slowly. Each of the wagons would cross the water that day, and they would not be spending any extra time to wait. Luke left the team of oxen in Olivia's hands and backtracked to the leader of the company who had stayed by the river shore to help folks who needed it. The pastor spoke to Mr. Mills about his idea and was given permission to hold a worship service.

"But not yet," Luke explained to Olivia that evening

over supper. "The next phase of the terrain is going to be the hardest yet, he says, and he doesn't want anyone's focus to be split."

Olivia nodded. "The guidebook says the most wheels break in this next part than anywhere else on the trail. It's going to be difficult, but I'm sorry you can't start right away."

"But it's probably for the best," he agreed amiably.

Not even half a day on the other side of the Platte, the terrain grew rocky. Olivia had never seen anything like it. It was as though God had rained down another plague of boulders on this country. The rolling green hills of Virginia were a continent away from this rugged landscape. At times it seemed a miracle that the wagon drivers could even find a path through the deep ruts and small boulders. They would have to make sharp turns to avoid the worst of the terrain, at times even forcing the wagons to roll over some of the smaller rocks. Just as the guidebook had predicted, three different wagons broke in the crossing, and the company was again delayed as the men frantically worked together to repair them.

Once the worst of the boulders had been passed, a small chasm opened between the rocks. The Sullivan-Mills company headed for a campsite at the bottom of the ravine where they would find fresh water. The narrow trail that had been cut into the side of the gorge didn't seem quite large enough for all the animals and wagons that needed to make their way slowly down it. Men chained the wheels of their wagons to keep from rolling down uncontrollably, and they clutched the reins, tensely holding back their teams from darting all the way to the bottom.

Olivia walked down on her own, staying out of the way of the enormous vehicles. As she made her descent, she wondered about the first men and families who had cut this trail, marveling that this was, in fact, the easiest way to get to Oregon. How badly they must have wanted a new start to risk such a crossing.

Once they reached the bottom, the emigrants could have a small break. The company would be granted a full day near water and grass for the oxen to fill up and take a break after the harrowing journey thus far. This was the first fresh water they had found in days, and Mills and Sullivan sent word around that they would stay here for two nights.

The first thing Olivia did once they made camp was to carry as much water as she could back from the small stream and fill her washtub. She felt as though she was caked in dirt; their clothing must be heavy with it.

"Here," she said to Luke, handing him the last clean shirt from the trunk inside the wagon. "Give me what you're wearing so I can wash it."

Luke took the clean shirt with a bemused smile on his face. "You don't want to, maybe, sit for a minute before getting right to work? You've been on your feet all morning."

"Of course I want to sit," Olivia said, "but I also want to take care of this while there is still daylight. And while I still have the energy to. If I sit down I'm afraid I won't get up again."

He pulled on the new shirt and handed Olivia his filthy one, already drenched in sweat from the effort of guiding the team down the steep trail.

"Well, don't wear yourself out, Livvy," he said.

"Tomorrow night will be my first church service out here. I've already cleared it with Mills. We'll have a full day in camp and then anyone who wants to can come worship. There's a spot right by the stream where we can fit a few dozen people, at least. If it won't put you out none, I'm going to make the rounds this afternoon to let everyone know. I think most folks are excited at this prospect."

"Well, of course they are." She smiled at him as she began to build her campfire. "Everyone loves you. I'm not at all surprised that you're going to draw a crowd."

"And you'll be there too, won't you?"

Olivia felt a jolt—whether it was guilt or surprise or fear or something else entirely, she couldn't be sure. Somehow, she had blocked from her mind the possibility that she would be attending this service alongside him.

She hesitated in answering, just a beat too long. He could read in her expression her doubt and withdrawal.

"It's fine," he said, saving her from having to answer. "I understand. You have plenty to occupy you."

The hurt in his eyes when he turned away from her surprised Olivia, but he didn't fight her. He squared his shoulders and walked off to the Sheldons' neighboring campsite to tell them his news.

How could he understand, Olivia wondered, watching her husband walk away. She didn't understand herself. But she couldn't deny being relieved that he didn't expect it of her. Just as she tended to take a while to think over a situation, so too did she need to take her time to get used to the idea of helping lead worship.

She would go some time, she told herself. Just not that time.

That first service was held the following evening after a long day of both chores and teaching (for the children) and resting. It only took until that following morning for Olivia to hear firsthand from someone who had been at her husband's church service.

She was fetching a bucket of fresh water to make coffee before they all left camp and ran into a couple of women at the spring. Though she didn't know their names, she knew they were somehow related to one of the company's captains.

Olivia cleared her throat, trying to talk herself into approaching the women and introducing herself. But before she could muster the courage, the younger of the women turned back to head up the trail and spotted her.

"Why! Mrs. Montgomery, we didn't know when we'd be running into you," the younger one said.

"We were wondering if you were maybe feeling poorly," the older one queried. The two looked so alike, and with the deference afforded the older, it was clear they were mother and daughter.

"It's... Mrs. Sullivan, isn't it?" Olivia asked cautiously. "And Miss Sullivan? Am I...? I'm sorry, I don't want to be presumptuous."

"Yes, yes, yes!" the younger woman exclaimed, hurrying toward her. Her buckets of water splashed over the side as she took incautious steps up the trail. "My name is Hannah. Please do call me that. I'm no Miss Sullivan. Besides, you can't be more than a year or so older'n me."

Olivia smiled at this girl's frankness. "Then I suppose you must call me Olivia." She let out a self-conscious laugh. "I'm sorry we haven't met before now—"

"Nonsense," Mrs. Sullivan insisted. "We see how Pastor Montgomery fills his time, morning, noon, and night. You must have plenty to keep you busy, supporting a man like that."

Olivia caught a look in the other woman's eyes that seemed to tell her that she understood. It still wouldn't do to complain about her husband to virtual strangers, but she certainly didn't feel the need to justify or make excuses.

"Yes, well," she said, "I wasn't feeling sick last night, but I just ... I thought I might be in the way. Tired as I am, and not knowing folk as well as he does. The last thing I want to do is be a liability for him."

Hannah smiled understandingly. "That's real thoughtful of you. He must be powerful busy if you haven't even had a chance to meet folk." She glanced at her mother, who nodded slightly. "Could I... Would you want me to help you with that? I can take you along wagon to wagon to make introductions. I know just about everyone by now."

"Oh, I— That is, I..." Olivia unconsciously stepped back, as though trying to put more distance between herself and the idea that hung in the air. "I couldn't."

Both women stared at her as though expecting her to elaborate.

"I just... I'm not..." She felt helpless, unable to explain exactly why the prospect of having to meet dozens and dozens of people all at once made her want to crawl back into bed. "Not all at once."

Both Sullivans laughed. "No," Hannah assured her. "I wouldn't do that to you. How about you come find me when you're ready, and we'll see how it goes."

Olivia nodded, knowing there was little chance she would make the time to do that. "But tell me," she said, pivoting, "how was the service? I haven't gotten more than a few words out of the pastor. He's all wound up. I think it took him hours to get to sleep."

"It was lovely," Mrs. Sullivan said sincerely. "He's a great speaker, and I think most of the families around here have really been missing their home churches and communities back east. Having a gathering point like this, and having a man of the Lord to lead us, really heals a lot of hurting hearts."

"You really should come next time," Hannah said. "Whenever he gets a chance to do it again. You must miss hearing him preach."

"Truthfully, I hadn't had a chance to hear him preach all that much before we came west. It would be almost as new to me as it is to all of you." With that, she moved past the women to fill her bucket in the spring. That was possibly the most personal detail she had revealed about herself since they had joined the wagon company, and she wasn't sure how she felt about it. When she stood and turned back, both of the Sullivans were watching her.

"You didn't get to hear him preach?" Hannah asked with a frown. It seemed as though she had been turning this fact over and over in her mind as long as she had been waiting. "I thought he had said he's been a pastor for years." She looked to her mother for confirmation and received it.

Both women looked at Olivia, who tried to respond nonchalantly. "Well, he was a traveling pastor, going from town to town..." They nodded, as though this part of the story was familiar to them. "We met when he came to my church in Charlottesville."

They still nodded.

"Last December," Olivia finished. "Just before we left for Independence."

Hannah's eyes went wide excitedly. "December? You met in December and left straight for Missouri? How romantic!"

Both her mother and Olivia laughed.

"Oh, maybe," she said, thinking back to that first afternoon when they had met. "Want to hear something else romantic?" She leaned forward, lowering her voice as though what she was about to say was highly confidential. "He also defended my honor against those wanting to harm me."

"He did what?" Hannah's eyes widened.

Olivia laughed again and told the women about how Luke had been invited to supper at her own house, and she had not been included. It had been a long time since Olivia had thought about that night, thought about what it had meant to her. Relaying these stories about her husband reminded her how amazing he could be.

As Olivia finished the story, Mrs. Sullivan nodded. "That doesn't surprise me at all. That man has been so compassionate with so many people these last few weeks. Why, what he's done with Jefferson Carter just proves it, doesn't it?"

Olivia couldn't hide her surprise and curiosity. "Jefferson Carter? I'm not sure... Remind me again what he's doing with Jefferson?"

"Why, the way that Pastor Montgomery has stepped in when Jefferson found himself at odds with the

Schmidt boys. Of course, I'm not sure it's common knowledge. Maybe he didn't want to be gossiping, but Dolly Carter told me all about it, so grateful she was to him."

"Oh, yes, of course," Olivia said, wondering what precisely her husband had done. "He's so thoughtful that way."

"Well," Mrs. Sullivan said, picking up her bucket of water from where she had set it at her feet, "shall we walk back together? It's lovely to finally get a chance to speak with you, Mrs. Montgomery."

After Olivia parted from the Sullivans and made her way to her own campsite, she found herself marveling at what her husband could be doing and not telling her about. Maybe it was just selfish of her to expect him to stay by her side when he could be doing such good for others.

CHAPTER EIGHTEEN

That morning once she had returned to her own campsite and before they left to travel west for the day, Olivia set about to really learn what her husband had been doing with his time. Now that she had heard more than one person giving their impression of the man, she was finally willing to admit to herself that her limiting view could be hurting them. Her rigid expectations could be holding them back. She was missing out on fully appreciating this amazing man that she had found herself married to. Olivia wanted to correct that before it was too late.

And she could start that moment. Something about Olivia's conversation with the Sullivan women made her think that if she could just get Luke talking, she might learn a lot about him. Not only what he had done for Jefferson Carter, but also what she had overheard Mrs. Thompson say about him at the river a couple weeks back. He must have so many stories, so many invest-ments in their neighbors, that he hadn't yet shared with her. She had to assume this was because she had made him feel like she didn't have time or didn't have the interest.

She hated to think she was bribing her husband just to talk to her, but a full meal was the best she knew to offer. Olivia put a little extra effort into the breakfast she made for herself and Luke, banking on his good mood to keep him talking. She made the bacon-biscuits that he had so enjoyed previously, added in a side of beans flavored with some wild onions she had discovered the day before. She splurged with a bit extra sugar to make a small apple tart for them to share. Running out of sugar before they reached Oregon wouldn't be the end of the world—that small sacrifice would be worth it if Olivia could somewhat resolve the tension and distance between her husband and herself. This would keep them fed all day.

Luke had been away from their campsite almost the entire previous day, only returning just before a quick supper before his worship service. His day must have been quite full, ministering to the people who had attended his worship service and following up with the spiritual needs of each of them. When he finally rose—the sounds of the campsite getting active all around them were difficult to sleep through, he smiled at her with the look of someone well satisfied with his work. He wiped his brow and washed his face and hands as she served up their meal. Over breakfast, after Luke heaped praise on her for all her skills and thanked her for all she did, Olivia tried to broach the subject.

"I heard from Mrs. Sullivan that the service last night was just what folks needed. You seem to be a lot of people's new favorite." She took his dirty plate from him and set about to the washing while he leaned back, full and content after the meal.

Luke grinned at her. "I think maybe getting the chance to preach again has just about made my whole week."

It was endearing, really, like a child with a new toy, the way he kept going once prompted. Luke had only excitement for all the adventures in his life.

"You know, Livvy, I forgot how much I feel like the Lord is speaking through me," he explained, after he had gone point by point through the sermon he had given. "Everything else that is part of this work is wonderful. The serving. The listening. The comforting." He sighed deeply. "But it's the preaching that really has convinced me that this is my calling."

"I'm really happy for you," she said softly, starting to pack up their dishes to return to the wagon. "It's nice to hear you talk about it. It sounds like you're doing a lot of good for a lot of people."

He looked slightly uncomfortable at that—both knew there was plenty still being left unsaid.

"That reminds me!" he exclaimed.

Before she could ask anything further, Luke had darted over to where their wagon rested. Olivia peered past him, curious about what he was doing. "What reminds you about what?"

"Do we have any glue?" he asked, sticking his head under the canvas flaps at the back of the wagon.

"Glue? I don't think so. Why?"

"I told Jefferson I would teach him how to rebind

books. It's no matter. I can also teach him how to make the glue."

"You did? But… Jefferson *Carter*? Why would a boy of that age care about such a thing?"

Luke took a deep breath and looked as though he were weighing his next words carefully.

"My dear." He took her hand and gestured for her to sit on the back lip of the wagon. Once she was comfortable, he stood before her, clasped his hands in front of him, and all in all acted as though he was about to offer a deep, heartfelt sermon. "There is quite a lot happening over the last few weeks that I have not shared with you."

"Oh?" she said, though inwardly relieved that he was finally sharing with her what it seemed that everyone else in the wagon company knew.

"You know I've been doing my best to make myself indispensable to the families here." She nodded. "And at times that has meant comforting the grieving, helping with their work, or even occasionally teaching the children. And you know— Or, rather, maybe you don't know. You're so innocent and hard-working the gossip might not have reached you."

"Know what, Luke?"

He looked somber. "The Schmidt boys run a poker game nearly every night. Only a few of the men participate, but the stakes have been high enough that it's not all just a way to entertain themselves. Paul Schmidt, for one, is becoming quite a rich man."

Olivia frowned. "But that would mean that others are losing money. How can they afford to? With as much risk as we are taking to get to Oregon, how can they do that to their families?"

"I know. I feel the same as you do. But of course, you know that we can't make a grown man do anything they don't want to do. John Harper and I have had words, for example, but he's going to make his own choices."

"And what does this have to do with Jefferson Carter?" she asked cautiously, not sure she wanted to know the answer.

He sighed. "Jefferson is old enough to be included in the game, old enough to have some cash saved up to gamble, but absolutely not old enough or experienced enough to be able to win against those men."

"Oh no..."

Luke nodded. "He's in deep. Much more debt than even his father can rescue him from. So deep, in fact, that there was a question of the boy being disowned, thrown out on his head, Morris was that angry."

"What?" Olivia couldn't imagine Mrs. Carter being so cold, but then she couldn't believe her own Aunt Bea had grown so cold.

"But you know, I couldn't let that happen if there was anything possible to be done. So, I... I stepped in."

"But, Luke, you don't have the kind of money to pay those debts, do you?" Olivia felt suddenly panicked. This was the man who had decided to move to Oregon before consulting her, after all.

"No, no. Nothing like that. But I'm not completely useless, either." He grinned. "I spoke to the men the boy is in debt with and they agreed to give him more time. And I spoke to the boy's parents, and we all agreed I would teach him a marketable skill that he can use to help pay off the debt." He beamed.

"Rebinding books." Now that he was explaining it all, Olivia could see how brilliant it was.

"Yes, as well as other various labors as needed. Jefferson is a strong young man who grew up on a farm and has plenty of abilities that many families can use. I believe he's helping Mr. Cole rebuild a wheel in the coming days for starters."

"Yes, I can imagine another pair of hands for work would be quite helpful." She thought wryly how nice it would be if Jefferson came to drive their wagon while Luke was off helping others but didn't voice her thoughts. They certainly didn't have money to spare. "That's wonderful, Luke."

"An eighteen-year-old has plenty of energy for his own chores and others," he went on with a smile. "The fact that he was playing that game every night proves it."

"So, then, is everything between him and his parents settled?"

"I think so. It's hard to know. Mrs. Carter was angrier than I think I've ever seen a woman. You can't really blame her. After everything they gave up to come out here, and her oldest almost throws it all away."

"But you calmed her down."

It wasn't even a question. Olivia knew without a doubt that Luke had made himself indispensable and changed that family's life for the better in the meantime. The more she heard about the details of his activities, the more she could see all the good he was doing. She felt honored to be married to such a man, even to the point as to feel ashamed of herself. She didn't deserve such a selfless person in her life.

How did she even get here?

"What?" he asked when he saw the expression on her face.

She shook her head, unable to fully explain herself. How to tell him that she finally just saw him again? How to admit that she had been so selfish and proud and controlling that she had thought his every action was somehow a judgment on her?

Olivia might be able to admit she was wrong to herself, but having that conversation with her husband was a very different matter.

"I'm very proud of you," she said simply.

He beamed. "I appreciate that. I'm sorry if my work—"

"I understand." She sighed. "It took me a while. And I'm sorry about that. But I see what you're trying to do, and I understand. You're really helping people, Luke. You're doing far more for that boy than anyone else is. You're changing the course of his entire life, and... I am proud of you."

Olivia leaned forward and kissed her husband on the cheek. The pleasure and surprise in his expression made her feel like she could have been showing him such gestures of affection long before now.

"We should get packed up," she murmured. "Surely Captain Mills will be wanting to leave soon. You can't change the world from here in the middle of the prairie."

He grinned at her. "Thank you, Livvy. I'll take care of the animals. I appreciate what a helpmate you've been for me over the last few months."

After climbing into the wagon to quickly organize their supplies, Olivia sat on the narrow corn husk mattress and looked around at her space.. It had been an eventful morning, and she almost could not believe she was now expected to pack up and walk another dozen miles. She had learned so much, and she was having a difficult time quieting her brain to focus on the tasks at hand.

A tiny hint of movement caught her eye, and even in the dim light under the canvas, Olivia could see a spider making its way from the middle wooden rib to the next. Where did it come from, she wondered as she watched. Did it know it was hitching a ride to the other side of the continent? Or was this spider like her, somehow swept up in someone else's plan without rightly knowing how it happened?

And, like the spider, Olivia could embrace the new life she had found herself in, making a home where she found herself.

CHAPTER NINETEEN

Olivia had only just finished her packing that morning when the Sullivan-Mills wagon company left camp after having a full day to rest up. They had stayed longer than they could really afford to, with still so much of the two thousand miles to go until they reached Oregon. After their conversation that morning before, Olivia was thrilled that Luke stayed with their team, helping her pack up the wagon and driving the oxen for the day. Without even being asked, he made his excuses when Charlie Cole had come to ask for a second pair of hands and instead stayed by his wife's side.

It was as though they had wordlessly reached a new agreement, that each would try harder to be part of the team. Together. Olivia was grateful, and though she dreaded what she needed to commit herself to, she knew that this was the right choice for both of them.

As they began the new day heading west, up and out of the ravine, the Montgomery wagon fell into line behind the Carter wagon. Olivia again fell into step next to Luke as he drove the team along the trail. They walked in silence for much of the morning, each alone in their own thoughts, but finally, Olivia's curiosity could hold no further.

"Luke," she ventured. "Don't misunderstand... I'm pleased you're here, but hadn't you promised Jefferson Carter that you would teach him how to repair books?"

"I will. Not today, though. He's got plenty of other work lined up before he needs to bother with my silly little skill. Not much call to repair books on the trail, is there?"

"No, I suppose not. I think we actually walked past a whole crate of books left at the side of the trail the other day. Folks are more likely to let the book go than try to keep it."

"Until we get to Oregon," he said with a knowing smile. "As the oxen get more tired and dehydrated, and folks are trying to drop weight from their wagon to ensure they get to the Pacific, books will be one of the first things to go. They're a luxury, and not many have time to read anyway."

"But whatever books people still have when we get to Oregon must be pretty special," she finished for him, seeing the logic. "How clever, Luke. You're right; Jefferson should be able to earn some extra money in time. But are you sure he won't be getting back into debt?"

"Well, I suppose I can never be sure, but he did give me his word. Only Jefferson Carter can say for sure what the value of his word is."

Olivia slipped her hand into her husband's as they continued walking. She knew the value of his word, at least, and for the second time that day, she was grateful she had married Luke Montgomery.

For the first time since they had left Independence, Luke did not leave Olivia's side for several days. She had him with her for every meal, for every step along the trail, for help with every need Nebuchadnezzar and the other oxen had. Though she wasn't used to it at all, she even started asking him for help. It was a bit ridiculous how much mental preparation it took her to ask her husband to fetch firewood, but she did it, vowing to get better at it.

As they continued traversing the plains, the heat bore down on them, and yet she felt lighter than she had in a long time.

"Phew!" Luke exclaimed. He fanned himself with the brim of his hat as the sweat poured down. "What I wouldn't give for a glass of ice-cold lemonade."

"Or just some ice by itself," Olivia teased. "Seems like a long way to winter."

"Maybe I'll get me a bonnet like you've got." He eyed the calico stretched over and blocking her face from the sun.

"Just hold on till we get to Oregon," she said dreamily, looking into the distance. "Trees for miles and more rain than you could ask for."

"How do you know that?" He looked at her with interest.

She blushed, as though she had been found out. "From reading the guidebook. I figured I should want to know something about where we're going."

"Tell me more about Oregon." He reached for her hand and held it as they walked.

"You already know plenty, I'm sure."

"I want to hear it from you."

She looked at him carefully and decided he wasn't teasing her. He really did seem interested in her opinion, or her telling, at least. Olivia spent the next ten minutes telling her husband all about the rich land where they were headed. Rolling farmland and the perfect amount of rain. Forests full of lumber. Rivers full of fish. Anything a person could want was in Oregon, not even excepting a newspaper.

"The *Oregon Spectator* started just a couple years ago in Oregon City. Even way out west... who would have believed it. And when we pick out our farm," she finished, "I'm hoping there's enough room for an orchard. I've always wanted an apple orchard."

"An orchard, huh?"

"Like the one we walked through at my aunt and uncles? It doesn't have to be large... Just... Enough that I can make apple pies all winter. Enough to keep us busy. Enough that our children have trees to climb in."

"Children?"

She blushed. "Oh, I..."

He lowered his voice, though there was no one nearer than Shadrach and Meshach. "We'll pick out a farm large enough for our children to have plenty of room to play and run."

"And pick apples?"

He laughed. "And pick apples." His tone returned to normal, light, and casual. So much so that Olivia wondered if she had been mistaken to hear the serious tone a moment ago. "But you know, Livvy, I don't know anything about running a farm. That will have to be your department. I follow directions as well as the next man, but you'll have to show me how."

Olivia didn't know why she should feel so much pride at having her skills acknowledged, but she blushed again. "I'll handle the farm sheep, and you handle the Lord's sheep."

Luke laughed so heartily that Olivia was startled. He dropped her hand, wrapped his arm around her shoulder, and pulled her tightly to him. She felt his stubble tickle her cheek as he planted a kiss on her temple.

"I will handle the Lord's sheep. Olivia Montgomery, you do beat all."

That was the day that Olivia remembered all the reasons she had fallen in love with this man. She had been trying so hard to make sure they merely survived that she had forgotten all about what a man needed to *thrive*. As she sat watching him over the smoldering coals, a feeling came over her so new that she almost didn't recognize it. It was a feeling of such peace and gratitude that she had not felt since he proposed. That feeling of being safe with Luke, of being secure, sent a wave of warm contentment through her. This handsome, kind man was her husband, and she had not done anything in her life to deserve such a gift.

Though it seemed as though they still had a long way to go before they could truly come back to each other, Olivia decided that she would be brave and take that first step to bridge the gap between them. Quickly, before she changed her mind.

"I was..." She was suddenly embarrassed. This was

her husband, she reminded herself. He must be waiting for such an invitation. The only thing to do was say it quickly, get it over with, and hope that she wasn't too embarrassed by his response. "I was going to go to bed."

He looked up at the sky, where the last rays of the sun still lightly painted the landscape. "Already? It's early."

She nodded. "Do you..." She cleared her throat. "Do you want to join me?"

He stared at her for a moment before a smile broke over his face. Without taking his eyes off her, Luke kicked dirt over the last of the smoldering campfire before crossing the space to where she stood outside the wagon. Olivia blushed deeply as her husband wrapped his arms around her waist and held her close to him.

"Why, Mrs. Montgomery," he murmured, his eyes darkening as he looked down at her. "How forward."

Even his teasing was back, she reflected with satisfaction, as she took his hand and climbed into the dark privacy of their wagon.

CHAPTER TWENTY

Olivia was up with the sun, waking to find her husband's stubbled face mere inches from her own. She smiled to herself, remembering his skin against hers, his lips on her own. Last night had been exactly what the two of them needed—and who knew when they would have a chance again. It had been far too long that she had allowed resentment to build between them.

Olivia sat up, tucking the blanket around his naked form, and dressed as quietly as she could. The space in the wagon was limited, but she managed. She quietly prepared for her day and climbed out of the wagon without knocking anything over or waking him.

As she collected fuel, built a campfire, and gathered water for their coffee, Olivia thought about how she could do better for him. For both of them. Though she still rather wished that she wasn't left to drive their wagon all by herself some days, she did need to admit that Luke was really doing good in the community.

Maybe there was a happy medium they could reach.

While she let her husband sleep, Olivia had an idea. She would take Hannah Sullivan up on her offer to introduce her to the other members of the wagon company. The pastor's wife had been alone far too long, and she had to make up for that. As she looked around at the rest of the camp, she realized that she was one of the few that seemed to be ready to leave the site soon. Figuring she would have time to go there and back before Luke woke, Olivia made her way to the Sullivan camp.

The sounds of the birds chirping, and the smell of the dew-covered prairie grass filled her senses. Olivia took a deep breath as she walked and tried to remember all the things she had to be grateful for. Though she recognized that she never would have chosen to travel to Oregon without Luke, she had to admit that having him by her side made this adventure worthwhile.

It seemed like this could be the start of a beautiful day out on the frontier.

But once she reached the Sullivans' wagons, she realized not all was going as planned.

The campsite around the Sullivans was hushed quiet, with Hannah looking frantically through the canvas flaps out the back of one of their wagons. She didn't seem to notice Olivia at all. The younger woman looked past her, then lit up when she saw someone else approaching.

Olivia turned to see who had made her react so.

It was Dr. Martell.

When they first joined the Sullivan-Mills wagon company, Luke had told her how lucky they were to have a doctor as part of the group of emigrants. Few doctors were willing to give up their practices and head west;

company leaders outdid themselves trying to tempt one to join.

Dr. Martell hurried to the wagon and climbed in as Olivia watched.

Whatever was happening, whatever the cause of such quiet and stillness, it must be serious for the doctor to find himself there. If this was something that Mrs. Sullivan couldn't treat on her own, Olivia knew it must be time to worry.

As she closed the distance between herself and the Sullivan wagons, another woman approached from the other direction. She was a petite, pale woman, and though Olivia surely had seen her once or twice, she couldn't say what the woman's name was.

"Mrs. Montgomery?" she asked as she approached. "I was just coming to see if Mr. Sullivan could tell us when we needed to be ready to go. Cyrus is feeling a bit sick this morning, so I thought if he could rest up a little longer, that'd be better."

"I haven't seen Mr. Sullivan yet," Olivia answered, "but Dr. Martell just went in." She pointed to the wagon, and the other woman's eyes widened.

"Oh, no. I hope it's nothing terrible."

Olivia looked around, wondering if there was something more she could do to help, someone who could tell them what was going on.

One of the Sullivans must be sick, and until they knew for sure what it was and how contagious, it was likely they wouldn't be leaving camp just yet.

"Well," Olivia said resolutely. "I don't have any children waiting for me back at camp. I can stay and help with what they need. If you want to return to your son, Missus..."

She smiled. "Hatchley. Opal Hatchley. And Cyrus is my husband, not my son. Occasionally he is just as much of a baby, though." She laughed awkwardly. "I'm sorry. I'm just so nervous. Whateverr this is must be bad if it's worth holding up the whole company."

Olivia nodded, the anxiety growing in her belly.

She felt helpless and useless, and yet she instinctively knew she needed to stay. If nothing else, both of the Sullivan women had been so kind to her just a couple days earlier. She could make an offer. She could do... something.

After another few minutes, Hannah came climbing out of the wagon and was startled to see the two women nearby.

"Oh! Heavens," she said. "Excuse me, I just... I need to get cool water to help bring down the fever."

"I'll do it," Mrs. Hatchley said. "You will have plenty to do later. Let me do this."

Without waiting for an answer, she was off, leaving Olivia with Hannah. The young woman's friend—Caroline Harper—approached then, concern evident on her face.

"Are you all right?" she asks cautiously. "I don't like to pry, but if there's anything I can do..."

"No, there's nothing. Or, rather, well, I don't know, to be honest. Dr. Martell says it's measles," she finished with a wail. "Jeremiah has measles in our camp! I can't think of what will happen. Mr. Mills may want us to stay behind all together, rather than bring measles along the trail with everyone else. I just..."

She slumped against the wagon, defeated. Caroline wrapped an arm around her shoulder in comfort.

For a brief moment, Olivia mentally recoiled at the measles. Such a disease could be deadly and could spread like wildfire. Maybe they *should* leave the Sullivans behind. She took a half step backward before rebuking herself. Such fear and selfishness were not only unChristian, but they were the polar opposite of what she had resolved that very morning. What would Luke do in this situation? Though Olivia felt overwhelmed by everything that could go wrong, she knew what she had to do. She would step up and take on the responsibility that was needed.

"I'm sorry," she whispered, shaking a little. "What can I do? How bad is he?"

"It's bad. Dr. Martell wants him to stay put, but Pa said that we have to go. I just— Ma is doing her best, but Jeremiah has been a little sickly since he got pneumonia last year, and I'm not sure he ever recovered."

"The thing to do," Olivia said resolutely, "is to get the rest of you young ones out of the way until this all is settled. Caroline, I can take Patience and Martha into my wagon. Could Hannah stay with you?"

"Of course." The young woman nodded. "Yes, of course. Please, Hannah. Let me do this for you."

"Thank you," Hannah said. "I didn't want to ask, but it'd be a mighty big help. Junior will be fine since he usually sleeps in a tent anyway, but me and the girls could use the offer. I appreciate that, Mrs. Montgomery."

Olivia nodded and followed the girls to the other wagon, where she could collect the young ones.

She knew what it meant to have measles in the community. When she had been only nine or so, there had been a rash of measles spreading quickly around Charlottesville. Though she had been so young, the fear and uncertainty had wracked the community, leaving a deep impression on her. Aunt Bea had done everything she could to keep them safe, but Olivia had still contracted it.

The weeks that had followed were some of the scariest ones of her life.

She had some idea of how Mrs. Sullivan must be feeling. But not only that, this young boy now could threaten the life of every person in the company. George Mills could very well ask the Sullivans to leave to better protect everyone else.

But to head that off, Olivia would take the two youngest girls with her. Keep them safe.

"Patience? Martha? Can you come out here, please?" Hannah called into the family's second wagon. Though Olivia didn't know her well, it was clear how hard she was trying to keep her fear out of her voice.

Two small girls climbed out of the wagon, the littlest one rubbing her eyes as though she had only recently woken.

"I have some news for you," Hannah said brightly. "This is Mrs. Montgomery. You two get to be big girls and stay with her for a night or two."

"Like Pastor Montgomery?" the older girl asked.

"That's right," Olivia said. She squatted in the dirt so she could look them in the eye. "Pastor Montgomery and I were hoping you would be our guests for a couple days. Think of it as an adventure. Would you like to have an adventure?"

The littler one—Martha—nodded, now fully awake.

"Can we say good-bye to Ma?" the older one asked.

Olivia and Hannah looked at each other.

"I'll tell her you said good-bye," Hannah said finally. "You know how busy she can be. And this way she'll be that much more excited when you come home, all right?"

Both of the little girls nodded warily.

Olivia's heart hammered in her chest. The fear of the measles, plus the fear of somehow harming these blessed children. But she would do it. She knew this was the right thing to do, no matter how much it scared her.

"Let's go find Pastor Montgomery for breakfast, girls."

Olivia took the girls by the hand and set off back to her campsite, unsure what she had just gotten herself into.

CHAPTER TWENTY-ONE

Holding the hand of a young Sullivan girl in each of her own, Olivia led the children across the site back to her own campfire, past at least a dozen other wagons. She felt the eyes of many of the other families on her, but she kept her chin up and her eyes straight ahead. They must be wondering why the company hadn't left yet, or what the pastor's wife was doing with two children who were not her own. For all Olivia knew, they could be wondering to themselves who she even was, seeing as she hadn't been rightly social in their journey thus far. Olivia took a deep breath and squared her shoulders. They could think whatever they were going to think; this was the right thing to do.

And she knew that for the first time since they had left Charlottesville, she and Luke would be in accordance with this.

When she reached her own campsite, she found Luke shrugging on his coat as though getting ready to leave.

"I just heard," he said hurriedly. "I'm going to go see if—"

The pastor cut himself off as he finally recognized what he was seeing—his wife, previously reticent and shy, holding the hands of two little girls whom she barely knew.

"Patience!" he exclaimed with a wide smile. "Martha! Girls, I'm so pleased to see you." He offered Olivia a grateful look before crouching down in front of the Sullivans. Patience was nine years old, and Martha was six. Both were plenty old enough to understand that something important was happening in their family. "Have you come to visit?"

He had directed the question at the children, but Olivia knew he was asking her.

"I thought it might be nice if they had a bit of a holiday from their own wagon," she said carefully. "More space here."

"Fewer chores too, I bet," Luke said to the girls with a wink. They both smiled shyly. "That sounds like a wonderful idea." He stood and looked his wife full in the face. "I can't tell you how happy this plan makes me."

He said it lightly, though, to Olivia, it sounded as solemn as their wedding vows had been. She warmed under his praise, though admittedly had little idea how she would entertain two girls for the day.

"We don't have much time, though, girls," she said. "We'll be leaving the campsite soon, so we'll need to get everything put away and ready for the trip. Do you... Well, do you usually ride in the wagon during the day or...?"

Olivia had not the slightest idea how to talk to small

children or what they needed in a situation like this. Did they need her to be their friend or to be an authority? She supposed the best she could do was try.

"No," Patience said, with an expression that implied Olivia was being silly. "Riding in the wagon just makes you sick. We mostly just play while the wagons are moving, but we're supposed to pick up any sticks for firewood we find. Sometimes when we get tired, we'll ride on the seat, but only when Pa or Junior is there."

Olivia nodded solemnly. "Oh! I didn't know it was like that inside the wagon. I only ever walk outside. There are probably lots of things you can teach me." She smiled down at them, and the bright smiles she got in return reassured Olivia that this was the right choice.

"We'll walk with you!" Martha exclaimed, bouncing up and down on her toes.

Olivia looked dubiously at the little girl's size and then exchanged a look with her husband, who shrugged.

"Let's walk together," he suggested. "I'll walk with the oxen, and you girls walk with me. How does that sound?"

"Thank you," she said to him.

"Do you want to help me get them all yoked up?"

Luke directed the girls and held their attention while Olivia finished with the last of their campsite. He had already taken care of much of it since he had so much time waiting for her. Soon their wagon was ready to hit the trail.

Olivia didn't like to think about what it meant to move Jeremiah if he was so sick, but she believed the doctor was doing everything he could. The alternative would mean leaving the Sullivans behind as the rest of the wagon moved on, and no one wanted that. Even aside from the fact that Mr. Sullivan was one of the captains of the company and they needed him, to be left out on their own on the prairie would put the family at risk of Indian attack, starvation, and death.

No. All in all, it was a better choice for all involved for the Sullivans to leave with the rest of the company. But even the better choice didn't mean that there was no risk.

All Olivia could do was take care of these girls and keep them out of harm's way as best she could. That was the task God had set for her, and she would do her best.

It only took until mid-afternoon for Olivia to admit that she was no match for these children. She may have grown up working on a farm. She may have spent every one of the last thirty or more days walking westward and doing even more manual labor along the way. But the entertaining of two small girls is what finally drained the last of her energy.

Olivia could almost laugh at the absurdity of it.

And yet, in spite of her utter exhaustion, Olivia hadn't come close to enjoying herself quite so much. The sheer joy on Patience's face when she got to feed Shadrach a handful of oats made Olivia laugh out loud. Martha's constant questions about Luke's childhood in Vermont or what Olivia's aunt and uncle were like in Virginia were endearing.

"Did you have a doll, like me?" the girl asked wide-eyed. "What was it like to have your own room?"

Olivia laughed and answered her questions as best she could.

Best of all, Luke stayed by their side the whole day.

She knew it wouldn't last—nor would she want it to if a family needed comforting—but it was such a delight to see him with the girls. He was patient, attentive, and absolutely joyful in every interaction he had with the children. They plainly adored him.

Olivia let herself daydream about what Luke might be like as a father.

By sunset, Luke was leading their team to the campsite for the evening, and Olivia promised the girls they could eat right out of the pan for supper. The Montgomerys only had enough dishes for two people, so if the children could think it a treat to not use any, all the better. It had been a long day, yes, but she was more than satisfied with how she had spent it. Patience and Martha seemed to not show any signs of sickness; hopefully, Olivia had been successful in keeping them safe.

Luke led the team of oxen to the nearby water while his wife set up their campsite. As she climbed out of the wagon with the rice and beans she was about to start cooking, Olivia spotted Junior Sullivan, the oldest son, walking across the open expanse toward them. When she caught his eye, she could read in his expression that he had bad news.

"Girls, why don't you go see if you can find me any wildflowers nearby? Don't go too far, though, please."

"Yes, ma'am," Patience said, tugging her sister's hand and darting away.

Junior reached her then, watching his sisters.

"They'll be back soon," Olivia said, indicating the two little girls running off. "But I wasn't sure..."

Junior shook his head. He seemed unable to speak for a moment, then cleared his throat. "He's gone. This afternoon."

Olivia wanted to hug the poor young man; he seemed so anguished as he relayed his brother's last hours. "Oh, Junior... I'm so sorry. Can I... Can we do anything to help? I'll ask Pastor Montgomery to pray for your family."

"Ma was hoping you could keep the girls overnight," Junior continued in a low voice. "She thought it might be kinder to them to give them a little more time in ignorance. We've got to get him..." Junior stopped, shook his head lightly, and cleared his throat before continuing. "Get him ready to be buried, and it's just better if they could be here instead."

Luke joined them then, just to hear the last part. "I'll come by your wagon later tonight to talk to your parents about the service tomorrow."

Junior nodded. "I'll tell them. And... Thank you. I don't... I don't know what to say to Patience and Martha. Thank you for keeping them for a night. Ma wants to tell them in the morning."

"I understand," Olivia said, placing a reassuring hand on his arm. "Go back and be with your parents. The pastor will see you later tonight."

Junior could only nod and duck away again, hurrying to his wagon.

"Where'd he go?" a small voice asked.

Luke and Olivia turned to see Martha running up to them, her hands dirty and clenching small weeds that looked like she had torn them up by the root. Luke turned to Olivia with a questioning look, and she could only laugh.

"These are the wildflowers you found?"

"Yep!" Martha said proudly. "And Patience found some too!"

"Why don't I go get some water to wash those hands? Mrs. Montgomery will find a vase for your flowers," Luke suggested. "And then you can help make supper. We'll have quite the night together."

"Thank you," Olivia said to her husband. He smiled sadly at her; they were bound together in this shared disaster.

This would be the little girls' last night before tragedy struck their young lives. She would do her best to make it as carefree as possible.

CHAPTER TWENTY-TWO

The following morning, when Olivia woke she almost got an elbow to her face before she realized what was happening. Patience and Martha Sullivan were curled on either side of her, in the narrow space of the Montgomery wagon between barrels of flour and crates of supplies. Little Martha, the youngest, snored lightly in her sleep. There were curls plastered to her sweaty face, and she lay on her back with her arms up over her head. Patience was curled up in a ball, tucked into the small of Olivia's back and all but pinning her in place. Olivia almost laughed, wondering how she had managed to sleep at all with such a monkey-child next to her.

In the still quiet dawn, Olivia lay between the two slumbering girls wondering how best to approach their morning.

The night before, she had put the girls to bed, and Luke had made his way over to the Sullivan camp to help as best he could. He didn't return to his own wagon until late. But Olivia was still awake, and they sat whispering together over the embers of their campfire.

Mrs. Sullivan wanted to be the one to tell the girls that their brother had died. She wanted to do it this morning before they had a short funeral service for the boy. And the service needed to be completed early, so the wagon company could set off again across the wide-open plains toward Oregon without losing too much time.

As Olivia woke, she steeled herself for such a difficult day. With a deep breath, she sat up, smoothed down her hair, and climbed out of the wagon, leaving the Sullivan girls to sleep just a little bit longer. She was surprised to see that Luke was already up, reading his Bible. The scent of brewing coffee welcomed her.

"Oh!" she said in surprise.

"Good morning," he said quietly. "I thought you might want to take the girls back to their camp this morning. They seemed to have such a great time with you yesterday, it might be nice for them for you to walk with them."

"Really?" Olivia had been so used to Luke just leaving her behind while he handled everything outside of their little home that it hadn't occurred to her that he would need her to do anything at all.

He nodded. "I'll finish my coffee, and then we can go back together for the service. But those little girls need to see their mother."

She nodded and smiled at his thoughtfulness. He was right—they needed to get the girls up.

Ten minutes later, Olivia was repeating her walk back across the wide campsite, with a Sullivan girls' hand in each of hers and with the eyes of their neighbors watching. This time, Olivia felt more sympathy than curiosity in their gazes—the news of Jeremiah's death must have spread. Both had gotten out of bed quickly when she told them they were going home.

Martha was full of questions, but also full of energy. She was ready to go home long before her sister. Patience seemed to be taking her time, preening and examining herself in the small mirror hanging from the bow in the Montgomerys' wagon. Though she knew they needed to get going, Olivia didn't want to rush her. These were the last minutes before they were told about their brother, after all. The last minutes before tragedy truly touched their young lives.

Once the three had woven through the campsite to where the Sullivans' two wagons were, they found their mother waiting for them. Mrs. Sullivan sat on the rear lip of one, shoulders sagging with the weight of her loss heavy on her. Olivia deliberately stepped on a small twig in her path, making noise to pull the woman's attention so they didn't startle her.

"Girls!" she exclaimed as her face lit up in seeing her daughters. Olivia could hear the hitch in her voice, but none of that pain was in her expression. She must have been immensely strong to be able to remain calm in the wake of what she had been through.

"Say thank you to Mrs. Montgomery," Mrs. Sullivan told her daughters.

"Thank you," they said in unison, though Martha hiccupped in the middle.

Olivia bent down and held her arms out, and both girls stepped into a hug. "I had fun," she said into their hair. "Thank you for spending the day with me. Be good for your mother."

The two little girls giggled, then waved to Olivia as she walked away. She was out of earshot already when she looked back to see Mrs. Sullivan pull both girls close to her and talk quietly to them. Olivia couldn't imagine how difficult the moment must be for that mother; her own throat closed up as a wave of despair crested over her.

Olivia had spent so much of the journey thus far tamping down her feelings and denying that anything was truly wrong. She wasn't sure how much longer she could keep that up. A child was dead. A *second* child was dead, and though Olivia had not known Jeremiah directly, the rest of his family that she was now close to showed her what a delight that young boy must have been.

And now he was gone.

By the time Olivia reached her campsite again, she had given up trying to hold back her tears. She couldn't imagine what her expression must have looked like to lead Luke to rush to her side and embrace her as soon as he laid eyes on her.

"Livvy," he whispered into her hair. "It's all right. It will be all right. I'm so sorry, my love."

She let the tears spill over and cried in his arms. The shoulder of his coat must be getting wet; others would see when he led the funeral service, but she couldn't stop herself. She had been trying to stay strong, trying to stay invulnerable for too long, and this was the last straw.

"Do you want to stay here when I go—"

"No," she answered abruptly, pulling away and

looking at him. "No, please, let me go with you. I want to pay my respects. I want…" She shook her head at herself, unable to form the words that filled her heart.

"All right," he said, taking her hand. "Do you want some coffee before we leave?"

Olivia shook her head again and wiped her face with her hands. "Just… give me a moment."

He nodded, and she made her way to the wagon where there was a small mirror hanging from one of the ribs holding the canopy. She peered at herself in the dim light, a bit dismayed at how red her eyes were. She combed her fingers through the knots in her hair, braided it again, and changed into her last clean dress before meeting Luke again outside.

With a gentle smile, he took her hand, and the Montgomerys made their way together to the Sullivans' campsite to help honor and bury another member of the wagon company.

It all seemed a blur—now that Olivia no longer denied herself the feelings of sorrow and grief, the world seemed overwhelming. But she knew better than to ask for any sympathy. She was there to support and offer her own sympathy, not to take from others.

Jeremiah Sullivan was buried in a shallow grave a few feet off the trail. Only twenty or so people came to hear Pastor Montgomery praise the boy and pray over his final resting place, but the heavy depression fell over everyone.

Not ten minutes after Jeremiah's father, brother, and another friend had piled heavy stones on top of the grave, the lead wagon had rolled out onto the Oregon Trail heading west again. There was no time to delay, and no time to mourn when they weren't moving. The Sullivan-Mills company had to make up some time—all of the recent delays had put them behind the pace they needed to set in order to make it over the Blue Mountains before the first snowfall.

But thoughts of snow seemed foreign to the wagon company now. It was all they could do to stay cool and shaded with every step west. The oppressive heat of late June added another layer of misery to the grieving emigrants.

All through that day, after burying Jeremiah, Olivia could not stop thinking about the Sullivans—how they must miss their little boy, how much love she witnessed between them. That was a family to be admired, and Olivia actually found herself wanting to be better friends with them. What must it be like to have dear friends that would support her in the event of such a tragedy? Olivia could only imagine, but for the first time in her life felt like it might actually be possible for her.

Traveling the two thousand miles of the Oregon Trail, however, was no place to start thinking about her social life.

Olivia's mind went blank to everything but the trail as the wagon company continued their trek west under the beating sun. One foot in front of the other, unceasing and unchanging. Olivia sweated through her dress each day, and each night slept uncomfortably, chafing her skin and hoping it would dry before the morning. All of her thoughts were distilled down to how she could stay cool. How she could find water or shade or firewood or time to rest.

The Oregon Trail filled all her senses.

From north to south, east to west, the great plains stretched to the horizon. The land was so flat around them that it almost made Olivia dizzy. She felt unmoored. There were no trees or even shrubs to break the unending flatness of the prairie.

Once, Olivia stepped off the trail into the grass, pulled off her bonnet, and looked up at the bright blue sky. She squinted against the sun. In the periphery of her vision, it felt like she was at the bottom of a great bowl, the sides slowly climbing with her in the middle. Stopping and feeling the land all around made her feel more anchored, more present on the trail than just the never-ending progress westward.

As she looked up, an enormous bird flew high overhead. She watched it head north, by itself, toward whatever nest or food it could sense. It was not the first vulture she had seen on the trail. Just the day before, the wagon train passed the rotting carcass of an ox that had been dragged to the side. Though it had evidently been dead for a couple days, the vultures had not yet finished picking the bones clean. Half a dozen of them perched still, ripping at the rotting flesh.

Olivia shivered.

Occasionally the monotony of the flat plains was broken by vultures and carcasses, but also by furniture. As though they had sprouted out of the ground, wardrobes or armchairs would be passed by the wagons. Grass had grown up around the legs, birds perched on top, and the surface of the wood had been faded and worn down by the wild weather of the plains. This furniture had belonged to families that had overestimated how much weight their teams of oxen could pull across the continent and found themselves having to give up treasured heirlooms.

For the first time, Olivia felt grateful that she and Luke had had virtually nothing to take west, and so nothing important she had to let go of.

Finally, after several days of such monotony, a new shape rose up on the horizon that remained in place day after day. Olivia studied the guidebook, learning all about the giant rocks that served as guideposts along the trail. This first behemoth they reached was named Courthouse Rock, after the county seat in Missouri.

This was the first, like a gate to a whole new part of the country. No longer just monotonous plains, now the wagon company would see enormous granite formations jutting up out of the grass at regular intervals.

In another couple days, another huge formation rose out of the plain. A round mound that narrowed into a tall spire. The company would stay overnight at Chimney Rock, and Olivia felt the presence of the immense stone over her the entire time they were there.

This longer stay and fascinating creations lifted the spirits of the emigrants. The monotony and the recent deaths had taken their toll. But now all seemed reenergized and newly confident that they would make it over the mountains before cold weather.

CHAPTER TWENTY-THREE

One morning soon after, Olivia went to slice off a couple strips of bacon for their breakfast and was met with a rancid smell. Frowning, she lifted up the slab out of the crate where it had been stored—the odor intensified. The entire bottom of the meat was vaguely green, putrid, and rotting.

With a gasp of dismay, Olivia dropped the bacon back into the box. She grimaced, wiping her fingers obsessively on her apron, hoping she could get the smell off of her.

She looked around at the interior of their wagon and realized that was just about the last of their meat. There was a small amount of jerky left, and there was still a chance Luke could hunt fresh meat for them, but what they had left was nowhere near enough to feed them for every meal. She would have to figure out a way to make it last.

Shaking her head, she climbed back out of the wagon, mentally planning what they could have for breakfast instead. She would deal with the rancid bacon later.

Later that day, Olivia hadn't yet found the fortitude to get back into the wagon and deal with the rotting meat that was starting to smell like death when a cry of joy sounded up ahead on the wagon train. The Montgomerys were in the latter half of the line of wagons and couldn't guess what had occasioned such a reaction from whoever was ahead of them.

But they didn't have long to wait. Before long, Daniel Mills, the wagon company's oldest son, was riding down the length of the train calling for the men to circle up.

"Making camp right here," he yelled out to everyone in earshot. "Grab your guns, men! There's buffalo on the horizon! Ten minutes."

He didn't stop for questions, but everyone moved their wagons into place. With only exchanging a look, Olivia and Luke guided their wagon into place, lips overlapping with the Sheldons' and the Carters' wagons, and unyoked the animals.

"Are you really going to hunt?" she asked him as he stuck his head under the canvas flaps and pulled out his rifle.

He nodded and chuckled. "Don't hold your breath for anything, though, Livvy. I haven't properly hunted in more than ten years."

"Do your best. We could use fresh meat. Besides, the other men all love you. They won't let you come home empty-handed."

"You're probably right," Luke said with a laugh.

He kissed her on the cheek and ran off toward the

north where the men were gathering to go after the herd. Nearly all the men and boys over fourteen had grabbed their weapons and moved away from the camp in a drove.

Olivia smiled to herself as she relished the quiet afternoon ahead of her. This break—and this bounty—would be exactly what the company needed to break out of the melancholy that had overtaken them in the heat and the monotony. They had luckily camped near a spring, so Olivia fetched a fresh bucket of water and set about to get things done. If she hurried, she could wash a few items of their clothing and set it out to dry while there was still enough sunlight.

Just under an hour later, Olivia was draping a couple of dresses, shirts, and underthings over the canvas wagon top under the baking sun to dry. Her hands were a bit raw from the water, soap, and scrubbing, but the work was worth it. It had been far too long since she had worn a clean dress.

She was about to dump her soapy water and empty her tub when she heard a piercing yell float across the prairie.

Though she couldn't see precisely what had made the sound, her blood ran cold. Looking around, she realized that very few of the others still in camp had heard the scream, let alone known how to react.

Olivia took several steps toward where she thought the cry had come from, watching carefully, listening, wishing she could shush the little boy nearby who was giggling out of control.

She heard something new. Something thunderous and pulsing. A half-second later and she realized that the sound she heard was horses galloping. But that couldn't be their men she heard. It could only be—

Indians!

Olivia froze, utterly uncertain of what to do. How could she stay safe when they were being attacked? Her mind leaped from possibility to possibility, thought to thought. One moment she was furious that Luke had taken their only firearm, but the next moment she realized the natives must have known the men had all left.

She stood rooted to the spot—dying grass and dirt under her feet. After walking a few steps away from her wagon, she was inside the circle of wagons that had been meant to be a barrier against any attacks. But as she watched, the dark, shirtless native warriors jumped down from their horses, and with little effort, pulled apart two of the wagons.

The men must have been in such a rush to get to the hunt that they hadn't taken the proper precautions. They hadn't chained the wheels together as they had at every other campsite. As Olivia watched, the wagons were pulled farther and farther apart, allowing the attacking party to pour into the center of the white emigrants' circle.

And still, Olivia did not move, even as the Indians spread out around the company, intent on raiding as many of the wagons as they could in as quick a time as possible.

There was a small part of her that felt outside her body altogether. She felt like she was just watching this all unfold, somewhere apart from her.

An arrow landed in the dirt, almost piercing her right

foot, and kicking up a small cloud of dust up around her ankles.

Olivia shook herself out of her reverie and forced herself to move.

Waiting and watching was how people got hurt. She would not be responsible for anyone else dying in this company.

No sooner had she taken a step back toward her wagon than she felt a strong arm wrap around her rib cage.

Shock and horror roiled through Olivia—her primal instincts screamed at her to fight back, even as her mind wondered what was happening.

Whoever had grabbed her gripped tighter, and Olivia felt her feet leave the ground. She felt her side pressed tight against the warm, muscular body of a horse. She heard the shouts and foreign words of her captor. And she suddenly realized what was happening to her.

But she refused to let it.

Using all her strength, all the muscles in her abdomen, Olivia twisted this way and that, trying to loosen the grip of the native trying to lift her off her feet and carry her away. She would *not* allow herself to be taken away from her husband, from her life, from people who she hoped were her friends.

She couldn't see where they were going; she only knew that she had to free herself. No one else would do it for her. Stretching her legs out as far as she could, Olivia realized she could drag her toes along the ground, slowing her captor even if only a little.

Standing in one spot as she had been, Olivia must have looked like an easy target. A petite woman all alone without even the presence of mind to hide when she saw they were being attacked.

Olivia was determined to prove that estimation wrong.

She had twisted around enough that she could see the man that still clung to her with one arm. He was counting on being able to brace his captive against the horse long enough to draw her up, but Olivia was quickly slipping out of his grasp.

And he had left her arms free.

Though she had never thrown a punch in her entire life, Olivia made a fist and swung her right arm around to hit as much of the Indian as she could reach.

"Let go!" she screamed, smashing her knuckles into the man's thigh. "Let go, let go, let me go!" She felt tears of frustration coming as she yelled and fought.

But this Indian was all muscle. He didn't even look down at her as he continued to ride—though slower now—holding her with one arm.

"Let go!"

Hitting him over and over again, not just his thigh, but she twisted herself even farther to reach his arm, his wrist. Anything that might be a weak spot that she could touch.

His hold faltered, and she slipped. Not totally out of his grip, but now both of her feet dragged on the ground. The horse slowed, thankfully, and Olivia felt certain she must be close.

"Let me go!"

The Indian looked down at her, frowned, shook his head, and then dropped her in the dirt and rode away.

Olivia lay crumpled in the dirt as horses rode around

her, women screamed in the distance. She was vulnerable. She knew she had to get up, to stay on guard. The man had only let her go because she had made things too difficult for him—there was no guarantee another wouldn't try it again if she looked too weak.

Pulling herself to her feet, Olivia felt her face coated with a layer of dust. She coughed and spit, trying to clear her throat so she could take a deep breath. She took a hesitant step toward her wagon and realized she must have twisted an ankle when she was being dragged by the horse. Putting weight on her right foot sent pain through her. She tested it again. It didn't seem broken; she could wiggle her toes inside her boot. It hurt, but it wasn't insurmountable.

Especially not at a time like this.

She looked up, peering through the sweat pouring down her and the clouds of dust the horses were kicking up, looking for her own wagon. Looking for where she could be safe.

There. To her left, all the way across the circle of wagons, she spotted her own wagon. Back before they left Independence, Luke had painted "Psalm 119:105" in big black figures on the side, and now she was grateful. She had never been far away enough from their wagon to need the visual cue, but now it called to her like a beacon. She looked all around her before taking another step. The sounds of horses—and now cattle—were all around her, and she didn't want to walk right into a stampeding herd.

As quickly as she could move on her injured ankle, Olivia darted back to her home. The campfire was still smoldering, her tub of water had been overturned, creating a wide puddle of mud, and her cast iron pan had been knocked into it.

Grateful it hadn't been taken, Olivia could none-theless see evidence that her wagon had been raided.

But before she could make her way under the canopy to assess the damage, she heard a scream.

This was different—not an Indian war cry but a young girl's scream. And it was near enough to her that Olivia looked around in panic.

The Sheldons' wagon was jutted right up to hers, and there at the back was a Native American with his arms full of supplies. From this distance, Olivia could just make out the faces of Mrs. Sheldon, Lily, Millie, and David in the dim light of the wagon. It was Lily who had screamed, Olivia realized.

Without a thought beyond righteous fury, Olivia caught up the only heavy thing nearby and limped the few yards to the Sheldons' wagon. Maybe she wouldn't have been quite so courageous if the thief was holding a weapon, but with his hands full of sacks of flour and a man's shirt, Olivia let her emotions rule the day.

"Drop it!" she commanded, though, in the back of her mind, she knew he couldn't understand her.

The Indian did, however, turn toward the interloper.

It was Olivia, limping, hair a mess, face streaked with dirt, carrying a heavy pan, and yelling unintelligibly at him.

"Leave them alone!"

But before she even got to him, he had darted off with his bounty.

Olivia had not yet stopped shaking.

CHAPTER TWENTY-FOUR

Still shaking, petrified, and drained from her near-kidnapping by their Indian attackers, Olivia sat in the shade of her wagon away from the afternoon sun. The men were still off hunting buffalo, and the women of the wagon company were trying to pull everything back together, calm the children, and stay on the defense. All across the ground around every wagon were strewn the rejects and broken pieces of whatever the Indians had seized or overturned but then not taken with them.

Though it was tempting to find someone to blame for the attack, Olivia knew that would be futile. The thing to do now was to move forward, not look back. There was too much still to do to waste time pointing fingers.

Olivia had returned limping to her own wagon after chasing off the warrior from the Sheldons. She waved off any thanks or offers to help, knowing that Mildred would have plenty to do with the children—adding Olivia's needs to her burden would only make things harder. So now she sat alone and injured, breathing through the pain and panic. She tenderly pressed her fingers to her ankle, feeling for the extent of the injury. She could already tell she shouldn't be walking on it—would she have to ride on the wagon? How long would she have to stay off her feet?

With slow, repetitive breaths, Olivia calmed her beating heart and stop her hands from shaking.

She stood, and hopped to the back of her wagon on her good foot, then leaned against the wooden frame to peer inside.

It was a complete disaster.

Crates overturned. Bags emptied and spilling out. Trunk opened with some of its contents still hanging over the edge.

Olivia willed herself to continue the slow, calming breaths.

As she assessed what might have been taken, Olivia supposed it was lucky that she and Luke didn't own much—there wasn't much for the native warriors to take from them. They had left Virginia with the bare minimum, and even the little they had wasn't of much interest.

Even with that caveat, Olivia saw that the clean clothes she had left out to dry on the wagon top had been pulled down. Both of her dresses now lay in the dirt, and since they had been damp, they were now muddy as well. She glanced up at the sun's position and realized if she hurried, she might still have time to wash and dry them before dark.

But hurrying meant she had to be on her injured ankle.

Olivia clenched her teeth and pushed through the pain.

She climbed to her feet, resting most of her weight on her good ankle, and set about gathering the laundry. Both dresses were draped over her arm when Olivia realized that all of Luke's clean shirts were gone.

"No," she whispered to herself, walking around the far side of the wagon to see if maybe they had been blown off. There wasn't much wind to speak of, but it wasn't impossible that she had missed seeing them float down to the prairie grass beyond the circle of wagons.

But even retracing her steps and double-checking the same places she had already looked did not yield her husband's clothing. The Indians must have stolen them. It could have been worse, but still, the feeling of dread and frustration coursed through her.

She rubbed her face and was reminded just how dirty she still was from being dragged around by the Indian's horse through clouds of dust kicked up. Though more work was the last thing she wanted to do, Olivia found her bucket—mercifully not also stolen—and made her way to the spring to gather more water.

As she limped slowly, she saw the molding side of bacon discarded in the dirt ten feet from her wagon; whoever had stolen it had noticed after a few steps it wasn't worth taking.

Oh well, thought Olivia with a sigh. She had intended to throw out most of it anyway.

It took her all afternoon, but Olivia spent the rest of the day working, in spite of her injured ankle. At times the jolts of pain brought tears to her eyes, but at least she knew that nothing was broken. She had washed her dresses again, washed her face, and cleaned up the scattered bits and debris that littered the ground around their campsite. A sack of flour had been ripped open and discarded, the ground coated in a thin layer of the white powder in a five-foot radius. She managed to rescue some of it; not an ounce could be wasted.

All around her, as she saw to her own campsite, other women were cleaning their own stores, bandaging wounds, and gathering together to comfort each other and exchange stories. Some of the cattle that had been corralled in the middle of the circle of wagons had been driven out and also stolen. There wasn't one family who had not lost something valuable.

As she sat watching everyone else, Olivia was approached by her neighbor, Mrs. Sheldon, carrying a bucket of something.

"How are you feeling?" she said, nodding to where Olivia had stretched out her right foot to elevate it.

Olivia smiled ruefully. "Hurts. But it's not broken. I'll live."

"Well, you know, with four children, I've done a bit of nursing in my day. I'm happy to help you wrap that ankle whenever you like."

"I appreciate it. Maybe tomorrow, before we start out?"

"I'll hold you to that." She smiled. "But the real reason I'm here is that I wanted to give you this." She set the bucket down at Olivia's feet.

Olivia was perplexed—she already had as many buckets as she needed. But when she took it from the other woman, she realized it was full.

"Is this... milk? I thought your cattle were all stolen. I can't take this, Mrs. Sheldon. You must need it."

"Nonsense. We still have some cows, and they'll make more milk. That's Sheldon dairy of the finest quality," she said with a wink. "I know this is not enough to thank you for stepping in as you did earlier. I hate to think what would have happened to us if you hadn't been there."

"Oh, I don't know if that's true." Olivia blushed at the praise. "I was just the closest."

"Maybe. And now you're the one I'm giving this to. If you leave the bucket hanging in the wagon, the swaying and jostling as we travel should actually churn it into butter."

"Is that so?" Now Olivia was intrigued. "Luke and I haven't had butter since we left Independence. What a treat this will be! Goodness, I... Thank you, Mrs. Sheldon. I'll return the bucket to you soon."

"Take your time." She waved dismissively. "Fewer cows, after all. Fewer needs for the bucket. Lily pretends to be disappointed, but we both know she'll relish having fewer chores now."

"Thank you," Olivia said again.

It seemed as though Mrs. Sheldon wanted to hug her but didn't know how she would respond. "I'll leave you to it, but you send the pastor over my way if you need me, you hear?"

It wasn't until sunset that the men returned from their hunt.

The sounds of emotional reunions and exclamations filled the air. Olivia looked up from her seat by her campfire to see women running to meet their husbands, hurrying to spill out the whole story of what had happened when they were gone.

Olivia's ankle was far more swollen by now, after an afternoon on her feet, and she didn't want to seem too needy to Luke. She stayed where she was. It wasn't long before she saw him hurrying across the open circle to their wagon.

"Livvy!" he called when he was still ten yards away.

She stood, awkwardly keeping her balance on one foot, though she tried to smile in greeting.

"Are you all right?" he demanded.

Luke had been carrying a slab of something—buffalo, hopefully—and his rifle, but set them down hurriedly. He caught her up in a tight hug. She lost her balance, falling into him.

"What's wrong?" Luke was immediately panicked and stood back from her, holding her upright with a strong hand on each of her arms.

"I'm fine," she said. "I'll be fine. Just hurt my ankle, is all."

"Oh!" He gasped his surprise and guilt, helping her to sit again. "Is it wrapped? Can I help? Tell me what to do."

It was endearing how badly he wanted to make things better for her, but Olivia knew that everything that could be done had been done. He sat in the dirt at her feet, looking up at her.

"You shot a buffalo?" she asked, gesturing at the bundle he had set aside.

He waved it off dismissively. "Oh, that's nothing. I didn't even shoot it. Mr. Cole just made sure I got a piece of the one he took down. What's more important is what happened here. Livvy... Indians?"

"I don't know... I don't know where to start, or what you've already heard," she began hesitatingly.

He took both of her hands in his and looked into her eyes. "What happened after the men left? Start there."

So she did. Her initial efforts in doing laundry, hearing the hooves approaching, and hearing the battle cry. Seeing the wagons pulled apart and the warriors pouring into the space. It was all so clear in her memory. Each moment that she had stood there watching was so visceral.

It wasn't until she had to explain how she had been attacked that Olivia faltered.

"I... um..." Her heart raced, and her hands went numb. "One of the warriors targeted me, and I... hurt my ankle, but he eventually left me alone. And then, I heard Lily Sheldon scream—"

"Wait," Luke said with a frown. "What do you mean he targeted you?"

Olivia looked away. If she forced herself to actually see and process the concern clear on his face, she might cry. She shook her head. "He just... He grabbed me, and then, eventually, let me go."

"Livvy," he said tenderly. "What happened?"

She looked at him and was overwhelmed by the events of the day. Try as she might to tamp down the feelings, tears spilled down her cheeks.

But she told him the truth. All of the truth.

All of her fear and her rage and her feelings of helplessness.

She wasn't sure she had ever in her life been as

vulnerable with another person as she was in this moment. It was too soon to know if she would regret it, but she knew she would never be happy being married to a man she had to hide things from.

But surprisingly, the more she talked, the easier it was. Luke had always been a good listener, and to have his attention focused solely on her was the balm her soul needed.

It was clear from his expression that there was plenty he had to say, but he didn't interrupt, he didn't explain. Her husband just heard her in her pain and her fear and was there for her.

When Olivia had finished her story, he simply whispered, "I'm so sorry," and drew her into an embrace.

CHAPTER TWENTY-FIVE

After hearing all about her harrowing day, Luke insisted that Olivia go straight to bed. He would handle everything that needed doing, all the cleaning up and settling. She had worked far too hard that day, even aside from the attack and her injury. He wouldn't take no for an answer, and she was grateful for the rest.

It had been a long, exhausting day.

Olivia was asleep the moment she closed her eyes.

The next morning, the families needed to be ready to leave as soon as possible. The longer they stayed, the longer they remained vulnerable to another attack, and there wasn't one family that could risk losing any more supplies.

By dawn, when Olivia woke, she could already hear some of the families moving about. All the wagons had been repacked with what supplies each family had remaining. The buffalo meat had all been processed and handled, to feed the company for another couple of weeks. The guns were all cleaned and ready in the event of another attack.

The Sullivan-Mills wagon company couldn't dawdle. There was too little time remaining to get to the mountains. Olivia knew she hadn't been the only woman injured—she had seen Dr. Martell's wife and a couple of the other matrons darting from campsite to campsite yesterday. She wasn't about to be a reason they were late leaving.

She heard Luke humming to himself outside the canvas and moving something around. He sounded like he needed help, and she wasn't sure he knew where all the supplies might be kept. Her body ached all over from the adventures of the day before, but she was determined to not be a burden.

Stifling a groan, Olivia climbed down from the wagon, holding herself awkwardly up with white knuckles, trying to keep her weight off her injured ankle while she lowered her good foot to the ground.

"Livvy!" Luke exclaimed when he saw her. "What are you doing? Get back in bed."

"I'm not riding back there, Luke. You heard the Sullivan girls say it makes them sick. I have to get up."

"Well—"

"And it sounded like you need help. Should I make coffee?"

She would have thought she had suggested breaking a wild stallion; she was met with an expression of utter shock from her husband.

"No! Livvy, no. Here." He grasped her arm, trying to take all her weight on himself. "Come sit, at least. I can handle this. Really. You need to heal."

"But—"

"Please."

He said it so urgently, and she had so few steps to rely on him that she agreed, secretly resolving that as soon as he was out of sight, she would get up again and tend to her own coffee. But he never let her out of his sight, not when he was making breakfast, not when he was hitching up the team. The only chance she had was when he collected Mrs. Sheldon and brought her back to bandage up Olivia's ankle. Finally, when all was ready, he returned to where Olivia was and helped her to climb up to the wagon seat.

"Don't even think about getting down on your own," he teased.

The wagon train rolled out of camp early, heading ever west. They still had several days before they would reach Fort Laramie, and every man, woman, and child was eagerly awaiting that respite.

If they hadn't managed to secure the boon of the fresh buffalo meat, Olivia had been worried the group of travelers would stagnate and fall into a depression. Fortunately, though, they had the treat to wake them all up a bit. Each member of the company was going through the motions of getting through each day and looking forward to the stop at the fort where they could rest, feel protected from further attacks, and most importantly, buy more supplies to fill their stores.

Fort Laramie had been purchased by the United States Army the year before, after starting as a trading post for Americans trekking across the wilderness. They should have at least some supplies to tide over the travelers and replenish their stores.

During the few days of travel to the fort, Olivia spent most of the time riding up on the seat of the wagon while Luke drove the team. Though she was grateful to have him around for days at a time, and she knew she should be even more grateful that he was finally taking the lead on driving the wagon, Olivia found herself unsettled.

She hated not being at her full strength and capability. She hated having to rely on another person for so much. She had never been good at it, and this new injury only shone a light on that fact. Even when they stopped at night, Luke insisted on being the one to gather water, to pull together whatever Olivia needed to make supper. She tried to protest that she wasn't helpless, but Luke wouldn't hear it.

"I don't want you injuring yourself further just because you don't want to accept my help," he said.

But the pastor wasn't the only one trying to make Olivia accept help. Mrs. Sheldon, Mrs. Martell, and Louisa Hudson all came by the Montgomery wagon more than once to lend a hand. Olivia tried to protest, but Luke gladly accepted every offer of food, cleaning, or kindness that the women offered. Louisa even brought Lawrence with her one evening to help unyoke the oxen and set up camp.

All the while, Olivia had to watch helplessly.

Over the several days that the company traveled to the fort, Olivia rested, though it was against her very nature to let anyone do anything for her. She was grateful she had, however, when they reached Fort Laramie.

As the wagons rolled up the trail to the fort, she

could see quite a ways from her perch upon the wagon seat. Fort Laramie boasted tall, fifteen-foot-high walls all around the large square. Olivia gasped to see them—this was the first secure structure they had come across since leaving Independence.

They would have a long afternoon here, enough time to make wagon repairs and refill their stores. Olivia climbed down from the wagon, grateful that she could finally walk under her own power. She stretched her limbs and tested her weight on her ankle.

"I'm going with you," she called to Luke before he could disappear.

He paused and looked back, watching expectantly as Olivia took the few steps toward him. His proud—and relieved—smile spurred her on, and she began to feel more confident that her injury had healed.

She approached the fort at Luke's side, where she could see Indian huts built out of straw and dried mud all around the outer walls. She slowed her walk, cautiously watching for anyone that looked like the warrior that had tried to take her, that had injured her only barely healed ankle.

Two guardhouses stood at opposite corners of the fort. Under the eyes of the soldiers watching, she was perfectly safe. She passed the Indian huts, seeing no more than a handful of older women, at least one of them wearing an army coat. She breathed a sigh of relief and entered the fort, eager to purchase what supplies she could find.

. . .

After leaving Fort Laramie, they had to cross another long stretch of terrain without water or even many plants. The ground was dry and dusty, and the animals had to press on with the little bit of brush they could scavenge and the handful of oats that Olivia could spare.

The days passed monotonously. Endless stretches of the trail under a clear blue sky, marching ever onward to Oregon with only an occasional abandoned piece of furniture by the trail to break the constancy. They needed to make at least fifteen miles every day. All of the springs along this section of the trail were sulfurous, and they needed to move as quickly as possible to get to more clean water.

Though such a punishing pace would be hard on the animals—hard on the whole company—anything less put them all at an even larger risk.

One such afternoon, the monotony was broken when everything stopped. The wagon ahead of them had paused completely. It scared Olivia—they were supposed to be hustling to make as many miles as possible. What could have happened to arrest that?

She and Luke exchanged a glance.

"I'll go," she volunteered.

After he nodded his assent, Olivia walked quickly up the trail to the Carters' wagon.

"Do we know what happened?"

Morris Carter shook his head. "Not yet. Hope it's not a broken wheel or anything. We can't afford to be stopped for too long."

Olivia nodded and kept walking up the trail. Ahead of the Carters, past several more wagons, until she came to the Sullivans, whose wagons were about halfway through the row.

Patience was the first one to spot her, a wide grin breaking across her face.

"Mrs. Montgomery!" She ran to Olivia and threw her arms around her waist.

"Hello, dear." She hugged the child back. "Do you know why we're stopped? If anyone needs help?"

The girl shook her head. "No. Nothing anyone can do. Ma says that the Gladwells have an ox that fell."

"Oh, no! How did it fall?"

Patience shrugged. "It just stopped walking? I think. I don't know. But then they had to stop, and everyone behind them had to stop, and we're stopped, and now they gotta move it somehow so the wagons can all keep going."

Olivia nodded, looking up ahead at the wagons waiting on the trail for the Gladwells to handle their oxen. She imagined that if their team was anything like her own, one of the animals had just... had enough. Gone too long without food or water.

And Patience was right; there was nothing Olivia could do about that. The only important thing for her—for any of the emigrants—was taking care of her oxen. Without these animals, they had no chance of making it all the way to Oregon.

Olivia returned to her own wagon and told Luke the news. All they could do was wait for the Gladwells to take care of their animal. In the meantime, Olivia leaned her forehead against Shadrach's head, petting her nose and talking softly to her.

She would never not be grateful for these four oxen,

all working so hard to help them get to Oregon, to help Luke achieve his dream, to help Olivia keep them all alive.

When the wagon train started moving again after a few minutes, they finally arrived at the scene of the perished draft animal. Olivia averted her eyes from the carcass that had been dragged to the side of the trail. Moments after the last wagon rolled by, the wolves and vultures would descend to claim it.

The following day as they made their way west, the train slowed again, though it didn't stop completely. The wheels kept turning, and the Sullivan-Mills company continued ever onward. Olivia was on edge, waiting to pass whatever it was that had slowed the lead wagon.

After an hour or so, she noticed a cloud of dust larger than she would expect and somehow coming toward them.

"Oh, no... It's a turnaround," Luke muttered, seeing the same dust-up she did. "They're going to pass us going the other way."

"What are turnarounds?"

"Folks who have changed their mind about heading to Oregon and are making their way back."

"But... why? They've already come so far!"

He shrugged. "Maybe they lost too many animals or too many family members. Maybe they just are tired of going without the niceties they had been used to. There's lots of reasons, Livvy. And we should be generous in our assumptions. We don't know what hardships they've been battling. Some of these folks have had to give up on their dream."

She nodded thoughtfully, though curious to see what people who have so completely given up would look like.

When the wagon reached the Montgomerys, the pastor took off his hat respectfully to the family passing them. It was an older couple, old enough to be Olivia's parents, and no children that she could see. The "turn-arounds" seemed dejected and grieving. Whatever had befallen them to make them believe that what was ahead wasn't worth the work required to get there must have been substantial.

"May the Lord help you find what you're looking for, ma'am," Luke called to them.

"We're looking for home," the woman said bitterly from her perch on the wagon. "There ain't nothing worth starving and being afeared of Indians every waking moment. We've had enough. Better the devil you know than one you don't."

Her husband said nothing but stared on ahead numbly.

"God bless you," Luke said kindly. "We'll pray for you."

"And we'll pray for you. You're as like to need it more than we do."

Though Olivia realized she also had no idea what the trip would be like when she had set off for Oregon, she knew that following through with the commitment was far better than anything she had left behind. They were just days away from the Divide, the halfway point in their journey. And everything following was sure to be more difficult. No wonder these families were turning back now when they could.

CHAPTER TWENTY-SIX

Olivia felt as though she had lived several lifetimes since leaving Charlottesville, Virginia, and they were not even halfway to Oregon. The monotony and constant struggle wore on her—even the thrill of fresh buffalo meat had long ago dissipated. But soon, the trail brought them to something that made her feel refreshed, like they had a new beginning. Among the landmarks and milestones that the Sullivan-Mills wagon company had passed so far, none were as impressive or significant as Independence Rock.

For several days before they reached it, Independence Rock rested on the horizon right in their line of sight and drawing them ever closer. The enormous granite formation rose slowly, steadily, in their view, the target of their journey. It was one of the most important landmarks that they would come across on their trek across the continent. Even the monuments they had passed in the previous weeks couldn't touch this one.

The wagon company finally reached the foot of the

granite in the early afternoon, and by prior arrangement, pulled the wagons into a circle. They would make camp for the rest of the day. Olivia had already heard Mrs. Carter, Mrs. Sheldon, and many other mothers warning their sons away from climbing too high. This half-day rest would be an adventure for most of the company.

"It's beautiful," Luke said, breathlessly after they had made camp at the foot of the rock. He took his wife's hand in his and absorbed the sight with her standing by his side.

Olivia couldn't take her eyes from the rock, either. It filled her senses; she imagined she could even smell the coppery undercurrent of dirt. "Did you read about why it's called Independence Rock?"

Luke shook his head, still gazing up at the granite behemoth.

"The guidebook says it's because we're supposed to get here by Independence Day," she said, unable to hide the worry from her voice.

"Oh, well." He squeezed her hand. "We're only a few days late. I'm sure Mr. Mills and Mr. Sullivan know what they're about."

"I hope so. If we don't make good enough time..."

She trailed off, not wanting to articulate all her fears. She didn't see the value in worrying Luke about things he couldn't really control, not when he was taking on so much of the emotional weight of so many of the members of the wagon company.

But Olivia's own worries were numerous. They were days behind the schedule they should be hitting in order to get over the Blue Mountains before the first snowfalls. The guidebook said the trip could take as little as four months, and that was what they had planned for. The Montgomerys only had so much food left, and Olivia was mentally calculating how she could start to ration their remaining supplies now. Though there were more forts between here and Oregon that they would be visiting, they couldn't count on having the funds to stock up. And that was even supposing the supplies were still available when they arrived.

In order to do her duty by her husband, Olivia needed to make sure this all ran smoothly, so he didn't have to worry about mundane things like flour. He wouldn't even know she was worried if she could help it.

"I'm going to go see if I can hold a church service while we're here," Luke said. "Just being at the foot of this incredible monument is like being in a chapel. I just know there will be some folks who will want to worship."

"That sounds lovely."

"Will you come? I've heard you sing, Livvy." He looked around to make sure no one was watching and then wrapped both his arms around her, pulling her close. "I want you to come stand by my side, please."

She took a deep breath and thought about if she could, but the amount of work she had to do was still overwhelming. And the thought of using the little energy she had to make friends with strangers made her feel even more tired.

"Maybe next time," she answered gently. "I'm sorry. We only have half a day here, and I'm only just on my feet again. I want to get the wagon reorganized and—"

"Of course," he said brightly. Though, at the same

time, he dropped his arms and had interrupted her. "You work hard. I understand. And I appreciate you."

She looked down, hoping he didn't see the relief in her eyes.

"I'm going to go talk to the men," he said. "I'll see you later."

And with that, he was gone. Olivia felt a sting of rejection, but she pushed it away. It was her own fault she was being left alone after all. She had every chance to say yes, to spend the day with her husband and not working, but...

She sighed and turned resolutely away from the breathtaking view that was Independence Rock. Some of the younger folks were already starting their climb up. She had read all about the carved initials and marks that previous emigrants had made as they had crossed the plains. There seemed to be a primal human urge to leave a mark, and the sheer relief at accomplishing such a trek as this would be more than enough to prompt it. No wonder the young men risked life and limb to climb to the top.

Olivia was almost tempted to hike to the foot of the rock, at least, to put her hands on the stone and to feel the centuries of nature underneath.

But she had more important things to do.

Olivia ticked through her mental list of chores. There was so much to catch up on, and there were always new projects to attend to. After washing their clothes and bedding and spreading it all out to dry in the sun, Olivia thought about what else she needed to prioritize this afternoon. It might be the best chance she had for a while to assess what supplies they still had and organize the wagon stores better around what remained.

As such, the first thing she did was pull everything out of the wagon. Stacked in the dirt all around their campfire were empty crates, a couple trunks, other odds and ends like blacksmithing tools, and the little bit of food remaining.

Olivia took a deep breath and got to work.

"Do you need help with that?" a pleasant voice called.

A couple hours later, she was interrupted by a visitor. But Olivia's arms were too full, and her balance was too precarious for her to turn to see who was speaking. "I'm fine," she said over her shoulder to whoever it was.

"I'm not sure you're fine." She heard a light chuckle.

Dolly Carter stepped into Olivia's line of sight and hurried forward to take the sewing box that had been about to tip over off the top of the stack. Though grateful it hadn't fallen, Olivia was nevertheless slightly irritated that her claim to be fine hadn't been heeded.

"Whoops!" Dolly said with a laugh. "Almost lost that one. You sure I can't help you?"

"I think I'm fine." Olivia carefully set the cornmeal barrel that contained and cushioned their more delicate dishes on the dirt at her feet. With hands finally free, she turned back to her guest. "What can I do for you?"

"Well, Pastor Montgomery came by earlier to tell us about the service he is holding tonight, but he mentioned you wouldn't be there because you had too much work to do. It seems a shame that you would miss such a soothing respite, especially as your own husband is leading. So, I came over to see if you might need help with something, or if I can take something off your hands so you can come join us."

She almost said yes. Standing there, before this kind, motherly woman, Olivia felt a strong pull to be part of something more than just herself. More than just her work. She could almost talk herself into it.

But not quite.

"I can't. I'm sorry. I'm just... Can I be honest with you? I'm worried about the rest of the journey. Everything seems so uncertain, and we're running late. I need to make sure that everything is taken care of so Luke— So the pastor doesn't have anything to worry about at home."

"I understand," she said, nodding. "Don't take too much on, though. You know that's the very reason that we cross in a company like this, don't you?"

Dolly looked at her with understanding in her eyes, as though this was a lesson she'd already had to learn.

"I know. Thank you. I feel like if I can get all this," she gestured to her piles and goods strewn about, "under control, I'll feel better going forward."

"All right." Dolly smiled brightly. "If you're sure. I'll leave you to it, then."

"Thank you." She let out a sigh.

It wasn't until the words were out of her mouth that Olivia realized she might have been a little standoffish to the other woman who had just been trying to help. But, she reminded herself, Mrs. Carter had three children at home that needed her. She couldn't be spending time taking care of the Montgomerys, too, cleaning up some other family's messes.

Olivia had expected her husband to come back to the campsite for supper and maybe even try to entice her again to go to the church service. In fact, she spent all afternoon marshaling her arguments and trying to find the energy and wherewithal to finally say yes when he asked her again.

But it was all for naught.

Luke must have had plenty of invitations to stay for supper as he had made his rounds telling everyone about his sunset church service. He didn't bother to come back for Olivia at all.

She kept looking up, looking around, looking everywhere but at the apron she was mending. She felt like she was on high alert, so she could know exactly the moment when her husband returned. Being so vigilant made her even more tired than she had been before. When she realized Luke was truly not returning, the rejection stung her all over again.

Though she was disappointed, Olivia wouldn't let herself wallow.

She told herself it was what she had wanted anyway.

She told herself, as she ate supper alone, that doing the laundry and reorganizing the wagon was far more necessary to Luke's work than merely standing next to him in front of folks.

She told herself, as she put away the extra biscuits for leftovers, that not being a burden was the greatest gift she could give him.

She told herself this was the best for everyone.

All her life, she had striven to not be a burden to her aunt and uncle, who had constantly reminded her of the charity they were offering by taking her in. Now that she had a home and husband of her own, the instinct hadn't ceased. She still felt as though she needed to go above and beyond to earn her keep.

But maybe, she realized, part of earning her keep was supporting her husband in the time and place when he asked her to.

As she wiped out the cast iron pan, brushing crumbs into the dirt, Olivia heard the faint melody of a hymn being sung by a group of earnest worshippers. Pausing, she looked around, trying to determine the location of the sound. There was a faint echo of singing; she wondered if the service was being held right up next to the rock itself.

Olivia took a deep breath. There was still sunlight for another thirty minutes or so, and she had spent all afternoon working and doing chores. There wasn't much to keep her here at the campsite. Recalling Luke's face when he had asked her to come to the service, Olivia resolved finally to go.

She wiped her hands on her apron, untied it, and tossed it over the back of her wagon. Taking a deep breath, she strode off toward the music.

Luke had found a clearing at the base of Independence Rock where other smaller boulders were scattered that could serve as seats. Most of the seats were occupied by women, with men standing around the perimeter and children sitting in the grassy patches in between. At a glance, Olivia would guess maybe three or four dozen people had shown up to this last-minute service.

They must have needed this just as much as Luke had predicted, she thought.

"Lovely," Luke called to the congregation as the first song finished. "And now, let us sing 'Joyful, Joyful, We Adore Thee.' "

The congregation began a cappella as Olivia slipped in between, and slightly behind, two of the men standing at the back of the crowd. They looked familiar to her, for certain, but she regretted that she didn't know their names. Maybe if she stood in the back like this, she wouldn't be called upon to be the hostess—and fill her role as pastor's wife—just yet.

No sooner had she opened her mouth to sing than her husband caught her eye. The look of pleasure and surprise on his face was unmistakable, and Olivia found herself blushing under the approval.

She remained standing in the back through the rest of the service. She had forgotten how peaceful Luke's preaching had always made her feel, as though she was already accepted and loved just as she was. As though she didn't have to work any harder to prove herself. This was exactly the message that Olivia had been craving for months and didn't even know it.

After half an hour Luke closed the service in a prayer. Olivia said a silent 'amen' and ducked out early. She would stay out of her husband's way while he said his goodnights and return to the campsite.

As Olivia crawled into bed that night before he returned, her stomach rumbled lightly. She hoped wherever Luke had been to supper, he had gotten plenty to eat, because with the rationing they would have to do in order to make their food last, she imagined there would be lots of occasion in the coming nights that they would go to bed early without supper.

. . .

The following morning, their brief rest was over. Not long after sunrise, the wagon company left Independence Rock for another long trek to their next goal of Pacific Springs.

They pushed hard and covered nearly fifteen miles each day for several days. They wanted—and needed—to get to Pacific Springs as soon as they could. The water and chance to rest was much appreciated.

Rest was just one on a long list of things that Olivia could not get enough of.

CHAPTER TWENTY-SEVEN

"Oh, blast!" Olivia swore under her breath when she smelled the smoke.

As soon as the word was out of her mouth, she blushed and looked around to make sure she had not been overheard. The pastor's wife cursing could be the end of Luke's career. She sighed in relief when she saw she was far enough away from the Carters' campsite that no one had witnessed her transgression. She was all alone.

Olivia had set a pan of beans to heating over the fire and then dashed off to get another bucket of water while she was waiting. Since the Sullivan-Mills company had gotten a longer day in place at Pacific Springs, she was taking the opportunity to do a little extra baking, and her hands were full. It seemed as though every time she had a spare minute, she was filling it with chores.

Luke had been so kind and loving during the previous days—really since she had been attacked and almost kidnapped by the Indians—and she wanted to do something nice for him to acknowledge it. She had promised him an apple pie weeks ago but had never found the time. This day, however, she would be able to take the time she needed to mix up the crust and borrow the cinnamon from Mrs. Sheldon and give the pie time to bake over the fire. It was going to take a bit more of their sugar than Olivia wanted to part with, but it would be worth it to see the joy on her husband's face.

But first, dinner and—while that was cooking—collecting water.

It happened, however, that when she returned from the spring, she realized she had been gone just a few minutes too long. She found the shallow pan smoking and smelled the sharp, charred scent of burnt beans.

Olivia hastily dropped her bucket, wrapped her apron around her hand, and caught up the pan, moving it away from the heat. It was all she could do to save as many of the beans as she could by transferring them to a clean plate. The bottom of the pan, however, was coated in a black, sticky layer of unsalvageable beans. It was at least half a meal of waste, all because she had been careless.

She was so angry with herself. They didn't have beans to spare. They didn't have *any* food to spare. She was hoping that the sight of an apple pie would be the salve over the fact that they were almost out of meat altogether.

Maybe Luke wouldn't notice that their meals were so much smaller than they had been a month ago, with the scent of sugar, apples, and butter. This was the last of their butter, that luxurious gift that she had made stretch as long as she could. After tonight Olivia would be able to return the bucket to the Sheldons.

She had a whole plan, a specific schedule of how she would be spending this last day of good camping, and then she had gone and burnt the beans.

As she was silently berating herself and scraping the burnt food out of the bottom of the pan, Luke returned.

"Oh no!" he said with a laugh. "I take it that wasn't what you intended to make?"

She knew he was teasing and that he didn't mean any harm, but the idea that she had wasted some of the precious food they had upset her terribly. Olivia couldn't even respond. She just shook her head and turned away so he couldn't see the tears she was trying to hold back.

"Oh well," he said. "I'm sure whatever we have instead will be delicious."

"How was Jefferson?" Olivia redirected his attention. He had just come from the Carters' wagon.

"He still has a lot to learn. His hand isn't as steady as I would like to see when restitching pages. But he's coming along. I think by the time we get to Oregon, he'll be ready to take on a paying client to repair some of the more well-loved books that make it there."

"That's wonderful." Olivia thought she had gotten as much of the char out as she could. With a deep sigh, she set about to dishing out their meal—what was left of it —between their two plates. "He hasn't gotten into any more trouble, has he?"

Luke grinned. "No, I think between his parents and me, we instilled the fear of God in him. But, then, most boys his age will do just about anything to keep from making their mothers cry."

"You should tell my cousin that," Olivia said with a sad smile.

"Do you miss him?" Luke asked quietly.

She shrugged. "I'm not sure. Yes, I think. He wasn't all that nice to me, but I never had anyone else. Every so often, I remember that I'm likely never going to see him again. Him or my aunt and uncle. The only family I've had, and to be honest, the only people I've ever been close to."

"Well..." He hesitated, and when she looked at him, he seemed apologetic for what he was about to say. "There are plenty of families in this wagon company who would be happy to be your new family. Annie Hudson was just asking about you, as a matter of fact."

"Was she?" Olivia felt flattered. Annie Hudson was one of the most well-loved young ladies in the company. "And how are the Hudsons?"

He nodded. "They seem to be doing well. Lawrence is kept mighty busy, I'll tell you. I think that small involvement with Jefferson and his lot was just an unfortunate chance. He's a good kid."

Even Olivia was surprised by the next words that came out of her mouth. "I should go see Margaret, see if there's anything I can do to help."

The brightness of Luke's smile at Olivia's simple statement could have lit up the territory. "I'm sure she'd love that."

"Oh, I don't know," Olivia said, already backtracking. "I don't know anything about raising a boy of that age. Or any age. I'm liable to put my foot in my mouth like as not."

"You don't have to tell her anything." Luke took his

plate from her but didn't take his eyes from her face. "Sometimes just being there is enough, just listening without judgment. There's no doubt she's gotten plenty of earful from Louisa. You could just be a friend."

Olivia nodded, thinking it over as she sat next to him by the campfire.

"I'll even go with you if you want," he added gently.

She smiled at her husband, grateful for his compassion and unceasing generosity.

The camp at Pacific Springs was possibly the last time that Olivia expected to feel truly comfortable until she finally had a home of her own in Oregon. She had plenty of water, she had time to rest, and she hadn't needed to ration her food too severely yet. She relished the break, knowing that what was ahead could be far worse. Every spare moment she had, Olivia pored over the guidebook, looking for clues and signs that she was prepared, that she would be able to handle what was coming.

Before they left Pacific Springs, each member of the company collected as much water as they could carry in every empty bucket, bowl, or canteen available. They would have to ration their water, both for themselves and for their animals. Later, Olivia learned that two days past the last spring, one of the Gladwell children accidentally upset one of that family's buckets of water. Mrs. Gladwell had to go begging among her neighbors for any water they could spare.

The day after leaving the comfort of Pacific Springs, Olivia woke before dawn curled up in a ball under her light quilt, nearly shivering from the cold. She hadn't expected that weather to set in so soon. It was summer, but they were climbing in elevation. It would only get colder still.

As they climbed higher into the mountains, the wear on their oxen was more apparent. It hurt Olivia's heart to see the ribs and hip bones jutting under Meshach's skin. The poor creatures worked so hard to pull the wagon over the mountains and into the new territory, and she could not even make sure they were sufficiently fed. As the trail climbed, each degree of inclination, each foot of elevation was an added strain on their already beleaguered teams.

Olivia wasn't the only one to consider how the trek was affecting their animals. As they climbed higher up the mountain, the wagon company passed more piles of discarded luggage, tossed off the side of the trail. Their own bacon was not the only meat to start to show mold and rot before it could be consumed. How painful it must have been to the woman who had to discard that pork or jerky that she had been saving and rationing all the way across the continent.

Olivia bore her hunger silently, proudly. The less she bothered Luke with her needs, the more he would be able to care for the members of his congregation and do his job to the best of his ability.

CHAPTER TWENTY-EIGHT

As the Sullivan-Mills company headed farther west, the wagon leaders set a hard, punishing pace, pushing the families to their limits. It was as though everyone was finally starting to realize what Olivia had known for weeks—they were far behind where they needed to be. Each day they fell a little further behind. By this time in the summer, the company should be much farther west, and there was only one way to make up the distance. They were constantly on the move, some days not stopping for a midday break. The animals were forced to keep hauling the wagons mile after mile. Olivia couldn't imagine that anyone was getting enough rest or enough food.

And yet, they had to keep going at the same relentless pace.

She walked alongside her oxen day after day, with a shawl wrapped around her shoulders as a guard against the chill. It seemed as though Olivia was always far colder than Luke, or even other women. Maybe she just wore thinner dresses or fewer petticoats, or maybe her constant rationing of food made her more susceptible to the weather, thin as she was getting. Whatever the reason, Olivia was grateful that she had to keep moving; it kept her warmer at least.

In the midst of the exhaustion on the rugged trail west, Olivia finally found a chance to visit the Hudson women as she had been intending to do for days, to check and see how Margaret was faring and how her son was coping. It was a choice she made for herself; Luke never nagged or even hinted that she should go. She could see it in his expression every time they talked, but he never pushed her.

Accordingly, one evening after supper, Olivia stood resolutely wiping her damp palms on her apron.

"All right. Here I go. I'm going to visit the Hudsons." She felt as though saying it out loud would make it more true.

Luke grinned at her. "The dishes will be clean when you return. Don't worry about me," he assured her. "Off you go. Mrs. Hudson will be thrilled to see you."

Wringing her hands nervously, Olivia made her way across the wide circle of wagons to the Hudsons' camp. They had brought two wagons west with them and painted "Norfolk" on the side of one of them; she was able to pick out their camp at a distance.

As she walked, Olivia reminded herself of all the reasons why she was doing this thing that felt so uncomfortable—to support Luke, to be a good friend to this woman who had been so friendly with her, but mostly to pull herself out of her self-imposed isolation. She didn't want to be alone; she wanted the kind of friendships that she had never been able to develop growing up.

Nevertheless, Olivia was dismayed to find that all four of the Hudson women were near their wagons when she got there. There would be no quiet, private conversation; she would have to be truly social. Lawrence was off somewhere else, thank goodness, but everyone else was here. Annie—the youngest—looked up at her approach and smiled.

Olivia smiled back. "Missus... Um, Margaret?" she called from her awkward position, a full ten feet from their campfire.

"Mrs. Montgomery?" Margaret was rummaging in the back of one of their wagons looking for something, but she stood up straight when she heard her name.

"Hi, yes, hello, um..." Olivia said before laughing awkwardly.

"Did you smell my sister's black currant whirligig? Don't worry, I think there's enough to share." Margaret winked at her as she came to greet her guest. "Come sit by the fire while it finishes baking."

"What, really?" Olivia asked. She took a deep breath, smelling in the tart berries and pastry. "Black currant whirligig over the campfire?"

"Would you like the recipe?" Annie asked kindly.

"Oh, yes, please," Olivia responded. This visit was already turning out to be worth her nerves.

"Now, Mrs. Montgomery," Margaret said, sitting next to her, "surely that's not the real reason you're here. What can I do for you?"

"I just wanted... That is, I was wondering..." She

cleared her throat and forced herself to make an effort. "How are you faring with Lawrence and all?"

Margaret's expression softened. "How kind of you to ask."

But before she could respond any further, Louisa stood from her perch at the front of their lead wagon.

"I can't stay up a minute longer," she declared.

Olivia saw Josie and Annie exchange an amused look.

"Sleep well," Margaret called to her sister-in-law as she climbed into their sleeping wagon. "She's been complaining all day," she said quietly to Olivia. "But you know Louisa. Won't take anyone's advice. Just like a toddler."

Olivia couldn't help but laugh at that. Louisa Hudson had the reputation of a forceful woman who insisted on always getting what she wanted, not unlike a toddler, she reflected with a smile.

She didn't stay long with the Hudsons—long enough to feel like she had made friends. Olivia heard all about Annie's plans to marry when they reached the Willamette Valley, about Josie's best recipes, and Margaret's late husband. As the younger Hudson passed around plates of her black currant whirligig, Olivia learned that Lawrence's reading had come along nicely and that his mother had extracted a promise to return to school as soon as he could. In turn, Olivia shared with them stories of the congregations Luke had preached to on their journey from Virginia. It was strange and exciting how much intimacy could fit into a short hour of conversation.

Eventually, Olivia realized she was so tired, she hadn't heard half of what Annie had just been telling her about the home they left in Virginia. She blinked wearily, trying to focus on the other woman.

"Oh, you poor dear," Margaret said kindly. "We've been keeping you here, jawing your ear off when you need to rest." She stood. "Thank you so much for coming by, Mrs. Montgomery."

"Please call me Olivia," she said, also standing. She was surprised to find that the sun had set long ago while she had been busy talking. The dark night sky was filled with stars.

"Olivia."

"I'll send Lawrence by with the whirligig recipe, just as soon as I have a chance," Josie promised.

"That's so kind of you." She yawned. "Goodness! Excuse me."

The three Hudson women only laughed.

"Get you home," Margaret said. "Tell that husband of yours thank you for sharing you."

Olivia walked back to her own campsite—eyes firmly on "Psalm 119:105" on the wagon's canvas lit from the fire below—thinking over the previous hour. Maybe it wouldn't be as difficult to make friends as she had thought. Maybe she had put down her very first little soul-root since leaving Virginia.

As the trail climbed in elevation over the following day, Olivia keenly felt the change in the weather and environment. The thin air seemed barely enough to sustain her as they rose higher toward the foothills of the Rockies. She thought about how exhausted Louisa had been the night before and sympathized.

The wagon company slowed as the trail climbed, and when they finally made camp that night, the entire group felt subdued, though Olivia could not point to why. It wasn't until later that night, when Luke had returned from seeing to Jefferson Carter's bookbinding training, that she learned what had happened.

Luke shook his head as he approached their campsite. "It's bad, Livvy. Real bad. We'll have to pray on it."

She looked at him in surprise. "What is it?"

"A fever all over the camp." He gestured with a sweeping arm. "The doctor says it's Mountain Fever. Tons of folks have come down with it. Weak, flushed, out of their heads. The Valentines and Findleys and Harpers. Many more." He shook his head again. "We've been lucky so far."

"Goodness," Olivia said under her breath. "Those poor families. What can we do?"

"We have to keep moving. That's what Sullivan and Mills have decided anyway. Since the sickness is common in high elevation, we need to keep moving till we're out of the area. Can you... Do you think you'll be able to drive the team yourself tomorrow? I'm going to go see how the Valentines are faring. Two of them have taken ill, and I'm sure they can use an extra hand in driving their wagons or cleaning or something."

Olivia wanted to say no. She wanted to keep her husband close to her, safe, away from any sickness. But she knew that was not a charitable response, so she set it aside.

"Of course." She nodded resolutely.

.   .   .

The next day was one of the hardest she had had to suffer through on the trail. Not only was Olivia driving their team of oxen by herself again, but she was doing so while cold, hungry, and exhausted from the previous week of rationing her food. All of that added up to a day where she felt barely able to put one foot in front of the other. Fortunately, Shadrach and Nebuchadnezzar knew enough to simply follow the wagon in front of them. If Olivia had had to make any real decision, the results could have been disastrous.

Luke returned to their campsite that night, and at the sight of him, Olivia realized how much of her energy that day had been spent worrying about her husband. She ran to meet him, throwing her arms around his neck in relief.

"You're back. Oh, Luke... I was so worried. How are you feeling? How are the other families?"

He smiled thinly. "I'm fine, Livvy. Don't worry about me. It's these sick folk we need to pray for. I tell you... I don't know how the doctor can do it, facing such suffering every day."

He walked past her to sit on the back lip of the wagon, looking dejected.

Olivia gave him space, moving slowly to gather the fuel she needed to build a fire for their supper. He would talk when he was ready, and in the meantime, it was enough that he was here and safe with her.

Even as she stoked the fire under the pan, she could tell Luke's attention was split. Olivia looked up to see a gangly young man with a worried expression approaching them. Her husband rose to meet him, speaking quietly to the boy out of her earshot. This was yet one more face Olivia recognized but couldn't name, but someone that knew Luke enough to come with a message. She glanced over periodically to try to gauge what they were speaking about, but the messenger wasn't there long enough for her to discern anything.

She stayed quiet as Luke crossed the space to her, his face somber, his hands stuffed in his pockets.

"Lewis Jameson came to tell me..." His voice broke, and Olivia looked at him sharply. He cleared his throat. "William Sullivan has succumbed to the Mountain Fever. He's dead, Livvy."

"No," Olivia whispered. "That poor family. Oh, heavens, what will they do? What will the rest of us do?"

"I'm going over there right now," he said. "Don't hold supper for me."

She only had time to nod before he was gone again, into the darkness to bring comfort to the grief-stricken.

CHAPTER TWENTY-NINE

For yet another morning, the Sullivan-Mills wagon company was delayed in leaving camp by a funeral service. More emigrants came to pay their respects at the grave of William Sullivan than any of the previous deaths along the trail, as Luke had told Olivia to expect. This man had been kind to each and every person under his charge. He had been a father figure to some, an authority, and a friend, and Olivia was proud to be able to stand by her husband as he preached the value of their leader.

No one in the gathered crowd had dry eyes as Luke began his eulogy.

"William Sullivan wasn't just a friend, a husband, and a parent, he was a leader of this company," Pastor Montgomery intoned. "He looked after each and every one of us. He wanted every member of this party to get to Oregon, and we can't let him down."

Olivia stood by her husband's side as he led the wagon company in mourning for their fallen leader. As a community, they had already been through so much, handled so many deaths, but this time was different. This was one of the men who had promised to get them to Oregon, and Olivia wasn't sure they could keep going without him.

She and Luke stood on one side of the grave, about twenty yards off the trail under an evergreen tree. The family of William Sullivan stood on the other side of the grave; the rest of the emigrants gathered closely around. The Sullivans had already lost a son to measles. Now they also had to bury a husband and father. Mrs. Sullivan kept her head down, eyes fixed on the wrapped form of her husband already lying in the shallow grave. Soon he would be under the earth, under the stones to protect the body from predators. Junior Sullivan had already etched his father's name and date of death on a hastily crafted wooden cross and was standing by to plant it at his father's head.

Olivia could sense that Luke would do everything he could to ease the Sullivans' suffering, though she couldn't say what that might be.

After the funeral service, the Montgomerys returned to their own campsite. The company would not be leaving for another hour yet, and the couple sat in silence holding hands, each alone with their own thoughts. For Olivia's part, she couldn't stop thinking about what it would mean to lose her husband and how heartbroken Mrs. Sullivan must be. She was beginning to learn that being married to a pastor meant learning to be okay with him repeatedly putting himself at risk. How else could he comfort the sick if he wasn't near the sick himself?

She squeezed his hand tightly and leaned her head on his shoulder.

"We'll be all right," he said quietly.

"Will we? It seems as though everything that can go wrong will."

"I know... I know... but we still have each other. And we have our health. And we're more than halfway to Oregon. We'll get through this, Livvy. I promise. Together."

Olivia was spared answering when Daniel Mills approached their campsite, hat in hand.

"Pastor Montgomery?"

Luke stood to greet him while Olivia watched carefully. Daniel was the oldest son of the now-only company leader. Whatever message he was bringing to them was sure to be important.

" 'Scuse me, sir. Ma'am. I don't mean to interrupt, but I have a message for y'all. Later tonight, my father would like a man from each wagon to come to a meeting. We have some decisions to make about the route and future plans for the safety of everyone, and we need to have a discussion. With Mr. Sullivan... gone, well, my father is hoping for other men's input."

Luke nodded. "I'll be there."

Daniel made his way to the next wagon as the pastor turned to his wife.

"We'll get through this," she said, echoing his words back to him.

. . .

Olivia turned the fabric sack inside out, shaking as much of the flour out as she could, even getting into whatever small grains were stuck in the seam. She had already managed half a scoop, and now a dusting of flour floated down into the pan. It might be enough to feed one of them—but not both.

She was making supper as she waited for Luke to come back from the meeting that Mr. Mills had called. That day had been difficult, but Olivia was grateful that Luke had stayed with their wagon, driving their team of oxen so all she had to do was walk with them. As soon as the company stopped for the evening, he left her alone to join the rest of the men to attend a discussion over the next steps. Olivia was relieved that she wasn't the only one who was worried about the company getting over the mountains in time—there had been times in the weeks leading to now that she had wondered. She hated that she couldn't go to the meeting as well. She had to trust that the men would make the best decision.

And in the meantime, Olivia had to figure out how to make a supper out of hope and air, it seemed.

She had been rationing her own food for a week or more. However long it had been, Olivia was well used to the constant gnawing of hunger. It was almost unnotice-able by now. She had been nauseated in the mornings, but with all the Mountain Fever and physical exertion and lack of proper meals, there were plenty of things she could attribute it to.

With one hand on her hip, Olivia looked around her campsite in despair. She should have been paying closer attention. She knew they were running out of food—she could have looked for wild onions while they traveled or asked Luke to go hunting or... anything. Even the Hudsons had found black currants somewhere along the trail. She could have eaten less in the weeks before. There were plenty of options that could have kept her from this situation.

Olivia wasn't actually sure that she could have eaten less and still managed to put one foot in front of the other. But it was much easier to berate herself for poor planning than to admit that maybe what she was trying to do wasn't possible.

"There she is, light of my life, queen of my heart."

Olivia looked up and smiled at her husband. He handed her half a strip of crispy bacon while he took a bite of the other half.

"What's this?"

"Oh, I stopped by to talk to Dr. Martell about what support the sick members of the company might need, and his wife gave me this. It might be the last of their stock, but who am I to turn down hospitality?"

"I can't take this." She held it out to him. "We can't take the last of their bacon."

"Eat it," he insisted. "It's not like I'm going to walk it all the way back now. And I'm certainly not going to stand here and eat a whole piece of bacon while you have none."

That was true. Though it racked her with guilt to do so, Olivia took a bite of the bacon, the first such taste she had had since before the Indian attack. She almost groaned in pleasure. Chewing as slowly as possible to stretch out the experience, Olivia prompted Luke with more questions.

"How was the meeting? What are we doing next?"

"Well," he chewed hurriedly and swallowed, "arguments were made on both sides, but it sounds like we're going to go south for a bit through more fertile land. Heading that way in the morning."

"But... There's a cutoff we could take," Olivia said. "It would save time."

Luke shook his head. "No, that's what the whole meeting was about. Mills put it to us, and the men voted to go the long way around."

"But..." Her heart pounded. She knew exactly how little food they had left and was already mentally recalculating how to make it stretch. "That... that's seven more days on the trail before we get to Oregon."

"I know, but it also takes us around by Fort Bridger."

"There might not be anything even at Fort Bridger. It's so late in the season. We're so much behind schedule already!" Olivia felt the desperation rising in her. She hadn't even gotten to vote at this meeting, and now she would have to bear the brunt of this choice.

"I'm sorry, Livvy," he said, though she didn't think he seemed nearly concerned enough. "It won't be easy, but we'll all be in this together. And this way, the oxen will at least get the water and grass they need. We need them to get the rest of the way."

"Hopefully," she mumbled.

She moved to fetch her big spoon and lost her balance. Luke caught her before she could fall, his expression all concern.

"Here. Sit." He guided her to the wagon where she could sit on the lip. "Are you all right? Are you sick?"

He placed the palm of his hand on her forehead. She closed her eyes. Even as she sat, the ground felt like it was rolling underneath her. That half of a piece of bacon had been the first thing she had eaten all day, but she wasn't about to admit that to Luke. He had enough to worry about.

"Take deep breaths. I don't think you have a fever, but... well, maybe I *should* go back to see Dr. Martell."

"No," she said, as firmly as she could. "No, I'm all right. The bacon helped." She tried to smile but still had not opened her eyes.

"Liv... Are you sure? What can I do for you?"

"Nothing. Nothing." She opened her eyes and stood again. The vertigo was fading. Being prepared for such feelings of dizziness made it easier for her to keep her balance. "I'm fine, really. What else did you talk about at the meeting?"

He peered at her as though trying to assess how much of what she said he should believe. "That's all, really. There was some discussion and then a vote. After the vote, things got more lively. That John Harper sure has a temper. A couple of the men yelled, but then they were part of the losing vote, and there's no doubt they feel put upon. It's understandable, I think. They're trying to do their best for their family and now have to go against what they think is right. But... well, this is what they agreed to when they joined the company. There may have been rumblings about a smaller group breaking off to take the cutoff, but I don't think that was serious."

"Which option did you vote for?"

"The long way. Fort Bridger. I remembered how hard it was for all of us—for you in particular—those days across the plains without water. I didn't want to have to put you through that again."

"Thank you," she said, while thinking that maybe she should have been more honest with him about how low their food stores were. "I hope you're right, and Fort Bridger has the supplies we need. But…" She stopped herself, and he looked at her questioningly.

"But what?"

"Forgive me," she said in a rush. "I don't mean to question you, but even if the fort has the food that we need, will we have the funds to pay for it?"

She knew as soon as she finished her question that this was the wrong thing to say. This was doubting him. This was implying uncertainty about his ability to provide for her. Casting doubt on his role as the head of the family. His face clouded with anger, but he held his temper in check.

"Thank you, Mrs. Montgomery, for reminding me of my duty," he said coldly.

"No, I… Luke, I'm sorry. I—"

"No, I'm sorry. You're right. I will make plans to earn the funds that we need before we get to the fort. I'll hold another service or… see about repairing a book, or maybe I'll just hire myself out as an extra hand to one of the families that has lost someone. Maybe I'll go hunting, even."

"Luke, please, I didn't mean—"

"No, it's fine. Livvy, you're right." He sighed and shook his head. "I got all excited about the idea of there being enough water for the next week that I completely forgot about what else we would need."

They stood in silence together. Although he'd said it

was all right, and it seemed his anger had abated, Olivia was unsure how to proceed.

"Can I help you?" she asked timidly.

"My dear." He impulsively kissed her cheek. "You help me every day. You are my heart and my right hand. I couldn't possibly have survived this journey if it hadn't been for you by my side."

She blushed under his praise but even so, thought about all the things she could be doing differently. While he was off trying to earn a little extra money so they could buy food at Fort Bridger, she would again be left to drive the team and take care of everything around their campsite.

But she could do this. For him. For them.

She was absolutely determined to not be a burden to him.

CHAPTER THIRTY

It was a harrowing several days. The Sullivan-Mills wagon company lost several of its members to Mountain Fever, but by the end of the week, most of the remaining sick had recovered. Olivia, however, didn't seem to be able to shake the weakness that had plagued her for the last several weeks. She woke every morning shivering and lightheaded but forced herself to push through it. There were expectations and responsibilities. There were miles to cover, and she couldn't rest until she got to Oregon.

Coffee was the only item that the Montgomerys still had plenty of, and she somehow subsisted that little bit of energy for most of the day. The Sheldons' cows had dried up long ago, so Olivia didn't even get milk to put in the coffee. Luke got a cold biscuit or a few spoonfuls of beans but was so caught up in the concerns of their neighbors that he didn't seem to notice that he was the only one of them eating.

As the wagon company had chosen the route that

would take them a full seven days longer, Olivia had cut her rations even more to make the food stretch. They would be taking the route that would keep them near water—and for that, she was thankful—but Olivia had spent most of her life planning for the worst-case scenario, and she had no way to know if Fort Bridger would have any food for them to buy, or the funds necessary to buy them.

To make up for the longer route, Mr. Mills spread the word around camp that they would be leaving each site at first light every morning. No exceptions.

And so, Olivia made her coffee in the dark, savoring every mouthful, not knowing when the next time she'd be able to get food would be. Even with the plentiful water, grass, occasionally even shade that they passed in those seven days, no one in the wagon company was able to enjoy it. Each person was far too busy moving ever forward, pushing their animals, taking care of the children and old folks who were having a hard time under this punishing pace.

Walking alongside Luke on the second day, Olivia started to consider the possibility that she might not be able to continue at this rate. It was early afternoon, and she had fetched a cold biscuit and the last piece of jerky from the back of the wagon for Luke to eat while they walked. She had found herself sitting on her narrow mattress, resting far longer than the time needed to find the food she was looking for. As though she lost time, her focus failed her and she lost herself, her mind unable to hang on to a single solid thing.

Olivia wondered if maybe she would have to tell Luke to leave her behind. She wouldn't have been the first pioneer to fail partway through the journey. She tried to push that thought from her mind—it was certainly overreacting. Some part of her knew that. But at the same time, she was so hungry and so tired, she didn't see how she could take another step.

She finally came back to the present when the wagon jostled over a rut. Blinking back her mental fog, she gathered up the food for her husband in a small towel and climbed back out of the wagon.

"You're not hungry?" he asked as he took the food from her.

"No." She shook her head. "I'm fasting."

He frowned. "Fasting? Is that a good idea, with as much work as you're doing?"

"It's in the Bible, isn't it?" She tried to sound casual and carefree as she fibbed. "I feel less weighed down. I'll eat something tonight. Don't worry about me."

She wasn't completely crazy; she knew she had to eat something at supper. But for now, she was able to make their food last longer if she skipped food in the middle of the day.

He smiled, shrugged, and ate the meal she had brought him.

Olivia couldn't be sure if Luke noticed how small his portions were getting or if he realized how little she was eating. She didn't think so. She hadn't had an appetite for a while, and now with them being on the move almost constantly, and his visiting other families all over the camp, they didn't really have time to eat together.

He didn't seem to notice a thing.

She told herself it was only a few more days.

As they walked that afternoon, however, Olivia

began to grow even weaker. The sun overhead was draining the little energy she still had.

She stumbled, grabbing onto Luke's arm to keep herself from falling to the ground.

"Are you all right?"

"I... I think so. I just..."

"You should eat something."

"I don't know if that's it." She tried to smile at him. "I think I'll just ride on the wagon seat for a bit if that's okay."

"Of course."

He slowed his animals enough that she could climb up top. Grasping the wooden bench tightly, Olivia settled herself up above the oxen and the trail.

"You set?" he called.

She nodded and waved her thanks but said nothing. Now she sat under the sun, holding tight to the swaying wagon seat while wondering how much longer she could last under such strain. To feel both nauseous and hungry at the same time was unsettling. To be so lightheaded that she didn't feel as though she could walk without stumbling was frustrating. To know that she was doing all she could, and it still wasn't enough, made her feel hopeless.

After all the sacrifices she had made for Luke—and for the people he was supporting—she had hoped for more of a reward, more of a sign she was doing the right thing.

Through the rest of the afternoon, Olivia simply rode along in silence.

It was such a pleasant change to have Luke around during the day to guide the animals that Olivia felt almost spoiled. How many days had she done all of that herself? How many times had she resented him or others for claiming his attention?

But now, so much less was being asked of her. All she had to do was ride along, keeping up her strength, and making sure their food lasted as long as possible.

There seemed to be only twenty or thirty minutes left of sunlight when Mr. Mills finally guided the wagon train to make camp. Olivia stayed where she was, holding on to the wagon seat so she wouldn't get in Luke's way as he guided the animals.

"Do you need help getting down?"

She shook her head, but she was so focused on holding her grip that she wasn't sure if he saw. The light-headedness from earlier had expanded to full-blown dizziness. She was reminded of the one time she had taken a glass of wine with her Aunt Bea the previous summer. The double vision and feeling of being out of control had been enough to swear her off of it, but now she felt the same symptoms.

Luke appeared at the side of the wagon in her line of sight and reached a hand up to her.

"Feel better after your rest?" he asked kindly. "I'll go collect water and build a fire if you want to make supper."

She nodded, still not speaking, but she let herself take his hand for the assistance climbing down. Other than the fact that should be eating more, Olivia didn't know what was wrong with her.

As her feet touched the ground, and she moved out

of the sun for the first time that day, Olivia felt a chill come over her. It shook her bones and rattled her teeth. Where were her shawls?

But Luke didn't seem to notice. "I'll be right back," he called over his shoulder, bucket in hand.

Olivia took a deep breath, reminding herself of all she had to take care of at that moment. Luke was counting on her. The wagon company was counting on her. She just needed to move the few feet to the back of the wagon to collect their meal, and then she could rest.

She took three steps before the dizziness overwhelmed her.

Olivia collapsed. The last thing she heard before she blacked out completely was the lowing of their oxen, waiting for Luke to return and take care of them.

CHAPTER THIRTY-ONE

The world was spinning.

Olivia awoke alone in the dark. She couldn't be sure where she was. Even with her eyes closed, even alone in the middle of the night, she still could not escape the feeling that the world around her was spinning. She tried lying flat on her back, feeling as though she were hanging on to the edge of the world, but it didn't help.

She turned over. The moldy corn husks in her mattress rustled under her.

That one motion was too much, and nausea overtook her.

Olivia retched. Somehow in the darkness, she managed to fumble around for a tin mug that had been sitting on the side of her bed. Water sloshed over her hand as she grabbed for it, bending her face close to the lip of the half-full cup.

But there was nothing in her stomach. Nothing to come up but bile.

After a few moments, she lay back on her mattress,

crying softly and letting the waves of dizziness roll over her.

She ached all over.

Her skin burned to the touch.

She had not eaten in so long, and now her body was too weak to fight off whatever this illness was.

And she had done this all to herself.

Olivia sobbed. She had no way to know what time it was, though it was clearly after dark. The quality of the silence around her told her that nearly everyone else in the wagon company must be sleeping.

Where was Luke?

Who had put her to bed?

How was she ever going to recover?

"Livvy?"

A whispering voice called to her from the end of the wagon near her feet. She didn't have the strength to sit up and look at him, but she smiled to herself, knowing Luke had heard her and come to check on her.

"Luke." Her voice was a weak whisper.

"Don't try to talk, darling." He was climbing into the wagon, then carefully approached her as though concerned she might break with just a touch. "You're awake. Oh, my goodness, I'm so glad you're awake. We were so worried."

She made an inquisitive noise but couldn't form any words.

"The Carters, the Martells, the Sheldons. So many, my love. Even Margaret Hudson came by when she heard you had collapsed. But you were out completely, and we had no... I didn't know..." He sat on a crate by her head and picked up her hand. Leaning far down to her, Luke kissed her hand. "But you're awake now. How are you feeling?"

She still couldn't answer. She just shook her head as chills came over her. Pulling her hand from Luke's, Olivia grasped for a blanket, pulling the quilt up to her chin, but she couldn't seem to get warm.

"Chills?" Luke placed his hand to her forehead. "You're burning up. Let me get you another blanket." His eyes fell on the cup next to her. "And fresh water. I'll be right back."

He squeezed her hand again and stood to open the trunk at the other end of the wagon where Olivia kept the extra blankets. Even through her sick haze, she was mildly surprised that he knew where to find another quilt. She had been operating so long on the assumption that he needed her to do everything, and yet here he was taking care of her.

Her mind swam with confusion, memories roiling and bouncing in her head.

She felt the weight of another blanket settle over her, and his strong hands tuck it in around her chin and shoulders. Olivia closed her eyes and sighed with satisfaction. Though she still ached all over, she was beginning to feel warm again.

Maybe she fell asleep, or maybe she just lost time, but when she opened her eyes again, she was alone in the wagon. It was still the middle of the night, but there was a fresh cup full of water next to her. Luke must have gone and come back again before she even realized it had happened.

Never in all of her imaginings would she have

guessed she would need her husband to take care of her, or even that he would be able to.

She fell asleep again with visions of Luke tucking a quilt tightly under her chin, soothing her to sleep.

Olivia slept soundly and fiercely all through the morning, not waking until the wagon started to move.

She jolted in surprise, waking to the wagon swaying underneath her. For a brief moment, she panicked, thinking the brakes had failed or an axle had broken. But the next second, she heard the voice of her husband, calling to his team as he drove them westward.

He seemed to be trying to stay quiet enough not to wake her, and that sweet, though foolish, thoughtfulness would have made her laugh if she wasn't still so nauseous.

Sitting up as slowly as she dared, Olivia picked up the cup of water that was threatening to slosh over with the movement of the wagon. Sitting next to it, wrapped in a towel that she was sure did not belong to the Montgomerys, was a cold biscuit and half a piece of cold bacon.

She took a bite before she could talk herself out of it.

Chewing on the buttery mouthful, alternating with slow sips of water, Olivia let herself enjoy this first real meal she had had in several days. Later she would learn who had given it to her—who she now owed food from her own table. But she knew she would never be able to repay that debt unless she was well herself.

Halfway through her small meal, nausea again tried to take Olivia. She wrapped up the last of the food she still had left and set it back where she had found it. Willing her stomach to keep the food down, Olivia tried to gather the strength she would need to get out of the wagon.

It was kind of Luke to let her sleep in the way he did. She would be happy to admit she didn't feel well, but she couldn't stay all day in this wagon.

Not when there was work to do.

But not quite yet. Not when she could barely keep a few bites of food down. If she climbed out of the wagon now, she would just end up collapsing all over again and be a burden on Luke once more.

Olivia took a long, slow breath, stilling her stomach. Sleep was again pulling her down, and she succumbed. The sun's rays were beating down on the white canvas, but under the wagon's top, the shady interior was a soothing, even coolness.

Laying back down, relaxing into her narrow mattress, Olivia pulled the quilt up to her chin again and was asleep almost as soon as her eyes had closed.

She woke again in the late afternoon and was strong enough to finish the rest of the biscuit she had left that morning. Though it was so little, this was more food than she had had in so long. It sated her immediately, and she sat up listening to Luke calling to the team as they pressed on toward Fort Bridger.

Telling herself that she would get up as soon as the wagon stopped, Olivia lay back in on her bed and closed her eyes again. This time she didn't sleep but listened to the noises on the other side of the canvas and felt the wagon rolling underneath her. The Sullivan girls had been right; she could see how easily a person could get motion sickness by riding in the back of the wagon.

But it was either this or risk collapsing as soon as she set foot on the dirt outside.

She didn't have long to wait. The pause and jostling of the wagon as it pulled off the trail told her they were setting up camp for the day. She had a few minutes while Luke led the wagon to their spot for the evening, and she took the chance to run her fingers through her dark hair. It was a mess, utterly knotted from a full day and night of sleeping, tossing and turning.

Her dress was filthy since she had fallen in the dirt and then sweated through it. She would wear it one more night and then look for something clean. Putting a hand to her own forehead, she tried to guess if she still had a fever. No matter. It wouldn't be bad and she couldn't dawdle anymore. Luke would need her.

The wagon was pulled into place, and Olivia could hear Luke tending to the animals, murmuring to them softly and unyoking them for the evening. She pulled herself to her feet, though the effort almost undid her. The world spun again, and she had to brace herself against the trunk to keep from falling over entirely.

"What are you doing?" Luke cried, sticking his head between the canvas flaps.

"I was getting up." She winced at how weak she sounded, but her nausea had returned, and she didn't want to open her mouth.

"Get up? Olivia Montgomery, you must be crazy. You are going to stay right here until you're well again." He climbed into the wagon and wrapped an arm around her waist. Guiding her back to the bed, he took on most of her weight.

"I'm well," she insisted. "Well enough. The food

helped. I should maybe not fast quite as much as I have been doing."

"It's not the fasting, Livvy," he said gently. "At least, not entirely. Your not eating has absolutely weakened your body. Weakened you enough that you're now proper sick. The doctor thinks it might be Mountain Fever, delayed for some reason. So you will stay in bed until he gives you the go-ahead to get up."

"But—"

"Livvy. Please." His gentle voice and pleading eyes broke her heart. "For me. I need you. People... William Sullivan, Liv. Mr. Sullivan and Louisa Hudson, and I'm sure dozens more in other wagon companies. People *die* from this disease, and I won't have you one of their number."

She had no response.

CHAPTER THIRTY-TWO

Olivia spent another full day and night riding in the wagon under the canvas, despite the slight motion sickness it gave her. She slept as much as she could and dutifully ate everything that Luke brought to her. Though she wasn't back to her full strength, she begged him to send Dr. Martell to examine her, sure that she could get the man to agree to her leaving the sickbed.

That night when they got to camp, Olivia called to Luke.

"I'm tired, Luke," she said plaintively when his face had appeared at the back of the wagon. "I'm tired of sitting and lying around so much. I need to stretch my legs. I'd like to get out of here, please."

He shook his head. "Not without the doctor's say-so."

"All right. I understand. Can you get him? Please?"

"Tonight?"

"Goodness, yes. I want to be on my feet tomorrow."

He smiled, pleased at how much better she sounded.

Not twenty minutes later, Luke had done exactly as he had promised and fetched Dr. Martell to assess her. The doctor stood outside the wagon and asked Olivia questions, holding his hand to her forehead, his fingertips to her pulse, and nodding as he listened to her describe how she was feeling.

"Hm," he said. "Tell you what. Let me send my wife over to talk you through it. Sometimes a woman's insight is far more useful than an old man like me."

Though that response confused her, Olivia agreed and waited another ten minutes for Mrs. Martell to make her way over to their camp. Once again, she went over her symptoms and put particular stress on how sick she had been and how much better she felt now.

"And, you know, Mrs. Martell, the others all recovered from Mountain Fever much more quickly than this. I really think if I'm able to get some fresh air and exercise, I'll get well ever so much faster. Please tell my husband I'm fit to get out of bed."

"Well, now, Mrs. Montgomery... I'm not sure nausea is a symptom of Mountain Fever. There may be something else going on here," Mrs. Martell said kindly.

"Oh, that's true. Riding in the wagon hasn't been particularly comfortable." She tried to offer a smile. "And all my fasting has surely done a number on my insides."

"That's not quite what I mean, dear. Did you notice any sickness in the weeks before now?"

Olivia frowned, thinking. "A bit. But I had been rationing our food since... almost since Independence Rock, to be honest. Wouldn't it be related?"

"Perhaps, but... forgive me this indelicate question, Mrs. Montgomery, but when was the last time you got your monthly?"

Olivia gasped and paled, the realization of what the doctor's wife was asking crashing over her. She did some quick mental math. Even if she was wrong about what day today was—she had been asleep quite a bit lately after all—she could not be so much mistaken.

"I—" Her mouth hung open, and she didn't know how to respond to Mrs. Martell.

The older woman smiled kindly. "I think, perhaps, Mrs. Montgomery, that it would do you good to rest a bit more." She patted Olivia's knee. "And be sure to eat all the food your husband brings you. We can't be certain of anything. Not in this life and not under these harrowing circumstances. But if you promise to take care of yourself, I won't put up a fuss if you decide you're done being relegated to the sickbed."

"How do I... What do I..."

"Really, Mrs. Montgomery, it's best not to think too much about the possibilities just yet. It's likely very early. But you do need to promise me you'll stop fasting. You come to me if you feel any pain, if you see any spotting, or if you have any questions. But, again. Don't you worry. Everything will be fine, provided you take care of yourself."

Olivia nodded and was soon left alone again.

She put her hands to her abdomen, thinking over the previous months, over what she had done, how hard she had pushed herself in service of her husband and their family.

Their *family*. She had been so stupid; she could have ruined everything with her over-the-top martyrdom.

Olivia would have to make it up to Luke, but that would mean she would have to actually rest. And eat. She would have to believe him when he told her he didn't need all his shirts clean.

She would have to actually ask for help. And accept it.

She would have to be vulnerable.

She wasn't sure she could do it.

Going out and offering to take the Sullivan girls or checking on how Margaret Hudson was doing was far easier for Olivia to wrap her mind around than it was to ask for help for *herself* from someone. Anyone. Even her husband.

But she could start there. She had to start there.

Luke made her wait another two full days before he was satisfied that she had regained her strength enough to even get out of bed.

"The only reason we're even discussing this," he said that final evening, "is because tomorrow we'll be reaching Fort Bridger. I don't want you walking alongside me in the morning. If you want to be out of bed, you can ride on the wagon seat."

He was firm with her, though she could see the genuine concern underneath.

She nodded and smiled. "I will. I promise."

"And I want you to rest more. To take help when it's offered. Please, Livvy."

"I will. I'm... I'm sorry."

He nodded brusquely. "All right then. Mrs. Montgomery, may I help you to your feet?"

He stepped back from the wagon to give her room to step down and offered both hands up. She stepped cautiously over the side, gripping the edge. How long had it been since she had felt the earth firm beneath her feet? But Luke was there to collect her. With one hand on either side of her waist, her husband lifted her out of the wagon and set her gently on the ground next to him.

And he didn't let go right away. She relished the warmth of his hand on her body and leaned into him just a moment longer than she needed to.

Their tender moment was interrupted, however, by a joyous laugh.

The Montgomerys both turned to see that they had been visited by Dolly Carter, Margaret Hudson, and Mary Sheldon.

"Mrs. Montgomery! How good to see you on your feet again!" called Margaret.

Olivia beamed at her friends as they gathered around her for a hug.

She followed Luke's requests and remained riding on the wagon seat until they finally reached Fort Bridger. Olivia had been eagerly awaiting their arrival at this fort for so many reasons, including her still-lingering hope that there would be food that the Montgomerys could purchase for the last stretch of their trek to Oregon.

From the seat of the wagon, Olivia was high enough to see the fort as soon as it came into view at the end of the trail.

Fort Bridger was similar to Fort Laramie in that it was surrounded on all sides by a sturdy, strong wall, protecting those inside from attack. Unlike Fort Laramie, however, that wall seemed to be the only security present. Olivia only noticed a single guard the whole time they were there. Even the wall itself didn't seem as high. This fort was low to the ground, as though hunkering down, not offering any of the comfort or safety that Olivia had felt before.

But it was a fort. A fort with American soldiers and possibly—hopefully—food and supplies available to help them through the last of their journey.

Just over a hundred feet from the wide gate of Fort Bridger was a narrow stream. Each man, woman, child, and even animal in the wagon company would be able to finally drink their fill of the sweet, clear water as long as they stayed. They arrived in the middle of the summer afternoon and would remain the rest of the day. Olivia had a split second to choose between buying more supplies from the fort or filling her canteen at the river. She noticed fur traders striding through the gate and made her decision. The water, she reasoned, would always be there. The supplies would be subject to whoever had come there ahead of them.

Once their wagon was in place in the camp, Olivia climbed down and excitedly began to list all the things she wanted to get. Luke laughed at her energy as she linked her arm through his to walk together to the fort.

"Flour, certainly, and cornmeal if they have it. I would love more salt and sugar, but I think we can survive without those if we need to. We have coffee, but could always use more. Meat if possible, but beans if not. And, Luke... If we can find more linen or cotton, I can make you more shirts to replace what the Indians took."

He nodded. "We'll do our best. Thank goodness you're coming with me," he teased.

She nodded, and the two made their way to the small storefront within the fort's walls.

Olivia gasped as they walked through the door and pushed through the small group forming.

The room was almost entirely empty, save for the other members of their wagon company who had gotten there before the Montgomerys. Even the shelves had been pushed to the walls, leaving a wide-open space in the middle of the room.

There was an angry murmur from the people gathered. Olivia leaned closer to Luke and listened to the outrage and disappointment from the people around them. Mrs. Mills was at the front of the crowd. A tall, stern woman, she seemed to be informing the storekeeper of all the ways he had failed in his duty. Olivia cringed inwardly for him, but that didn't keep her from being disappointed.

"Sorry, ma'am," the weary man repeated to Mrs. Mills. "Our last shipment overturned in the Kansas River. We're hoping to get another before the end of the summer, but right now, we're picked clean. I'm so sorry."

As she listened, Olivia felt sympathetic for the man who likely had no control over what reached him and what didn't. He must have had this conversation dozens of times over the previous weeks as hundreds of wagons passed through here. But sympathy wouldn't fill her belly, and now she didn't know how they would be able to eat the next several weeks. They had added seven days to their trip for nothing.

Fortunately, there was still another fort ahead of them. She would pray those still had stores. Olivia didn't know what they would do in the meantime, but for the first time, she let herself trust that her husband would be by her side to help her at every step.

CHAPTER THIRTY-THREE

After leaving Fort Bridger, the trail headed almost due north to more safely cross the mountains and go around the Great Salt Lake. As they crossed through this territory, Olivia began her efforts to rest in earnest, as much as she could, though it felt against her nature to. The part of the Oregon Trail during which Olivia had to try to regain her strength were some of the hardest stretches of the entire journey, not even including the fact that the Montgomerys barely had food. Every day she woke up telling herself that she would do better, and every night she went to bed thoroughly exhausted again.

Leaving Fort Bridger without being able to purchase any additional supplies put a strain on both of them. But even before they knew how much help they would need, Olivia had resolved to accept whatever aid that was offered them. Luke tried to reassure her. He kept reminding her that the Lord would provide for them. They would be fine. They just had to trust, pray, do their best, and they would get to Oregon safely.

She wanted to believe that, she really did, but her primary instinct of over-preparing and worrying over every possibility was too strong in her. It was only through the combined influence of Luke, the doctor, and the women around them that Olivia forced herself to rest as she needed to.

That first evening after they had left Fort Bridger, Olivia was leaning on the back of their wagon, peering into the dim interior and wondering what she had that could make a full meal when she heard footsteps approaching.

She turned to see Luke laughing with Jefferson Carter, both approaching the Montgomery campsite.

"Look what we have for you!" Luke called to his wife.

She moved to meet them and realized that Jefferson was carrying a rabbit and a quail, both recently hunted.

Olivia gasped. "Where did that come from?"

"Me and a couple of the boys went hunting this afternoon, ma'am," Jefferson explained. "And I thought... well, seeing as how Pastor here has done so much for me..." He trailed off, as though not used to having to say so much to an adult at one time. "Ma said I should bring you these," he finished lamely.

"And we are mighty grateful for these, Jeff," Luke said, clapping a hand to his back. "Mighty grateful. Just like you and me talked about, the Lord works through those that love us, and I know my wife and I are going to thank Him in our prayers tonight for men like you."

Jefferson reddened at being called a man and ducked his head.

"Thank you, Jefferson," Olivia said kindly as she took the meat from the young man. Skinning, plucking, and otherwise preparing the animals for them to eat would take the rest of the night, but this was food that could last them for days. She began thinking through how she could make them last as long as possible. A stew, perhaps? Dried and jerky? "I can't tell you what this means to us."

After the boy had returned to his own wagon, Olivia turned to her husband.

"You know, you deserve almost as much credit as that boy does." She gestured at the quail half-plucked on her lap.

He chuckled. "I'm sure that's overstating it."

"Luke, you know how much you've done for him. And how much you've been visible in this community every day since we left Missouri. They love you. And me, by extension, but you're the reason that the Carters thought to gift us this food. I know maybe I've complained in the past, but I appreciate everything you've done for us. For our position."

He smiled, embarrassed at the praise for maybe the first time Olivia had ever noticed. "Thank you."

"Of course," she responded lightly, not wanting to embarrass either of them. She turned her attention back to her work.

It had been a long road to get here, and she had had to learn some hard truths about herself, but the real stirrings of love were beginning to make themselves felt in her heart. Olivia did not feel fully prepared to say these things out loud, though. They spent the rest of the evening treading carefully around each other. Kindly, considerately, gently, neither brave enough to approach the cliff of emotion they had been making their way to over the previous several months of travel.

Instead, Olivia showed her love for this man by plucking the quail, strewing feathers all over the ground, and cooking up a hearty stew with the last of their rice. She would be able to serve this for their supper as well as meals the next day, and hopefully, such a source of protein would help keep up their energy as they hiked farther west.

That generous gift from Jefferson Carter kept the Montgomerys fed for several days, enough to carry them on through the next stretch of the trail. They walked through dust and sun, pushing on ever farther to the next fort. Olivia knew there was every chance that Fort Hall would also have been stripped of food, but what other choice did she have than to hope.

They still had miles of trail to cover, and the struggle of life in the wilderness was unrelenting.

One morning Olivia woke up and realized it was well into August. They had been on the trail for so long already, but they had at least passed the halfway mark. There was more trail behind them than ahead of them, and Olivia began to let herself hope that they would reach Oregon without any further disaster.

Each day was still difficult, of course. She had to be the one to ration the water out to the oxen when they traveled days between fresh natural sources. She had to be the one to tell Luke that no, they didn't have any more food to share with neighbors when they didn't know if the next fort would have any supplies for them to buy.

But it wasn't insurmountable, and every day there was a bright spot.

Jefferson Carter wasn't the only one of the members of the wagon company to offer the Montgomerys food. Mrs. Sullivan made sure a half bag of flour found its way to Olivia's wagon. The Hudsons sent Lawrence over with the last helping of whirligig; once he left again, she mysteriously found two fresh eggs set on the back lip of her wagon.

Though it was difficult to get used to, Olivia knew that she owed it to Luke to accept this help that was offered. She tried to remind herself that it was selfish to deny these kind folk who just wanted to help, who wanted her to stay strong.

She suspected Mrs. Martell may have whispered of her additional circumstances around the women of the trail, but Olivia opted to let it go. The resulting generosity was a kindness that she may never be able to repay.

And in addition to that, they had the promise of Bear River Valley and the river ahead of them. Olivia kept telling herself that rest was coming. Just get through one more of these hard days, then one more, and then they crested the hill ahead of the lush valley.

"Oh!" she couldn't help exclaiming out loud as the trail wound back down into the valley.

The spring rain had grown a lush carpet of high grass, enormous trees, and a wide flowing river. Such a valley would support plenty of game for the wagon company to live on every moment they traveled through it.

"It's like heaven on earth, isn't it, Livvy?" Luke asked. "Maybe we should just stay here."

"All of Oregon is like this," she told him with a sly smile. "You'll see."

Ahead and all around them sat low mountains, not yet topped with snow, though she could imagine how beautiful this valley could be in all seasons. They spent two days crossing the valley, following the trail along the Bear River at a leisurely pace. Every animal in the company got plenty of time to fatten up again on the plentiful grass and water. Olivia felt energized as Luke darted off each evening to hunt with the other men of the company. He came home with all manner of birds and game that Olivia prepared as best she could to last them over the weeks ahead. She dried and salted the meat as much as she could with the time allowed her; she and Luke gorged themselves on what she didn't have time to otherwise prepare for a journey.

It felt like utter luxury, and Olivia treasured every moment. Her appetite was beginning to return, and she didn't squander it.

After climbing the trail out of the valley, they were on the road across high desert for two more days before camping outside Fort Hall.

The landscape around Fort Hall was different than any they had seen before. Black lava plains and barren ground stretched for yards around the structure. It was two stories tall, windowless, and built from roughly hewn logs. After the fine, white-washed wall around Fort Bridger, this structure was a disappointment. It seemed just as beaten down and barely surviving as any member of the wagon company, rather than the welcoming oasis Olivia had been hoping for.

But in spite of its outer looks, what they found inside more than made up for it. Again, she braved the storehouse with Luke, but this time found what they were looking for. The selections were minimal, but Olivia was able to stock up on at least a few things. Enough to feed them for another week or so.

Everything was difficult, but for the first time in weeks, with her ankle healed, stocks and belly full, and husband attentive, Olivia felt something like hope and contentment in her new life on the frontier.

CHAPTER THIRTY-FOUR

After leaving Fort Hall with their supplies replenished, the wagon company reached the Snake River. Over the millenia, the swift, rushing river had cut a path through a rock canyon, and now the trail wound around the top of the canyon. The trail itself was relatively level at this point, though not wide. It felt a bit risky, but Olivia walked next to her team, between the animals and the edge of the ravine, so she could be closer to the water.

From where they walked along the trail, she could hear the roar of the Snake River far below. It had been several days since the emigrants had gotten fresh water themselves. They were again rationing the little supply they had been able to carry with them. Olivia's mouth watered at the thought of the cold water in the Snake River, though it was too far down for them to be able to use it as a reasonable water supply.

Instead, she took a deep breath and looked around at the trail, the rocks, the canyon, the animals—anything to take her mind off how thirsty she was.

"The first thing I'm going to do when we reach Shoshone Falls," Luke said to her over the backs of their oxen, "is pour a whole bucket of water over my head."

Olivia laughed. "You could just stand underneath the waterfall, you know."

"Well, yes, I'll do that too, of course," he replied with mock seriousness.

"I wish the river wasn't quite so far down there," she said with a sigh. "Just the sound of it is making me more thirsty."

"I thought about climbing down—or maybe seeing if Jefferson would climb down to collect some water for us—"

"Don't you dare," Olivia interrupted. "It's far too dangerous for anyone to try."

"I might have already seen Junior Sullivan dart down there last night."

"Oh, heavens." Her eyes widened. "Poor Mrs. Sullivan. Don't you dare be putting any other boys at risk, Luke Montgomery. Neither of us needs water that badly."

"All right, all right." He put his hands up in surrender. "If you don't mind, I don't mind. But remember, if one of those boys *offers* us water, you promise you'll drink it, right?"

She smiled and rolled her eyes a little. "If anyone of those boys is lucky enough to climb down and back without killing themselves, I hope they keep their own water."

Luke chuckled at that, and Olivia tried in vain to put all thoughts of water out of her mind as they continued their hike along the top of the canyon.

Later in the afternoon, there was a slow-down in the wagon train. Olivia craned her neck, but she couldn't well see over the wagons in front of them. There was a cry, she thought, or a yell, somewhere far up ahead. Something was wrong.

Luke looked at her, and all she had to do was nod. He handed over the reins of their team—who had now stopped completely—and he ran on ahead to see if he could offer any assistance. Olivia soothed their team; the oxen had been a bit agitated all day with the edge of the trail and the depth of the canyon so close. Now stopped, all they wanted was to get past it.

Luke returned after a bit, pointing behind him to where Daniel Mills was making his way down the trail. The wagon leader's son rode his horse down the length of the wagon train spreading the news of why they had stopped.

"Sorry about this, folks," he called loudly to cover the sound of rushing water. "We're stopping here for the rest of the day. Go ahead and make camp." He gestured to the open plateau extending away from the water.

After he rode on to the wagons behind them, Luke took the reins back from Olivia and led their team off the trail to camp.

"What happened?" she asked breathlessly. "Did you hear?"

He nodded grimly. "The good news is, Mrs. Van Anda has gone into labor." He smiled, but she could see his heart wasn't in it. "We should have a new member of our company soon."

"And the bad news?"

"Well... Junior Sullivan wasn't the only one who thought to climb down to get water."

"Oh no..."

He nodded again, and lowered his voice. "John Harper died. It seems he had filled his canteen and climbed almost the whole way back up before losing his grip."

Olivia was stricken—John had left behind a sister, a young woman her own age who was now alone. "What can we do?"

"We can see if Miss Harper needs anything, of course, but I know she's close with the Mills boy and the Sullivans, so we can thank God for that. I was also thinking that while we're stopped here, I can hold another church service. I'm sure everyone must be terrified over everything we've had to deal with, and an evening of prayer and fellowship could be exactly what they need. Miss Harper may not be up to attending, but it might do the rest of the folks some good."

The peace and relief that Olivia felt at hearing her husband's plans surprised her, but at the same time felt inevitable. This was it. This was what she had traveled completely across the continent to do.

"I'll come too," she said, knowing as soon as she said it that it was right.

He looked at her in surprise and didn't respond right away. He bent down to rub some inconsequential dirt off his boot before finally responding to her.

"You will?"

She smiled, pleased to see how happy her offer was making him. "If that's okay with you?"

"Really, Livvy?" He closed the distance to her. "Are you sure? I know you—"

"Really," she assured him, heading off any reiteration of all the excuses she had made to him in the past. "I want to do this. I want to be part of this with you. Really. This is where I need to be."

Luke caught her up in a tight hug. "Thank you," he whispered into her hair.

They had a long, difficult afternoon in that camp—the far-off sounds of a woman in labor mingling with the ever-present grief over one of their own losing a loved one. As the word went around the camp that the pastor would be holding a service that night, to Olivia, it seemed as though a wave of relief had crested over them. Soon, they could let go of their worldly worries. Soon they could be safe in the welcoming love of the family of God.

That night, in a small clearing just outside the circle of wagons, Olivia stood at the front by Pastor Montgomery while he led almost sixty emigrants in singing hymns praising God in the wilderness. Where they had made camp, near the canyon where the Snake River ran, tall rock walls spread out into a canyon behind them. The loud, sweet voices of the congregation echoed through the ravine, sounding almost like church bells as they faded.

It had been nerve-wracking to make herself stand in front of the crowd to lead, to put herself in front of all these people, most of whom she didn't know, but once she had committed to it, Olivia knew this was the right thing for them. She was the pastor's wife. She was fulfilling her role by his side and in the community.

She was meant for this.

The evening seemed to go by quickly, leading worship songs and listening to her husband preach. He spoke from the heart, finding a depth of feeling that hadn't been there before. He spoke about forgiveness and loving your neighbor. He spoke about community and the kingdom of heaven, where they would all find each other again one day. On the surface, the worship service that night seemed like just another chance to give the travelers a respite, but deep down, Olivia sensed that this moment was the last big coming together that they would have as they entered the final weeks of their journey.

Up until that point on the trail, the nearly fifty families had been disparate, traveling in the same direction but all focused on their own concerns. After that evening atop the Snake River, there was a coalescence, a solidifying of their lifelong connection. The trials of the Oregon Trail were the fire that had purified and melded the individuals into one larger, loving family.

As Luke—and she—led the singing of the final hymn, Olivia was surprised to find tears trailing down her cheeks. The feeling of belonging, of being wanted and welcome, had overwhelmed her. She slipped her hand into her husband's, proud to be by his side at this moment.

Early the next morning, Olivia stood by her husband's side once again as Luke held a short funeral service for John Harper. The unfortunate man's sister stood quietly crying as Luke extolled the virtues of the former New

Yorker, praising his care for his sister and his bravery in this new life. Olivia watched the young woman carefully, knowing she was now all alone in the world. But even as she watched, Hannah Sullivan linked her arm in Caroline's and supported her friend in her sorrow.

Maybe she would be all right. Maybe she wasn't completely alone.

As ever, Olivia was surprised at the kindness and generosity of her neighbors, but for the first time, she didn't feel quite so disconnected from it.

The wagon company left camp soon after, Mrs. Van Anda and her new son recuperating in the back of their wagon. Olivia was more tired than she ever had been working on her uncle's farm. But each step took her just that little bit closer to their goal, to Oregon and their new home. Luke stayed with her, guiding their animals more often than he was away now. Olivia wasn't sure why, but she wasn't about to question it. Just having him near as they walked, step after step, was exactly what she needed.

She didn't give any thought to the river, the desert shrubs, the mountains around them. There was only Oregon in her mind. Each moment that passed was one moment closer to being done with this journey.

The final half-hour of trudging along the trail, though, Olivia had a more immediate goal. She could hear the roar of Shoshone Falls long before she saw it, and every step brought her closer to that blessed cool oasis.

CHAPTER THIRTY-FIVE

It was already after sunset when the wagon train reached Shoshone Falls, but Olivia could hear the thundering water even in the dark. Word went around that they would stay at this water source until the middle of the following day. Olivia was anxious to keep moving west—she knew how scarce their food supply was—but the chance to rest near such a pool was too big of a temptation.

When she woke the following morning, the first thing she heard was the crash of the falls just outside their camp. Olivia smiled to herself. Camping near Shoshone Falls was a treat that Olivia hadn't let herself anticipate. As soon as she climbed out of the wagon, she nudged her husband awake from where he had still been sleeping underneath.

"Let's go," she insisted cheerfully. "Get up! Let's go look at the falls."

He laughed at her enthusiasm and pulled himself to his feet. "I'm coming."

Olivia already had a bucket in hand and led the way down to the water's edge. They had camped at the top of the canyon, at the top of the falls, and the crashing sound of water only got louder the closer they drew. The trees and bushes blocked most of their view of the water until they were practically right on top of it. A gap in the greenery opened up, and Olivia's eyes widened at the sight of Shoshone Falls just over the edge of the rock.

It was enormous—Olivia's breath caught in her throat at the sight of such natural power. There seemed to be enough water pouring over to create three or four separate smaller falls. The wall of water extended for something like a thousand feet across. The morning sun cut across the cloud of mist kicked up by the falling water, and Olivia could see half a dozen rainbows floating above the surface of the water.

"It's beautiful," she murmured.

Luke said nothing but held his wife close to him as they marveled at the Lord's creation.

They didn't linger long, but soon returned to camp where the thundering sound of thousands of gallons of water crashing into the pool below offered a soft undercurrent of noise that soothed her as Olivia went about her chores the rest of the morning. It might be a good chance to bathe again, fully. It might, in fact, be her last chance to wash her hair until they reached Oregon.

She had just started looking for her bar of soap to take down the water when Luke returned from an impromptu meeting George Mills had called.

"I need your help, please," he remarked easily. "We need to find things that we can get rid of."

"More?" She peered at him. "We've already lost your

shirts and the rest of what those Indians stole. We've gone through much of our food. I don't know that the animals need that much less weight on them."

"It's not for the wagon weight. It's a toll."

She frowned, confused.

"We're on Shoshone land," he said. "Every day that we're rolling through here with our noisy animals and wagons is a day that we're scaring away their game and putting the native tribe out from their usual resources."

Olivia nodded, surprised to find herself sympathetic with the indigenous people. "Oh... That makes sense. That must be hard for them."

"So, they're charging a toll."

"Oh, no!" Her eyes went wide. "But we don't have anything, do we? What could they do with dollars?"

He shook his head. "No, Mills talked them down, made them realize that we don't have any cash to spare now that we've been on the road this long. Instead, we're to take them any of the spare goods or supplies we can part with. A sort of trade. They don't want us to die on their land. But they do want us off as quickly as possible."

Olivia wracked her brain, thinking through everything that she knew was in the back of the wagon. She shook her head. "I don't know what we have to spare."

"We'll find something," he assured her. "There are lots of things that are replaceable. And we'll just need to trust that we'll be able to replace them. Sometime."

She followed him into the wagon, where they stood shoulder to shoulder, looking at their meager belongings. This was their whole life, all in haphazard piles. She was twenty years old, and her entire life fit in this one wagon. And she was about to give even more of it away.

Moving to the back of the wagon, Olivia looked for the big trunk she had packed full of clothes and linens. Even after losing a couple of Luke's shirts to the earlier Indian attack, there might be something in there they could spare. She dropped to her knees to rummage through the folded fabric.

Behind her, Luke began to sort through the black-smithing tools, their gardening tools, and other pieces he had brought on the trail.

"I probably only need one dress for the rest of the journey, don't I?" she mused. "What about this quilt?" She pulled out a light blanket that she had made a few years ago and was becoming worn through in places. "How much do you think they expect us to give them?"

She turned to see if her husband was listening and saw Luke pick up the cast iron pan that Aunt Bea had gifted Olivia so long ago.

"Not that!" she cried.

Though she had plenty of hurt and pain associated with her memories of her life in Virginia, this was still the only thing she had left of her family, the only item that she had carried across the entire continent that spoke of the people she had come from.

"All right," he said carefully, setting it down again. He smiled at her reassuringly. "All right. This stays. I understand."

She nodded brusquely and looked around at the rest of their things.

"This," she suggested, picking up one of her dresses. She still had two to spare and could likely make a new one as soon as they reached Oregon. "And this quilt. And…" She looked around. "The smaller mirror that I've been saving. It was silly of me to keep two mirrors. That will have to be enough."

Luke nodded and gathered the items in his arms. "This will be enough. Thank you, Livvy."

She watched him head off back to the Mills camp where the toll items were being gathered. A wave of exhaustion hit Olivia, thinking about how much they had already given up and now how much they had to give up again. Fortunately, at least, the Montgomerys had something to spare.

But she would be more than grateful when they finally reached Oregon and no longer were sacrificing at every turn.

That afternoon, they pulled out of camp at Shoshone Falls and headed farther downriver. The trail wound away from the Snake River and down another canyon. The narrow road pushed Olivia to walk close to her oxen's sides, slowly, praying that none of the animals would run loose or panic and stampede down the incline. Once at the bottom, they needed to coordinate with their neighbors. The only way to climb the steep grade to get out of the canyon was to chain two vehicles together and combine the strength of both teams to pull them up the trail.

Olivia was happy to walk up the trail herself, but nearly everyone was also asked to carry some supplies, some belongings, up the trail behind the wagon to further ease the burden on the team. With such a harrowing stretch, she wasn't surprised to find piles of discarded luxuries at the bottom of the canyon. The detritus that had been discarded along the trail was left there by emigrants who were getting more desperate and less sure that they would make it all the way to Oregon. They could now only ask their teams to carry the bare essentials and leave the medicine chest or leather-bound books behind.

Looking at the belongings that had finally been abandoned at the foot of the trail, Olivia couldn't help but think of the native American tribes whose land they were crossing. If only the emigrants had been able to give up these things days earlier when they could have helped others. Perhaps the tribe would find them after all.

CHAPTER THIRTY-SIX

The Sullivan-Mills wagon company kept pushing, desperate to make it to Oregon before winter set in. After leaving the deep canyon and the Snake River behind, the wagon trail curled along farther west, stretching across flat plains to the Three Islands Crossing. Olivia had read all about this river in the guidebook. It was shallow, though wide, and the wagons would have to be forded carefully across the sandy bottom, stopping at three different tiny islands as they make their way. It would take two days to get the whole company to the other side, as each trek had to be done carefully and slowly, so as not to get caught in the muck at the bottom.

The Montgomerys spent a leisurely morning waiting for their turn to cross the river. Luke visited a few of the families, while Olivia sat up on the wagon seat just to watch, a stark contrast from the fear that plagued her before crossing the Kansas River. From that height, she could see the river, see the camp starting to form on the other side as one family after another made their way through the water.

The river was only a foot or two deep where the company was trying to cross. It had to be done at this time of year before rain and snow drove the water levels higher. Olivia watched several of the wagons being driven over before she decided how she would cross the water. Riding in the wagon, even up on the seat, seemed far too perilous, and she had never been afraid of getting wet.

"You're sure you don't need my help?" she asked Luke.

"Nope," he said cheerfully. "Enough of the boys will be helping the teams cross that I'll be just fine. It's going to be rough going coaxing those animals into the water and through the current. Best if you let the men handle it."

She nodded. "Then, I'm going to ford across myself."

He frowned, concerned, and opened his mouth to protest. Olivia held up a hand to stop him.

"I'll just be in the way if I ride on the wagon. I don't want to be extra weight that Nebuchadnezzar and Shadrach have to drag through the sand and water. Please, Luke. You know I'll be perfectly fine. I've done plenty of more dangerous things back on my uncle's farm."

He took a deep breath and nodded. "All right. I trust you. But you'll be careful, won't you?"

"I'm always careful. Don't worry about me."

Her husband nodded and smiled and turned back to his work, already preoccupied with what it would mean to have to ford the river with his whole team. Olivia wandered to the edge of the river to watch the men crossing and to gauge where she should ford herself. The surface seemed to come as high as the knees of the men guiding their wagons across. She knew that the weight of her dress when it got wet would be a hindrance, but Olivia was reasonably certain of her own strength and balance to believe that she could do this.

She could do this.

She could do this on her own and help her husband by staying out of the way of him moving their wagon over. Looking over the surface of the river, she could see a clear path across. There were places where the water was shallow enough that she could see the bottom and other places that seemed deeper that she would have to be more careful as she crossed.

But this had to be easier than when she was a child, in Virginia, when she had fallen through the ice. She and her cousin had gone ice skating too late in the season. The thaw was already beginning. Billy spotted his friends and left Olivia to her own entertainment. He wasn't supposed to, and he got a walloping from Aunt Bea later that night; nevertheless, he had left Olivia on her own, so when the ice underneath her started to crack, she had no one to rely on but herself.

It was petrifying, and Olivia didn't get warm for an entire day, but she had managed somehow.

Wading through a river on the great plains should be easier.

She just had to take that first step into the water.

Olivia lifted her dress in both hands, though she knew it was futile, and stepped the final few feet to the edge of the water. Her toes were just under the surface. She looked up to find that she was about ten feet downstream of where the wagons were crossing. The Carters were fording the river now. Her own wagon would be next. She should have just enough time to cross the river and meet Luke on the other side.

Then she would build a fire, change into a dry dress, and make their supper for the rest of their evening in camp. It would be simple.

One step into the water, and Olivia realized she had misjudged how cold it would be. No matter—that's what campfires were for. In this spot, the river was only about sixty feet across, and she could do this.

Two more steps across—Olivia accidentally stepped on a rock and almost turned her ankle again. She regained her balance and gritted her teeth, determined to accomplish what should be a simple river crossing. It was just a little bit farther.

Several more steps, and she was near the center of the river. But here, the water ran more quickly. Stronger than she had expected.

Olivia's hands had been gripped in her skirts, but now she held her arms out wide, trying to maintain her balance in the rising water. Here, near the middle, the water was above her knees, almost to the middle of her thighs, and the strength of the water threw off her center of gravity.

Two more halting steps.

The current pushed her a little farther downstream. Olivia lost her balance completely, falling into the shallow water and soaking her dress all the way through. Her teeth started chattering from the chill, but she dug deep into the last reserves of her strength and pulled herself to her feet again.

She was already halfway across the river. Though she was ready to admit to herself now that maybe this wasn't going to be quite as easy as she had expected, she wasn't about to turn back.

She may not be able to turn back.

Olivia looked upstream to where the wagons were crossing and realized that the current had pushed her even farther away. It was almost enough to make her feel alone out here in the wilderness. She could no longer make out what the men were yelling to each other as they guided the oxen across the water. She could no longer see precisely which family it was that was waiting to cross on the far bank.

It was just Olivia and the water now.

She took another three steps before the strengthening current became too much for her.

It was pulling her under. She couldn't get her feet on the floor of the river. The current pushed her this way, that way, dragging her farther and farther downstream. Olivia's heart was in her throat as she felt all her control, all her strength, all her ability leave her.

She had only one choice.

Despite what she might be able to tell herself, Olivia Montgomery was not alone in the wilderness. She was not on her own. There were men and women all around that could help her, that wanted to help her.

She just had to ask for it.

Olivia took a deep breath, the cold stabbing her lungs as she filled them with air.

"Help," she called, her voice weak from the cold. No

one even looked her way. She balled her hands into fists, determined to survive this. "Help!"

This time she was loud enough to catch the ear of Lily Sheldon, who sat on her wagon's seat up front, next to her mother. Olivia saw the girl tug on Mrs. Sheldon's sleeve before the water pulled her under again. How had she so mistaken the depth of the current? She pushed off of the unstable bottom, barely managing to stand up out of the water enough that she could be seen.

"Help," she called again. "Please!"

In her haze of panic, Olivia dimly sensed people coming toward her, wading into the current after her. All she had to do was not drown, not allow the river to wash her away.

The chill of the water began to reach her core, her bones. Her strength was fleeing her even more quickly, but help was coming.

She could not survive this if she didn't ask for help, and now it was coming.

It was here.

A strong hand grabbed her upper arm; a voice yelled instructions. An arm wrapped around her waist, dragging her back out of the strongest part of the stream.

"I'm going to tie this rope around you, Mrs. Montgomery," Michael Sheldon said in her ear. "We'll get you to shore, but this is just in case."

She nodded numbly and felt her neighbor, her savior, wrapping her with the rope. He fumbled with the knot, tugged at the rope, and shouted for someone else to help. Another man—Morris Carter—appeared in the river on her other side, taking her arm and propping her up.

"You're all right," he assured her. "You'll be fine now. Michael, take her other arm. Let's get her out of here."

The two, man and boy, neighbors, strangers, Olivia's saviors, guided her through the most treacherous part of the river, far downstream from where the wagons were safely crossing, and up onto the bank on the other side. They all but carried her out of the water and sat her gently on the grass. She shook from the cold, from the fear, but she could get out a few words.

"Thank you," she said softly. "Thank you. Thank you so much."

"It's no problem, ma'am," Michael said.

"Just set here a bit," Mr. Carter said. "I'll get— Oh, here he is."

"Livvy!" Luke exclaimed, running to her. "What happened? How did—?"

The other two faded away, giving them privacy, but Olivia almost didn't wait before she interrupted her husband.

"No, I just—" She held up a hand to stop him. "Please. Give me... I need a minute. Please, Luke."

Something in her tone or face must have told him how deep her shame was because he didn't argue. He looked pained that he couldn't help her, but he stood back, nodding.

"I'm going to go make camp, get these fellows some food." He gestured to the oxen. Daniel Mills was holding their team a few yards away, waiting for Luke to return. "Come when you're ready."

She nodded and didn't look at him; she just broke down crying and sat in the grass at the edge of the wide river that had almost taken her.

CHAPTER THIRTY-SEVEN

Olivia took deep breaths to calm her heart. When she was most in danger of being swept away by the river, Michael Sheldon and Morris Carter had tied a rope around her waist to keep her from getting dragged farther downstream. Her strength had left her, and she needed help to get across. And now they had deposited her on the banks to rest and recover while they continued to help other wagons ford. Luke was taking care of their own wagon, so now all Olivia had to do was get a hold of herself.

Crossing the river was difficult. It should not have been such a trial, and yet somehow, she was grateful for it. Grateful for the chance to ask for help and receive it, and teach herself that the world didn't end because she couldn't take care of something by herself. Grateful to find that the people around her were watching out for her and willing to step up to help.

She knew she still had miles to go before she could truly believe, without a doubt or hesitation, that her loved ones wanted to help her, wanted her to lean on them, but she could make a start now.

Trying to ford on her own, away from others, was an instance when she had done everything right, had felt safe and sure, and yet still had needed help.

She could do this.

Olivia still shivered from the cold and the wet and the fear, but she was slowly calming. From where she sat on the bank of the river, she could see where some of the families had made camp. One woman had already finished laundry and had stretched out sheets and shirts across the brush. At least one other woman had started coffee brewing—Olivia took a deep breath, enjoying that warm, bitter scent.

With that fortifying reminder of what awaited her, Olivia climbed to her feet and began making her way through the campground. Many of the women and children she passed smiled at her; Mary Sullivan even called out to her, offering a mug of tea against the chill, but Olivia shook her head.

Not now. There would be time enough to make up for the coldness and stand-offishness she had put out through the journey. Now, she wanted to get to her wagon, to her home. To wrap herself in a dry blanket. To sit at her own campfire with her husband, and think about her day.

Luke had led their team out to the far side of the circle of wagons, unyoked them, and was starting to light the fire when she approached. He smiled up at her.

"Do you hear that?"

She tilted her head to one side and listened. "Is that... a fiddle?"

He nodded, blew on the spark to encourage it, and then sat back as the first flame began to eat at the dry fuel he had gathered. "Martin Jameson will play any chance he gets. Luckily his brothers don't mind doing a few extra chores." Luke chuckled and looked back up at her. "Let me get you a quilt."

Olivia almost protested that she could do it herself, but then she stopped herself. She nodded gratefully. Luke squeezed her shoulder as he walked past her to the wagon, and Olivia lowered herself to sit by the now-growing fire, her dress already starting to dry. The lively, comforting music floated over the company, mingling with the sounds of laughter, good-natured scolding, and muffled conversations that filled every night when they were in camp.

For the first time since they had left Virginia, Olivia felt like she was part of it all, instead of just watching. The crowd and love seemed to be all around her, rather than something she was outside of.

Her feet warmed as Luke returned and draped the quilt over her shoulders. Olivia pulled the edges together, wrapping herself in the dry, warm blanket, and sighed contentedly.

"You feel better?"

He sat down next to her, close enough to touch, but leaving an inch or two between them. Olivia felt an urge to lean into him.

"I do feel better. This fire is nice, thank you." She knew she was acting formal with her husband, but the alternative was acknowledging and feeling all the emotions she had been pushing down for so long. Olivia didn't know if she was ready for that.

He was silent for a moment before he continued. "Morris Carter told me about how they found you. Being pushed downstream and shivering with the cold. Livvy, I'm so sorry. I thought... I didn't realize the water would be so strong or so cold. This is my fault."

"No, it's not. Luke... I appreciate your trying to take care of me, but this was my choice. I thought I was stronger than I was. I thought..." She shook her head. "I thought I was doing the right thing by going off on my own and staying out of people's way. I didn't want to be a burden. But instead, I... Did the Carters get over the water all right? Did I ruin everything with my stupidity?"

"Oh, my darling girl." His head hung down, dejected. Taking a deep breath, he looked back up at her. "No, you didn't ruin anything. All the wagons got through the river. All the people made it safely. I think Miss Harper's axle might have broken, but I haven't heard of any other problems."

She sighed in relief.

"But I'd like you to do something for me," he continued, more seriously. "Olivia, I... I don't know how else to say this, but I need you to recognize how much you are cared for by this community. Not a single person here would ever say you're a burden."

"But—"

"No, not even Morris Carter. Pausing his crossing the river for a few moments, putting Jefferson in charge, to make sure you survived is *not* a burden. Olivia, please."

He looked at her pleadingly, and her heart broke a little. She saw now how selfish it had been for her to try to do everything on her own. To put Luke through this pain of knowing she might be in danger and be too proud to ask for help.

"I'm sorry, Luke," she said quietly. She leaned against him, sinking into his shoulder, and felt his arm go around her.

"You are more than forgiven, Livvy. But now I want you to relax and warm up. I'll figure out what we're having for supper. Don't you lift a finger."

"Thank you," she said again. "I appreciate you thinking of me."

He pulled away from her slightly and forced her to turn to face him. "Olivia Montgomery, I am always thinking of you."

She was surprised by his sincerity. Her shock must have shown on her face because he continued.

"Do you doubt me?"

She could have immediately said no. She could have reassured him with empty words, but instead, she paused and gave it thought. Did she doubt him?

"I think," she began hesitatingly. "I think... maybe a few months ago I might have doubted you. I think... well, you know. Every step along this journey, I have felt like I might be a burden—to you and to the wagon company as a whole. My uncle made me feel like I was a weight on him my entire life, and I haven't been able to get past that, it seems."

"I'm so sorry you grew up that way."

She shrugged. "Me too. But..."

Olivia didn't know what else to say. So many months ago, she had chosen this life with this man almost impulsively, not thinking about what expectations she was bringing with her, not thinking about how her own needs and quirks might affect him.

"I'm sorry," she said finally. "I'm sorry if you felt like I doubted your affection, Luke. I'm trying. I really am. I'm so grateful to you for helping me to leave Virginia, and I don't ever want you to regret doing that. I'll do better. I want to be worthy of you and of being your wife."

He frowned. "Olivia... Do you know how much I love you?"

Her mouth fell open. "I..." She gestured helplessly and shrugged. "I know that I'm useful to you... And, I know that you're fond of me. I do believe that you're happy you married me. I think. Probably."

"Probably?"

"The truth is, Luke... I'm not sure I ever let myself think about it. There was always something else to worry about, from finding a boarding room to buying enough flour to not getting kidnapped by the natives. All along, I've just been trying to do my best, trying to make sure you had everything you needed and that I wasn't in the way. So... love? Love was something I kept telling myself I'd think about later."

He chuckled, but somehow, she knew he wasn't laughing at her. With his arm still around her waist, he pulled her close in a hug, dropping his head to her shoulder. Luke kissed her neck before he gently, carefully, sought out the edge of the quilt that she had clasped around her. Olivia relinquished her hold on the blanket, and her husband unfurled it to wrap around himself.

He scooted closer to her, closing the distance between them, until they sat together by the campfire, hip to hip, with the quilt wrapped around the both of them. Under the blanket, Luke wrapped his arm around her again, pulling her close.

"Olivia," he murmured into her ear. His breath on her neck gave her goosebumps. "I love you devotedly. I'm so glad I married you. And now it's time to think about it."

CHAPTER THIRTY-EIGHT

Olivia was on cloud nine. It had taken traveling almost to the other side of the continent, but it now seemed as though everything was falling into place. Every day they were still fighting for survival, but she and Luke and all of the other emigrants they traveled with, were doing it together.

The wagon company still had several days of travel to go before reaching the next milestone—Fort Boise—and they pressed hard to get there as quickly as they could. Several days of difficulty was worth even the chance to purchase something that would sustain them another stretch of trail. Olivia held out hope that the shelves of this fort would be stocked. She couldn't help herself. She, as usual, planned for the worst, but if she was pleasantly surprised, all the better.

Fort Boise was just a few small buildings behind a stockade wall, but fortunately, it hadn't been completely picked clean, even this late in the year. Luke had taken a small offering the last time he had held a worship service, so the Montgomerys were grateful to be able to buy a little rice, beans, and jerky to squirrel away for the coming days, along with a couple yards of fabric so Luke could finally have a new shirt. They almost were not able to snag the linen, but Mrs. Sheldon noticed Olivia reaching for it at the same time she was and let the pastor's wife have it.

"You might as well take it," she said with a smile. "Goodness knows David is growing so fast that the shirt will be too small for him by the time I finish sewing it."

Gratefully, Olivia clutched the fabric to her chest. Her poor husband had been living with just a single shirt, now filthy and threadbare, since the natives had stolen his others. He deserved a new one.

The fort was near the Boise River, and once they had made camp and packed away the new supplies they had bought, Luke went off to fish with Jefferson Carter. The river was a couple hundred feet across in places, and the banks were already lined with men hoping to catch a fresh supper.

That evening, Olivia almost laughed in delight to see Luke returning with so many salmon.

"Goodness," she exclaimed. "I'm so glad we were able to get more salt. This will last us a while. Thank you so much."

He kissed her. "My absolute pleasure."

Olivia's hands were full salting their fish and finishing sewing Luke's new shirt, but such hard work set them up in as good a position as they could be in for the last final push over the mountains into Oregon.

The following morning, the wagon company left Fort Boise for another long, difficult stretch of terrain. The next big obstacle would be the Blue Mountains, and Olivia was more grateful than ever that Luke had caught so many fish. Her stomach was full for the first time in weeks, and the blue sky overhead felt like a gift rather than a punishment.

Each step they took brought them closer to Oregon and closer to the life that she was now truly looking forward to. The rest of the journey would be difficult, but with Luke by her side, it would still be exactly what she would want.

For the next few days after leaving the fort, Mr. Mills pushed the company harder and faster than ever. They didn't stop for a midday meal but kept moving westward. Olivia would climb into the wagon as it moved to retrieve salted salmon or beef jerky for Luke and her to eat as they walked.

Any time they saved was lost, however, when the sky opened up in mid-afternoon of the third day. The storm seemed to swoop in on them out of nowhere. Each and every person was caught out in the torrential rain. It was the kind of storm that immediately soaked through the topsoil, getting boots and hooves stuck in the mud as the caravan tried to move forward. The clouds had completely covered the blue sky; it was as dark as twilight even in the afternoon, but still, they pressed on.

Olivia had been too slow in grabbing her oilskin and shivered under the layer, cold to the bone. The rain didn't let up for several hours, finally slowing just before sunset and after they were into the foothills.

This was the coldest she had ever been on this trail,

and it was still late summer. They had so far to go, and soon the weather could turn on them again. Their trail through the Blue Mountains put a strain on Olivia's feeling of contentedness. The mud underfoot didn't completely dry for another full day. Once it did, the hard-packed earth was full of potholes, stones, and tree branches that had been blown across the path. More than once, the whole company had to stop when several men worked together to move a fallen tree from the trail.

Days passed. Miles were traversed. The Montgomerys finished their store of salted salmon, and they still kept going. Their journey westward was now well into September, and they had been on the trail for weeks longer than Luke had planned for and had bought food for. Olivia kept her eyes on the snow-capped mountains, using that goal to drive her forward every day, every morning, more and more steps to carry them west.

Olivia had walked so far that she had almost worn through her boots and had started thinking about what of their other belongings she would have to cut down to patch and fill the holes. The alternative would be riding in the wagon if she couldn't walk, and she already knew she didn't want to do that.

She wouldn't ride in the wagon for many reasons, but adding her own weight to the nearly two thousand pounds that the oxen had to pull would be too much for them. Not this late in the journey. Now that they were so high in elevation, there was not enough grass to feed them. The little plant life that had been accessible earlier in the summer had long ago been devoured by the wagon companies that had crossed this way before them. The wagon companies that maybe had not had delays from untimely deaths or Indian attacks.

Watching the oxen—Shadrach, Meshach, Abednego, and Nebuchadnezzar—work so hard to pull the Montgomerys' wagon uphill while barely having enough to subsist on was heart-wrenching. Olivia murmured kind words to them as they walked, knowing that she couldn't do any more. She barely had enough food herself. The salmon they had been able to catch when they had camped at Fort Boise had lasted them as long as possible but was now long gone. Luke managed to trade Ed Ellis for small birds in exchange for another pair of hands. That family had two wagons and not nearly enough strength for some of the larger repairs needed. Occasionally, Luke spent a little time teaching the Carter children. In turn, they would bring acorns and wild onions they had scavenged from the woods they passed through. Even with all their neighbors' generosity, more often, both Montgomerys had to go to bed with grumbling stomachs.

But they were together. And they were making it. And there were hopefully only a few weeks left to survive before they finally arrived home in the Willamette Valley.

CHAPTER THIRTY-NINE

They were so close. They were so very close to Oregon, especially when Olivia reminded herself that they had only left Virginia at the beginning of the year. They had come so very far, and yet she could never let herself forget that they could lose it at any moment. So many folks had already died trying to get to where they were now. Olivia vowed she would not take it for granted.

Every morning they woke before dawn, teeth chattering in the September cold. Olivia had brought her heavy coat all the way from Virginia, but Charlottesville cold and Blue Mountains cold were two very different things.

Every morning they climbed higher and higher under the heat of the rising sun.

Every morning, Olivia remembered stories she had read and warnings they had received of the companies that had passed through this part of the country in years prior. Families that lost members to the cold or gotten stranded in the snow. Companies that had to leave behind a sick man in order for the rest of them to keep going and survive.

It was easy to forget, when they were leaving Independence with a wagon full of food, how treacherous the trail could be. It was easy to underestimate how exhausted this would all make her.

But this far into the journey, her only job was to survive. To be an aid and comfort to her husband and to hang on long enough to get over the mountains into Oregon. To survive for her husband and for the child that would be joining them in only six months. She could do this.

One foot in front of the other, for only a few more days.

She was conserving her energy, sitting huddled in her coat on a stone just off the trail as they waited for the lead wagon to set the group moving for the day.

"We'll get some relief soon," Luke promised her as he offered Meshach a handful of oats he had been gifted from the Sheldons. The family had lost another one of their cows and so had fewer mouths of their own to feed. "Samuel Findley told me that Daniel Mills has been sent on ahead as a scout to get help."

"What?" Olivia looked up sharply. "We can do that?"

Luke nodded. "That's the word. I guess the people down in Oregon now remember well how difficult their own crossing was and are ready this time of year to lend aid and come up the trail to meet struggling caravans."

Olivia gasped in surprise. "Why, that's... that's... I can't believe it." She almost cried from the relief of just the possibility. She had been so hungry for so long.

"One of these days, Livvy," Luke said with a chuckle,

"I'll finally be able to convince you that people are inherently generous and kind. It might take a while, but one day you'll believe it."

Olivia laughed in spite of herself.

"I don't know how long it will take, though," Luke warned, helping Olivia to her feet. "It depends on how far he has to go and how quickly they agree to come back."

"Honestly," Olivia said, "even the chance that we're not alone up here on the mountain is an encouragement."

When they had been on the plains coming westward, the mountains had seemed so high. They had towered over the trail, and Olivia imagined the steep incline that would be required to cross through them. But here, it seemed as though every day they moved forward and every day they didn't get anywhere closer to the top of the mountains.

The company had stopped for a midday break, though almost none of the families had anything close to a meal left to eat. There was water nearby, springs trickling out of the rocks, and everyone could use a rest, but most were just sitting quietly, dejectedly, worn down from the months of constant stress.

Olivia heard unfamiliar voices and looked up. Strong voices. Calling out and spreading throughout their camp. She and Luke exchanged a look, but he shook his head. He didn't know who that was either.

For a brief moment, she worried that they were again

being attacked by Indians, but the tone seemed so welcoming. The words seemed to be in English.

She pulled herself to her feet. Luke took her arm, and together they walked toward the sounds. Only a few steps past her small campfire, two strange men approached them. They led a horse that was laden with what seemed to be heavy saddlebags.

"We're friends," the taller of the men said hurriedly, hands up in a symbol of surrender. "We've come up from the valley and brought you supplies."

Olivia choked out a sob before she could stop herself.

"Supplies?" Luke said weakly while still offering his charming smile. "Are you angels?"

"No, sir." The shorter of the two also seemed younger; maybe they were father and son. "Just common men, doing the right thing."

"We'll stay with you for the next few days as you make your way down the mountain, too," the tall one assured them.

"Goodness," Olivia said. "Who... Who are you?"

"Our group is from Dempsey, down in the valley. The last few years, around this time, we keep an eye out for emigrants coming over the hills. There was a... a tragedy a few years back. A lot of folks died real close to here, and we aim to not let that happen again. You must be hungry and weak, so we'll lend a hand. Like good neighbors."

"Thank you. Sir, thank you so much," Luke said, offering his hand eagerly. "My name is Pastor Montgomery, and this is my wife, and... well, I can't tell you quite how much this means to us."

"I know, Pastor. I understand. I've been there too. My name is Harvey. John Harvey. This is my son Mark. Let me get you all set up with a hearty meal first and foremost."

Fifteen minutes later, Olivia and Luke were sitting by their roaring campfire, each with fingers wrapped around a cup of hot coffee, each with stomach rumbling at the scent of bacon sizzling over the flames. The Harvey men were as good as their word and had brought more than enough food to keep them sated through the last few days of their journey.

It had been a long, hard road. They had made choices along the way that had made things even more difficult for them. But now, with the end in sight, all Olivia could think of was how much closer the journey had brought her to her husband. And to who she was meant to be in this new world.

She watched Luke's face in the campfire light while he looked elsewhere, his thoughts consumed by something she was not part of.

Watching her husband like this—thinking, planning —brought Olivia a sense of joy and contentment she would not have thought possible at this point in their journey. She had been far luckier than she realized when she had married this man. Not only did he understand her needs whether she voiced them or not, but he saw her for all her flaws and loved her anyway.

Sitting here in the twilight, high in the mountains above Oregon, Olivia saw clearly a vision of her life for the coming years. Decades. Working by Luke's side as he ministered to his flock of emigrants, farmers, and families who had come west seeking a better life. She would be called on a daily basis to allow herself to be cared for, to anchor herself in the present, in this community, and work alongside her husband.

This life was precisely what she had needed, and she didn't even realize it until she was here.

Luke looked over at her then and smiled.

CHAPTER FORTY

When Olivia woke the next morning, she almost couldn't contain her excitement. This would be the day, the day she had been looking forward to, the day that Luke had promised her all those months ago when she had agreed to be his wife. As she climbed out of the wagon and set about making them coffee and breakfast with the blessed food that their rescuers had brought, she could hear the bustle of the families all around her too, all eager to get moving and finish their descent into the Willamette Valley.

As Luke had so many times been wont to do, he was missing from their campsite up until the last minute when Olivia had to put out the fire and put away their dishes. When it had happened before, she had been angry and frustrated, but now she was far too happy for what lay ahead to complain. Now she understood all the ways he was adding to their lives by tending to those around them.

Instead, she laughed as she handed him the cooling cup of coffee.

"Drink this fast, husband. We have places to be."

He grinned at her over the top of the cup, watching as she made all of her last arrangements. The last time she would have to make them breakfast on the road. The last time she would have to cobble together a fire from scraps of worn-through shirts. The last time she would pack their cast iron pan away safely hidden from possible thieves.

Olivia knew that they still had many weeks or even months of work ahead of them as they found their future property, built a house and made it their home. She wasn't so naïve as to think that this was the last meal she would cook over a campfire. But there was a marked difference between living out of a trunk, a few crates, and a rickety wagon, and living in the place you would make the rest of your life.

As Olivia was putting away the last of their life in the wagon, Luke was hitching up Meshach and Abednego. This was one day he would be sure to drive their team himself, so as a family, Luke and Olivia could enter Oregon together, walking side by side as they had for so much of the journey west.

As she finished tucking away the quilt, she felt a light fluttering in her abdomen that surprised and then pleased her.

It was time to tell him.

When the wagon company started leaving camp, rolling one wagon after another into a line heading down the mountain, Olivia fell into step next to her husband, next to their team of oxen, and slipped her hand into his free one.

"How was your morning?" she started hesitatingly. The mysteries of married life and intimacy were still so new to her, she wasn't sure how to begin.

"I have good news!" he exclaimed, squeezing her hand. "I've been bursting to tell you."

"I have good news too," she said demurely. "But tell me yours first."

"Well." He lifted her hand to his lips and kissed it casually, eyes dancing with the joy of what he was about to say. "This morning, Daniel Mills came to fetch me and tell me his father needed to talk to me. I thought, oh no." He chuckled. "What have I done?"

Olivia smiled and shook her head. As if there was anything that Luke Montgomery could do to get in trouble with George Mills.

"So, I made my way over there, hat in hand. And though, of course, the Millses were all running around getting ready to leave like we were, George took me aside to tell me..." He laughed again. "I tell you, Livvy, I can't rightly believe we are so blessed as this. It seems just a miracle to me."

"What did he say?" she prompted.

"Seems he's been talking to a lot of the men, a lot of the families, about what we all need when we get to Oregon. George Mills is a great man. He wants to make sure every member of this wagon company lands on their feet and isn't left behind or left to suffer in this great new world of ours. So... So he's been talking to all the families. Right from almost the very beginning he started taking up a collection for me. For *us*."

"A collection?" she whispered, overwhelmed by the implication.

"And each time I held a service, he got more and more funds, all intended for us. All meant to help build our church when we get there."

"I don't... I don't understand, Luke. Are you saying...?"

"I'm saying that we have trusted in the Lord, and he has provided. I'm saying that between the cash money and the promises of labor and materials that Mills has collected on our behalf, that we will be able to start building our church right away. The Church of the Redeemer, I'm thinking. Our new life in the Oregon Territory is surely part of God's plan."

"I'm so happy," she said. "I'm so happy for you."

"For *us*," he insisted. You're part of this with me. This is our work together, don't you know that by now?"

"I do. I think I do. I'm just... Luke, you know." She shrugged and looked at her feet, taking step after step alongside his. "I don't want to be a burden. I only want to... to help."

"Livvy," he said softly, turning to look into her eyes. "Olivia Montgomery. You are not a burden. You are a gift. You are the only thing that kept me going for the last few months. How could I have ever made this journey without you?"

She blushed under his praise. "Thank you. I'm glad. I'm grateful. Luke... I ..." She took a deep breath. "I'm glad you think I'm not a burden because I'm going to..." She cleared her throat. "I'm going to need your help soon."

"What?" he cried in mock-surprise. "Olivia Montgomery needs somebody's help? I thought I'd never live to see the day."

She didn't even mind his teasing, so pleased as she was with what she was about to tell him.

"I'm going to need your help because my hands will be full." Olivia placed her free hand against her abdomen. "Making meals for three people instead of two."

"Olivia!" he yelled, startling the oxen. "A baby? *Our* baby. Our family. Oh, my goodness." He seemed breathless and utterly overcome with emotion. Tears welled up in his eyes as he looked at her. "When? How soon? Shall we name him George?"

She laughed, awkwardly, excitedly, happier, and more in love with this man than she had ever been. "A few months, yet. We'll have time to build him a proper home, instead of this rolling one."

"And I will build him the best home," he assured her. "Build one for all of us. Oh, my love. My heart. Thank you." He faced forward as they continued their walk down the mountain. Still holding his hand in hers, he pulled it up against his chest, holding her tight against him. "Thank you for making my life just perfect."

Olivia didn't respond in words but allowed herself to lean against her husband slightly as they walked into Oregon together. From this vantage point on the mountain, it felt as though the new territory was rising up to meet them. As far as she could see was green. Green fields and forests and grasses and lush rolling hills. Everything that Luke had promised her had come true.

Olivia breathed deeply of this new world, the scent of damp grass and evergreens heavy in the air.

She sighed contentedly. It had been a long journey, but this was precisely what she had wanted when she had chosen to leave Virginia almost a year ago.

THE END

Download your free book — *HANNAH'S HOPE* — at ATButler.com/Hannah

When Hannah Sullivan's family decides to head west to the Oregon Territory, she's exhilarated. The small town where she grew up was fine when that's all she had to choose from, but as soon as the horizons and opportunities open up, Hannah finds a whole new world, just built for someone as competent, kind and warm as she is.

Sign up for A.T. Butler's mailing list today and receive Hannah's Hope for free! Dive into a story where romance blossoms against all odds, and be the first to hear about new releases, exclusive content, and special offers. Don't miss this chance to fall in love with Hannah and Benjamin's story.

ATButler.com/Hannah

AUTHOR'S NOTE

Thank you so much for reading *Faithful Trail*, the second book of the *Courage on the Oregon Trail* series.

I admit, when I wrote *Westward Courage*, I had no intention of continuing the book into a series. I just kind of fell into this backwards because I could not get enough of the characters, the setting, and the whole experience. The Sullivan-Mills wagon company is populated with characters from a wide spectrum of American life and I couldn't help but want to continue.

So why did I start with Olivia's story? I grew up in a church and saw first hand what was expected of women in that system, how much they give and sacrifice and how hard they work. It is my own personal struggle to have a difficult time asking for—and accepting help—and I imagine that would only be exacerbated in a situation like Olivia's when really each of her own sacrifices does benefit other people. It's easy to talk yourself into running yourself into the ground when you can see how much your work is doing good.

But—like Olivia—I had to learn the hard way that destroying myself with work and not asking for help when I needed doesn't help anyone. There have been times when I was too exhausted to do anything, too emotionally spent to be there for a loved one.

Taking that same lesson and placing it in the extreme, perilous setting of the Oregon Trail seemed perfect. I suspect it might be a lesson we all need to learn and relearn throughout life.

Luke and Olivia's story continues in book four of the spin-off series — *The Pastor's Baby* available now.

Thank you so much for being on this journey with me. The excitement and the hardship and the heart that our pioneers go through every day. We'll be with the Sullivan-Mills wagon company for a long time still.

— A.T. Butler
October 2024

FREE PRINTABLE OREGON TRAIL MAP

Sign-up to download a FREE custom printable map of the Sullivan-Mills wagon company's journey on the Oregon Trail.

You'll also get news of future releases, updates for promotions and discounts, as well as occasional other exclusive goodies, created just for my subscribers.

https://atbutler.com/ot-free

The next book in COURAGE ON THE OREGON TRAIL series is available now.

**Grab FRONTIER SISTERS here!
(on Kindle and Kindle Unlimited)**

Oregon has to be better than what she has now.

Annie Hudson already has one foot out the door. She has responded to a mail order bride advertisement and now needs to figure out how to get all the way to Oregon.

When her older sister Louisa learns about her plans, she enlists the other two Hudson sisters to her side.  They refuse to let Annie make the trip alone, and soon four women--and one teenage boy--are driving their wagons westward.

Each of the Hudson sisters has to reconcile what she had expected her lives to be with the adventure she is now choosing.

Will the sacrifice be enough to give them the future they've always wanted?

All the books in the Courage on the Oregon Trail series take place within the same wagon company's trip west and run concurrently. They can be read in any order.

She thought the hardest part was behind her.

The Oregon Territory, October 1850: After nearly a year of living out of a covered wagon, day after day of grueling work and heart-breaking tragedy, Caroline Harper has finally reached the Oregon Territory where her new life will begin.

She thought she had given all she had to give; she thought she had become the strong woman the frontier requires. But every day brings a new challenge for the settlers.

When unexpected obstacles appear that keep her from getting married, from finally finding her security, Caroline learns that becoming the woman she needs to be will be far more difficult than she had realized.

Can Caroline find her new path or will this journey be the end of everything she thought she had achieved?

For all the stories of how these brave pioneers got to Oregon, look for the book series Courage on the Oregon Trail by A.T. Butler.

Oregon At Last Series:
Journey's End (Caroline's story)
Christmas in Oregon (Annie's story)
Snowbound Promises (Nora's story)
The Pastor's Baby (Olivia's story)
Frontier Fortune (Rebecca's story)
Reluctant Spring (Sadie's story)
Summer of Promise (Margaret's story)

ALSO BY A.T. BUTLER

Courage On The Oregon Trail Series:

Westward Courage

Faithful Trail

Frontier Sisters

Unyielding Heart

Wild Promise

Fierce Dreams

Seeking Home

Trouble and Grace

Oregon At Last Series:

Journey's End

Christmas in Oregon

Snowbound Promises

The Pastor's Baby

Frontier Fortune

Reluctant Spring

Summer of Promise

Juniper Falls Series:

The Juniper Hotel

Building the Dream

Snowflakes and Sugar Cookies

Jacob Payne, Bounty Hunter Series:

Trouble By Any Name

Danger in the Canyon

Justice for Jasper

Blood on the Mountain

Outlaw Country

Death By Grit

Desert Rage

Arizona Legend

Fool's Demise

Silent Night

Bountiful Justice Series:

Loyalty's Price

Riding for Justice

Trail of Redemption

Other Western Novels by A.T. Butler:

Hawke's Revenge

Short Stories from Juniper Falls

I grew up in the southwest—California Missions, snakes and constant threat of drought weaving the backdrop of my childhood.

But it wasn't until I moved to Texas a few years ago that the magic and mythology of the American West began to seep into my soul.

I'd love to write about western adventures, strong women and noble men for a long time.

If you enjoyed this book, a review on your favorite retailer would be greatly appreciated.

- A